ROUGH

ROUGH

A NOVEL BY ROBIN VAN ECK

Stonehouse Publishing Inc. is an independent
publishing house, incorporated in 2014.

Cover design and layout by Anne Brown.
Printed in Canada

Stonehouse Publishing would like to thank and acknowledge
the support of the Alberta Government funding for the arts,
through the Alberta Media Fund.

Alberta◼
Government

National Library of Canada Cataloguing in Publication Data
Robin van Eck
Rough
Novel
ISBN 978-1-988754-26-0

For Mom and Dad

"There is nothing like looking, if you want to find something. You certainly usually find something, if you look, but it is not always quite the something you were after."
J.R.R Tolkien, The Hobbit.

DAY ONE

THE RIVER

The river meanders, slow and steady, about to descend and embark on a great adventure. Through fields and mountain passes, it widens and slims, widens and slims, ducking under fallen limbs, rubbing against massive boulders brought down by a mudslide, an avalanche not so long ago, a block in the path, easily maneuvered. There is no stopping it. Its knuckles scrape the river bottom, fight against the upward battle of the spring salmon seeking a place to repopulate. A volatile home to so many, a sanctuary to more, the river creeps, gathering and surging, gaining strength. Its grumble echoes off granite walls, an illustrious bellow that no one can hear.

Bustling through town, the river stutters, waving a somber hello that goes mostly ignored. In retaliation it begins to gurgle and spit, tearing at banks, lifting itself up, daring them to notice. A quick glance around, there's nothing to keep it there. Angry and surging, gaining strength, carrying on to the next town and the next, where again, no one pays attention. Cigarette butts and beer cans are periodically tossed into the fray, along with garbage bags, sandwich wrappers and a bag of unwanted kittens.

Raging now, the river's force is no match; houses topple, roads are washed away. Now they're listening, and no one can stop it. Wedging outward the river steals dirt, debris, tree limbs, a child's sand bucket.

A city erupts along the banks, enormous buildings of glass and brick, higher and wider, until the sky is only a sliver of fading daylight. The river slogs along, nervous, edging under bridges, pedestrian walks. Cars slide overhead, an invisible haze emitting from their rear ends. Everywhere, the people, blissfully unaware of what lurks beneath, what's about to come.

Two men stand at the spot where two rivers converge. A jacket, too big, too heavy for this heat, hangs from a shrunken frame. Pant legs disappear into boots. Hair unkempt, dirty. The other younger with eyes black as coal, hair tucked back under a ball cap, shoulders squared.

The river lingers, watching, listening.

SHERMETO

What would Harlow do?

Shermeto stands on the bank, listening to the steady hum of the water. The calming murmur usually sets him at ease, but today has been a bad day. First, he couldn't get a meal at the drop-in centre because he'd been there too many times this week. He tried begging for money, but everyone seemed impossibly distracted today or gave him a hard *no*, one guy even told him to get a job. Then a dog peed on his shoe. Eventually, he'd scrounged up enough cans to get a cup of coffee, but that was this morning and try as he might, it's hard to ignore the hunger gnawing on his insides.

The water cuts over the rocks, polishing them to a sheen, edging up closer to their feet. Only last week the river was at least a foot farther out. It's angrier now. Frothing.

Against the backdrop of Fort Calgary, Jagger sways beside him, playing with something in his pocket, like a fidgety child. A plaid work shirt hangs open over an ACDC t-shirt, worn from black to gray, the logo faded and peeling. Jagger's eyes are as dark as his hair and he wears a grin that puzzles Shermeto.

The rain let up a few hours ago, leaving the pavement stained black and the air as soggy as the ground under their feet. Before all this, he'd spent countless mornings in this very spot—didn't matter the season—stooped over his camera, waiting for the sun to round the corner, casting its soft morning glow over the water. The perfect image. The perfect shot. Those memories are murky now, choked under layers of mud and grime, scars and busted lips. Blisters. Sunburns. Frostbite. The trivial, the mundane, doesn't matter no more. Best to leave the past buried where it belongs. Focus on the now. Keep the shiny side up.

The clouds have spread wide and the sun is glowing. The surface of the river looks muddy. On the opposite bank a slope of rocks is surrounded by police tape.

"What do you think happened?" Shermeto asks.

"Beats me."

Jagger is very little help in the best of times.

"Why was he even over there?" Shermeto shifts from one foot to the other, the ache in his joints making it hard to stand. Emergency crews still mill around, talking to themselves, studying the rocks, the grass, looking for any clue.

"It's not your fault."

"I know that." Shermeto snaps, his words sharper than he intends. "Still makes no sense," his gaze travelling back to the rocks. He can't shake the feeling he's being watched. It's been like this for weeks, maybe months. Since Harlow died, he supposes. Something surging under the surface: in the water, in the air, in the murky clouds floating overhead. Harlow would have known what was going on, would have known what to do.

"If you can't fix it, don't sweat it." Jagger adjusts the cap on his head.

Shermeto shrugs. Jagger has a point, but this is different. "Doesn't feel right."

"What you ducks looking at?" A woman appears, crosses the bike path and stands beside them, tugging at the neck of her shirt. Her hair is long, black, with stripes of gray that seem painted on. She's breathing hard, wheezing, each breath desperately scraping air into her lungs. She punches Shermeto hard in the arm.

"Jesus, Scissor. What the fuck was that for?" He holds his arm, the sting spreading out around his bicep.

"Wimp." Scissor waggles her finger at him, then drops to the ground, sitting cross-legged on the rocks. "Didn't mean anything by it. You know that, right?"

Doesn't change the fact that his arm still hurts. Shermeto pulls on a smile anyway. Scissor stretches her legs out in front of her and slowly lifts one and then the other. Over and over again. *Until the kinks are out*, he thinks.

A seagull dips low, dashes into the river and out again. The bird circles then flits away until the dot of its existence folds into the lingering clouds. For a blink he wishes he had his camera. He misses the way it felt in his hands; the weight, keeping him still, patient. Seems like a lifetime ago now.

Shermeto turns his attention back to the other side of the river, the emergency crews seem to be packing up.

"Nothing you can do about it," Scissor says, now pulling her knees to her chest, alternating legs. "We all gonna bite it sometime."

There's more to it than that, he's sure of it. "I want to see what's going on over there."

"What for?"

"He was my friend," Shermeto says. That's a loaded word. Friends. He hasn't had a lot of people who mattered in his life, before or after. No one understood. Harlow did. He was a good one. After Harlow came Jagger, but it's never been the same.

Jagger grunts, begins to cough and then spits on the ground.

Scissor laughs. "No one's your friend out here. Not really." Her exercises complete, Scissor settles back cross-legged. She rolls a small pair of metal scissors in her hand, uses the pointed end to dig dirt out from under her fingernails. "Everyone wants something." She digs deeper then wipes the blades on her pants.

Shermeto finds it hard to believe those little contraptions stabbed a man to death. Barely big enough to trim a nose hair. One rumour claimed she'd fought a guy over the last taco, another said someone had tried to steal her shoes and lost. That's the thing about rumours, they balloon until…poof. Maybe the scissors could skewer an eyeball, but doubtful they'd rip through layers of clothes and skin. Nothing more than a flesh wound.

"You believe in Creator?" She's moved on to the next finger.

"What's that?" Shermeto asks.

Jagger rolls his eyes and yanks up his pants. "You're crazy, lady."

Scissor raises her head. "Suppose she would be like 'God' to you." She lowers her head again, focused intently on her pinky finger. The moon casts a glow across the side of her face, illuminating the mottled skin on her cheeks and around her eyes. Her lips tighten, serious.

"No God would let us live like this." Jagger spits again.

"You're a fool. Where do you think we came from? You think Creator made houses and jobs and alcohol? We did that. She gave us know how. We abused it."

"Doesn't matter," Shermeto says.

"Then why you care so much what's going on over there?" She nods to the opposite bank.

Shermeto's gaze strays back across the river, knowing there's not a damn thing he can do about it. She's right. Why bother?

Scissor keeps talking. "I was ten when my uncle stained me with his whiskey breath. My mother knew and did nothing." She tucks the scissors into her pocket. "Look out for you." Scissor pushes herself up from the ground, grunting, gasping. "Watch out for those crazies. They're everywhere." She shoots a glare in Jagger's direction and stalks away.

Shermeto nods, smirks. The scuff of her shoes lingers long after she disappears. The other bank calls him.

"Going over. You coming?"

"What do you hope to find?" Jagger asks.

Shermeto shrugs. "Will know it when I see it, maybe."

Harlow would have assessed the situation first, stood back, learning everything he possibly could. That man didn't have an irrational streak in him. Straightforward, methodical. There was a purpose to everything he did.

Shermeto is still in the assessing phase.

KENDRA

Kendra kneels in the middle of the aisle, the ground under her damp, the cold seeping through her pants. The procession has barely begun. First the bridesmaids in their lavender gowns, spaghetti straps hugging their shoulders, their hair piled high in ringlets and innumerable bobby pins. The chairs on either side of the aisle are sinking into the wet grass and the guests look uncomfortable, sweating in their suits and blazers, dresses and shawls. Kendra usually loves outdoor weddings for the quality of light, but not for the unpredictable weather.

It's been an unusually soggy summer, the past week the worst and yet no last-minute changes were made, at least not ones Kendra was made aware of. Every bride she knows would be frantic, planning for the worst. Not this one. Sheila was her name and she'd been a problem right from the beginning.

Kendra remembers the terse emails, the demands. When she met with the couple to discuss specific poses: duration, shots, angles, guests, Sheila sat there with her arms folded across her chest, unwilling to give a little when Kendra suggested an alternate location for light and scenery, chance of rain. The husband-to-be, Brian, tried to reason with her, that Kendra was making a good point, it was important to have a backup plan. *It's my wedding and it will be how I want it to be,* Sheila had said.

And then, Kendra had been ten minutes late because no one told her of the change of venue and there was no time for the mother and bride shots in the bedroom. Sheila stood in the doorway, anger webbing out from under her tiara. She muttered something to her mother and then slammed the door. Kendra managed to get a couple of shots but the light coming in the window was harsh, a slap upside the bride's cheek and the mother was squinting. Not much Kendra was going to be able to do to fix that.

The bride begins her procession, a wide smile stretched across her face, the light catching her princess crown. Kendra hasn't seen a dress quite this extravagant in a long time. The sequined bodice catches the sun and shoots it in varying directions, the skirt rustles at her ankles. At least there is no train to get tangled in. She knows the glare is going to be hard to overcome, likely slicing across the lens, if she's lucky a few light bobbles will emerge and will lend to a more enchanting effect, but she's not hopeful.

Kendra gets a few more shots of the bride and groom under the lattice arch then slides into the background taking some candid shots of the guests, the scenery and then pauses to watch the vows, the happiness that fills this space.

"Aren't you supposed to be in there?"

Kendra glances to her right, at the woman who has come up beside her. She's never seen this one before.

"You're paid to be here," the woman continues.

"Who are you?" Kendra asks.

"Bride's sister and she told me to keep an eye on you."

"I'm sure she did," Kendra mumbles, loud enough to be heard, but low enough to be garbled. Then louder, "Thanks for your interest, but I've been doing this long enough."

Kendra raises her camera and catches the first kiss as a married couple and a few more shots as they make their way to a table off to the side for the signing of the documents.

"Get in there," the woman prods, pushing on Kendra's arm.

"Don't touch me," Kendra says, making her way up the aisle. *Who the hell does this woman think she is?*

The woman hangs back, the same know-it-all smirk plastered across her face as her sister earlier this morning. Obviously, the smug arrogance runs in the family. Kendra gets off a few more shots of the happy couple signing their lives away. *For richer or poorer. Until death.*

Sheila gathers the family, the bridesmaids, the groomsmen and beckons to Kendra. "We're going to do the photos at the pond."

Kendra nods and follows them along a cobblestone pathway, down some stairs to a narrow bridge. The sun is right in front of them.

"Right here," Sheila says.

"We need the sun behind you or to the side. Otherwise you'll be squinting," Kendra says, scouting out the area for a better spot. The bridge is the prettiest, would make for great photos if the sun wasn't hanging the way it is.

"We won't all fit that way," Sheila says. "Make it work." She leans over and whispers something to one of the bridesmaids who gives Kendra the side eye and begins to laugh.

Kendra has just about had it with these people and the bride-knows-best attitude. What the bride wants the bride doesn't always get. She knows this from her own experience. Love doesn't last. It's an enchanting idea that we struggle to achieve but will never actually get there. She glances at her left hand, at the ring she hasn't been able to take off even though James left months ago.

She guides the bride and groom, instructs them to stand close, facing away from the sun. The shots might not be bad, a few adjustments in photo editing and they would be passable. Sheila insists the bridesmaids and groomsmen get in the shot now.

"That's not going to work," Kendra says. "Here." She points to a grove of trees; a water fountain is set off to the side and the sun is perfect from that angle.

"I don't like that backdrop," Sheila says.

The groom, Brian, finally steps in. "Let her do her job," he says. "The photos will be perfect."

"No they won't," Sheila spits back. Adamant. Defiant.

"You're being unreasonable."

Brian pulls Sheila to the side and they whisper. Fury spreads across Sheila's face and there's the hint of tears about to erupt.

Brian shakes his head and makes his way over to Kendra.

"I'm really sorry," he says. "Is there any way to make the bridge work?" He's desperate at this point.

"Not with that many people," Kendra says. "Too much glare."

"Do your best," he says.

At what point does she allow her art and reputation to suffer simply to appease a woman who doesn't have a clue? "I won't do it," Kendra says.

"We paid you to do it." Sheila is back by her husband's side.

"If you want garbage photos, take them on your iPhone. I'm done." Kendra begins to pack up her camera and reflectors.

Sheila's mouth drops open. "You can't leave."

"I can and I will."

Kendra swings her camera bag onto her shoulder and stalks away. In the last decade, she's never walked out on a wedding before and she knows this is going to hurt her reputation.

SHERMETO

"You think you're some kind of detective now?" Jagger asks, leaning against a tree.

"It makes no sense. What was he doing here?"

It's an obscure area with jagged rocks and no place to really sit. Across the water, Fort Calgary stands wide and proud, the city to the left dwarfing its very existence.

Yesterday, Gerard had come into a little coin and bought lunch for them both from Spolumbo's, taking it to go.

"The river's getting mad," Gerard had said, as they made their way back to the river, looking for a spot out of the rain. They eventually settled under the 12th Avenue bridge, watching the river nip at the bank and tug at bushes dipping too close to the surface.

Shermeto had nodded in agreement. "It'll pass."

"You remember that flood years back?" Gerard took an enormous bite of his sandwich.

"Sure. Wasn't nearly as bad as people expected it to be." Shermeto unwrapped his sub. The girl with the green hair over at the restaurant had drizzled extra sauce on his sandwich without him even having to ask. People like her with her pretty face, made some days bearable.

Gerard spoke with his mouth full. "Different this time. I can feel it in my bones."

Rain curled along the pathway, forming puddles in the degraded concrete.

"That's the arthritis." Shermeto laughed. "There's nothing to worry about."

"High, wide and handsome."

"Huh?" Shermeto glanced up at his friend, taking in his far away gaze out onto the water.

Gerard laughed. "Something my old man used to say. Never did understand what it meant." He shrugged away the memory.

Shermeto rewrapped the other half of his sandwich and stuffed it into his pocket. "What's the plan for today?"

"Thought I'd go find some work. How are you feeling? Looking a little green around the gills."

"Not so bad. Gut's acting up a little. Probably go sleep it off." Shermeto stood.

"You should get that looked at," Gerard had said.

"It's nothing I can't handle." Or rather, it was something he didn't want to handle. Shermeto had left him there under the bridge and made his way back to his camp to take a nap and wretch up his stomach contents. Somehow, by the end of the day, Gerard ended up over here, with the animals snorting from their enclosures in the nearby zoo. What happened in between was anyone's guess.

Police tape flaps in the rising wind. Dark clouds are moving in again, making their way across the sky. It's going to be another wet night.

"Is that blood?" Shermeto says, pointing to a spot on the rocks, darker than the rest.

"You think the animals ever get out?"

"What?"

"The zoo. The wild animals. Man, that would be a disaster," Jagger says.

Thunder rumbles, still far away.

"Not sure what you been smoking."

"Find anything?" Jagger asks.

"Nothing worth anything."

"Told you."

KENDRA

Kendra sits in her car watching the front of the house. She doesn't want to be here, but she can't stop herself. James was supposed to come for his things today but didn't show up. She glances in the back at the boxes laying across the seat. *She's doing him a favour.*

The house sits at the end of a cul-de-sac, gray and foreboding, hidden partially behind a large pine tree. A yellow glow spills from the window. James is happy, comfortable without her. Found happiness with that skunk-faced whore from his office. Kendra knew too, long before he admitted it. All from the way she sat behind her desk, chewing on the end of her pens, spitting the fragmented Bic shards onto the floor, or squishing the lids until they were so flat they wouldn't fit on the end of the pen. Who does that? Disgusting. "You must go through a ton of pens the way she eats them," she'd remarked one day.

"It's cute," he'd said.

Kendra gathers the boxes and heads to the front door. She considers just leaving them and walking away, but she can't.

Buttery light streams from the window. There's no movement in the living room but the TV is on, a news reel played over and over, warning that the river may jump any day, the city on evacuation alert. It won't affect her any, she lives in the suburbs. A red couch that looks too puffy to be comfortable stretches along one wall and beside it, a matching chair with a diamond patterned throw lying across the arm. Reds and blues and whites. Did Skunk-Face make it herself? Is that what made her so goddamned special? Little Suzy Homemaker. The real Martha Stewart. Domesticated. Tamed.

A floor-to-ceiling bookshelf stands against another wall with more knick-knacks than books. Photos, flowers, ornaments, mementoes from faraway countries. Kendra recognizes the Paris globe cup James brought back from Vegas the last time they were there. Must have been two years. He loved that thing. Drinking slushy drinks in the afternoon heat. She'd called him a pussy for drinking the girly drink, but she didn't really mind, and they'd laughed and made love later with the flashing neon lights of the Flamingo splashing across their room. It felt dirty and hot and sexy. As Vegas should be. *Why did he keep it? Or worse, is it a new one?* A memento of vacations since. It's only been a few months. How many vacations could they have taken?

A shadow moves in a back room but she can't see anyone. Kendra takes a small step backward, forgetting she's standing on stairs. She loses her balance and screams as she hits the ground hard, knocking the wind out of her. The front door opens and Skunk Face appears. Her surprise fades away and she rolls her eyes.

"Jimmy, your ex is here."

A moment later, James appears in the doorway. "Are you okay?" he asks but doesn't offer to help her.

Kendra pulls herself off the ground and brushes off her clothes. "I'm fine."

Skunk-Face is watching her from the window, arms crossed, probably counting the seconds until she leaves.

"I brought some of your stuff."

"You didn't have to do that. I said I would get it."

Kendra shrugs. Why does this have to be so hard? Why can't she just get over it? Move on. What the hell is she holding onto anyway? "You said you would come today and you didn't."

"Sorry. Had a brief I needed to finish and one of my clients needed me."

Skunk-Face mutters something from the living room. James nods, steps outside and shuts the door. "She doesn't like it when you come around."

"I would think she'd prefer it to your coming to our house, alone."

"Your house," he says.

"It's not official yet," Kendra says. She glances back at the street. "I should go." She's fighting back tears.

"Are you okay?" James asks.

"It's just been a really bad day."

"You want to talk about it?"

"Not really." What she wants is to fall back into his arms and have him tell her everything is going to be okay. They will be okay.

"I've been meaning to tell you something," James says. "The divorce papers are being drafted. You'll get them as soon as they're ready.

"What's the hurry?" she asks.

"Caroline and I are getting married."

Kendra's heart begins to stutter, she can't breathe. Why is he doing this to her? Why now? It hasn't even been a full year. "I see," she says.

Her phone vibrates in her pocket. She plucks it out and glances at the display. It's Gary. The guy from the other night. They had a good time, but he seems far too serious. Too nice. Never trust the nice ones. She hits decline and tucks the phone back in her pocket.

"I should go. I think there's more stuff of yours in the shed. Let me know when you want to come get it."

***

Back in the car, Kendra's throat hardens with the expanding knot, each swallow more painful than the last. She can't smother the truth, can't pretend it doesn't exist. She pushed him away. It's on her. He moved on. So should she. But get married? He can't do that. It's not fair.

Her knuckles stretch and expand. Rain begins to splatter the windshield. Soft at first, then more impatient. An incessant hum that won't go away. The wipers whisk back and forth, trying to keep up. Between the tears burning at the corners of her eyes and the downpour, it's hard to tell where one ends and the other begins.

SHERMETO

Shermeto scours the sidewalk in front of The Blues Can, pocketing cigarette butts from the cracks where the rain can't reach. There's a goldmine in the planter outside the door. He digs through the cool, wet dirt while music crashes through the open doors. It's not raining hard, but it's raining.

He left Jagger about a half hour ago. Couldn't take the incessant chatter about how the tigers go for the throats, how the rhinos would trample anything in their path. Is that what was happening out here? Some menace ripping out the throats of his people? Shermeto buggered off as soon as Jagger asked who he thought would win in a fight, a tiger or a gorilla.

In the alley beside the pub Shermeto crouches in the weeds, listening to the thrum of music. Muddled with the rain, the vibrations course through the walls, pound at his feet. The air is thick like warm milk. No one should be alone out here, especially now, but he'll take his chances if the alternative is a drug-induced battle of feline vs. primate.

Sweat pools inside his jacket but Shermeto refuses to remove it. There's few things sacred in this world, and a man's clothes are one of them. He digs the butts from his pocket. Some have lipstick stains around the filter, but he doesn't care. Women never smoke the whole thing. Those squished or burned down to the nub, he flicks into the dirt; he works to straighten the others. He pulls out a lighter and begins to light one butt after another, drawing in long nicotine breaths until only the filters remain, then crushes them into the dirt. It's been a long night. Seems like he hasn't slept in a week. He leans his head back and closes his eyes, his knee throbbing to the beat of the music.

Everything hurts but there's nothing he can do about it. The pain is a welcome reminder of why he's here; all the hurt he caused now his to bear. As it should be.

An airplane descends, blue and red flashing lights arching towards the airport. Electricity buzzes, hums. He can never quiet the noise. Life goes on around him no matter what. Hell, he could die right now and no one would notice. Drown face down in a gutter. *There's worse ways to go,* he thinks.

Shermeto finally peels off his jacket and rolls it into a ball under his head. He closes his eyes, listening to the cars pass by 9th Ave, the muffled words of the bar hoppers spilling onto the sidewalk. They're worried they can't find a cab, bragging about the way the blonde with the big boobs was sizing them up. *They don't know how good they got it*, he thinks, returning to Gerard; the fourth death in as many weeks. The police won't take them seriously.

Most homeless, himself included, burned every possible bridge as they scuffled away, spitting on the doorstep of convention or offering a well-intentioned *fuck you* as the door slammed shut. At least that's what Shermeto did and there's no going back.

Gravel crunches. Shermeto opens his eyes a crack. A woman rushes into the alley and by the look on her face, she's crying. Two men follow close behind, jeering, taunting. They don't see him stretched out, or don't care.

"Leave me alone." The woman picks up speed, stumbles but doesn't fall. Her words slurred, meaningless.

"Come on. We just want to talk." Their laughter sounds like snarling. Shermeto thinks of the tigers, lying silent, circling their pray, then mauling it to death, or worse.

The woman reaches the end of the alley. There's nowhere for her to go. She digs in her purse. "I have a gun." The words stutter out.

The men pause a second. "Let's see it then." They reach for her.

She screams.

Shermeto glances up and down the alley. No one notices. Now they have her pressed up against the fence. She kicks and scratches and claws. It's no use.

Shermeto scrambles towards them, faster than even he expects. He grabs one of the men by the collar and pulls him off the woman. The other man is stunned. Shermeto knocks the first one to the ground and lands a sound fist up against the side of his skull. The second one recovers from his confusion and jumps on Shermeto's back, dropping him like a sack. His ears ring as the side of his face explodes in pain.

Then his knee, his stomach. A rib cracks and a shower of stars radiates out. Shermeto curls and groans, sucking in the milky air.

The woman screams and darts back up the alley.

"Help. Help."

Her words dissolve into his skull, become his words.

A car door slams.

An engine grumbles awake.

Police sirens wail.

Shermeto squints as the alley erupts with light.

Footsteps crunch gravel. Dark figures running away, moving towards him.

Muffled conversation.

"He didn't hurt anyone." A female voice.

Soft breath against his face. "Thank you."

"Get up." Baritone.

He groans. His voice won't work.

Hands grip him under the armpits, lifting him off the ground. The last thing he remembers is the stars creating trails across the sky.

KENDRA

Kendra clicks through the photos on her computer screen. One after another. An endless display of holy matrimony. They aren't as bad as she expected. She selects a photo and plunks it into her photo editor. A bit of extra light here, shadow there. Warmer, cooler. She sits back, studies the image. It will do. Click and save and on to the next.

Her wedding had looked a little like these. Ten years ago. A lifetime. Baby Spice curls around her feet, meows and stretches up, paws on Kendra knees. *They have no idea what's coming*, she thinks. Right now, it's perfect bliss. If she hears the word soulmate ever again she will shove her tripod down their throat. Blah. Blah. Blah.

Baby Spice meows and rubs the desk leg, peers up with big orange eyes. "Come on then." Kendra pats her lap. The cat jumps up, noses Kendra's hands apart. The cursor flits across the screen, the cat's eyes dart after it. Her butt begins to wiggle.

"Don't even think about it." Kendra shoves the cat to the floor and pulls the chair up closer to the desk.

An email comes in from Sheila. She's been expecting it but had hoped for a couple more days. She's demanding her money back and Kendra doesn't blame her.

Another notification flits across the screen. *Sheila has left a Google Review. 1 Star.* Kendra doesn't read it. There's no point. Then a Yelp alert. This might be worse that she first imagined.

How long has she been doing this anyway? Sometimes it feels

like she was born with a camera and tripod strapped to her back; she doesn't remember ever wanting anything else. Only now she's bored and growing increasingly bitter. Maybe it's time to consider a career change.

Kendra shuts off the computer and leans back in the chair. "What would I even do?"

The cat parts her eyelids a fraction and closes them again.

"That's right. Nothing," Kendra says. Destined to be behind the lens the rest of her life because she doesn't have the balls to try anything else.

Books line the walls of her office. Coffee-stained photography books, uncracked novels.

James pushed too hard. This is as much on him. She'd become a squishy lump on a log. Don't poke it, it could be toxic inside. This is possibly the first time in her life where nothing demands her attention. No one to fix, no one to feel sorry for. Only herself. *Snap out of it*, she tells herself, over and over. This isn't who she's supposed to be.

She should call her sister. Go for a visit. Lily finally met a decent guy who packed her up and whisked her and Penny off to some suburb outside Toronto. Last report they were doing great. Good for her. She deserves some goodness.

Now it's just her and Baby Spice.

And the naked guy in her bed.

HockeyNut44, AKA Gary. They'd been out a few times, but this is the first time she'd invited him home. *Does that make her a slut?* What was she thinking allowing a man she barely knows into her house? A beer and chicken wings kind of guy. So different from sweater-vest guy, or that one with more product in his hair than she had in her whole house–what was his name? Right, Damian. So why is she downstairs working when there's a reasonably respectable man upstairs, who wants to put his face in her naughty places? Who hasn't yet drowned in her heaps of emotional baggage?

Well, fuck. She turns off the lights and heads upstairs to the bedroom. She hesitates in the doorway, eyeing the lump under her blankets, the subtle rise and fall with each breath. James slept like that. She envied his ability to fall into an unadulterated sleep almost the moment his head hit the pillow. She couldn't shut off that easily.

Kendra barely makes it back to bed when the phone rings. The home phone, not her cell phone. The only reason she still has it is because James insisted they retain a landline. Who does that anymore? No important calls ever come that way. Only telemarketers or bill collectors. *She'll call and disconnect it tomorrow*, she thinks as she grabs it on the fourth ring.

"Hello. Is this Kendra…? Sorry, I don't have a last name," says the woman on the other end.

"Yes, this is Kendra." She glances at the clock on the stove, incessantly blinking 12:00. "What time is it?"

"Almost 1:30am." The woman sounds out of breath. "Sorry for bothering you so late. I'm calling from Foothills Medical. We have a Delmore Shermeto in emergency. This number was with his belongings."

Breath catches in her throat.

"Is he alright?" Kendra's head spins, she can't think clearly.

"Yes. He's fine. He's been in an altercation." There's a crack in the woman's voice. "We're admitting him overnight for observation."

"Should I come?" That's the right thing to do, isn't it?

"I'm sure he'd like that."

"Thank you for calling." Kendra hangs up the phone and sinks into a kitchen chair. *Well, that's just perfect*. Right when she thinks life can't get any worse, her father worries his way back into her life. Gary emerges from the bedroom naked.

"Everything okay?" he asks. "Late night phone calls are rarely a good sign."

"You should probably go." Kendra can't feel her face. Her legs have gone numb. Her mind, a blur.

"Are you sure? I can stay."

The way the light catches his scrotum makes the whole package seem impressively larger. A shame she must cut it short, but does she?

Kendra shakes her head. "Stay." She slides her housecoat off her shoulder.

"That's what I'm talking about!" Gary disappears into the bedroom. Kendra follows close behind.

***

The Emergency doors slide open. She lingers outside, wishing she hadn't quit smoking.

Kendra stamps her feet on the mat and shakes rain off her coat. Fluorescent lights stab her eyeballs. The waiting area is surprisingly empty. A screen on the wall declares the current wait time to be nearly two hours, yet only three people fill the blue plastic chairs: a woman rocking a baby in a car seat with her foot, and a man beside her is flipping through a magazine too quickly to actually be reading.

It's been years since she's been in an emergency room, but nothing much has changed. Kendra makes her way to the information desk. The nurse looks up as she approaches.

"Can I help you?" the nurse says.

"My father was brought in earlier this evening."

"Last name?"

"Shermeto."

The nurse types something into the computer. "Is it still raining out?"

Surprised at the small talk, Kendra nods. Then, "I was told you were admitting him."

"There he is. Go through those doors and down the hall. Just past the station. He's in curtain seven. I'll buzz you in."

"Thanks."

On this side of the doors there's considerably more patients: sleeping in reclining chairs, waiting for beds, clicking through TV channels. A lot of coughing and gasping and the steady hum of machines. Doctors and nurses hover around a central desk. A nurse looks up without a smile. "Can I help you?"

"Curtain seven?" Kendra asks.

"Around the corner."

Through the part in the curtain a man lies on the bed, head lolled to one side. She gasps.

Jesus. That can't be him. Two years shouldn't leave him this unrecognizable. He's the right height, but it's hard to tell from this angle. She pulls the curtain apart, studies the monitor blipping silently beside the bed. The lines move evenly, perfectly spaced peaks. She doesn't know what the numbers mean.

A blanket is pulled up to his chin. She leans over him, hears a gentle wheezing. Not the man she remembers. Not even close. His face is bruised, swollen, one eye sewn shut. Stitches on his lip, his forehead. Where he used to be clean shaven, there is a full beard, matted and crusted with his own blood. More forehead than he used to have, gray-brown tufts of hair poke out behind his ears. She wants to cry out but is afraid to make a sound.

A nurse pops her head through the curtain. "Are you family?" she asks.

Kendra nods. "His daughter."

The woman enters, checks his bandages, jots something on a chart.

"They said he's being admitted?" Kendra says.

The nurse nods. "Waiting for a bed. He's going for a scan soon to make sure there are no internal injuries."

"What happened?"

"A fight, I guess." The nurse adjusts the IV bags, makes a note on his chart.

"Where'd they find him?"

"I don't know. Police brought him in. Said they found him in an alley. He was in and out of consciousness. Hasn't said a word to us yet."

An alley? Has he been living on the streets?

"That can't be right. He would never do that," Kendra says.

"Let's wait for him to wake up and he can tell us what happened." She squeezes Kendra's arm. "He'll be okay."

Kendra places her hand on the blanket at the foot of the bed and then pulls back. She's seen him in a bad state more times than she wants to admit, but never like this.

DAY TWO

THE RIVER

If the river could rewind, it would have heard the footsteps crackling through the brush and the ugly words bristling the leaves, slashing the air. "Dirty ugly skank. Come here, cunt."

The woman, dark tangles pressed against her face, gray streaks turned silver, staggered, sped up, slowed, tripping over her mistakes. She scrambled backward, elbows scraped, bloody.

"What did you say to him?"

Eyes blank. Confused.

"What. Did. You. Say?"

The river sputtered along the banks, lashing up on the shore. Not angry, but desperately wanting to help. The woman rolled onto her stomach and crawled away. Lost her balance again, mouth planting in the dirt. Blood sticky on her broken lip. The man knelt beside her, touched her cheek, soaking in the fear behind her eyes. She jolted, a hard right and hurled her body down the bank.

"Stop fighting. It will all be over soon." A soothing coo.

They stumbled through thick brush, the woman clawing through arms of knotted branches, the man blind in the darkness. He slipped but regained his footing.

Her heart pounded, a rhythmic drum, thrum-bump, thrum-bump. Back crawl crab-like. Branches grasped for her face, her hair. Legs turned heavy, the soggy earth slurping at her heels. She pressed into the hollow core of a tree, pulling the trunk tight around her. So much screaming. So much violence. Handfuls of earth ripped from the ground, dirt under her nails, in the creases of her hands.

"I only want to talk."

She groaned. "About what?"

"What you told him. What did you say?"

"Who?"

"You know who." He clutched a handful of her hair. She screamed. "Tell me."

"Don't know. What you're. Talking about." A glint of metal in her hand.

"Stupid, stupid woman." The man pocketed the scissors.

The moon retells the story while the river silently listens.

The rumble starts low, from the river bottom, and claws its way to the surface.

SHERMETO

Somewhere in between then and now, Shermeto was certain he died. There was Grace, as beautiful as ever, her hand to her face, pushing back a stray strand of hair. Beside her, Stevie dug in the sand, a big yellow Tonka truck burrowing holes bigger than his head. A flutter of laughter fell into the hole and Stevie quickly covered it with his hand, trapping it forever.

But Shermeto isn't dead. He's very much alive and his head hurts like a son-of-a-bitch. He's been slipping in and out of this dream state since he landed in the emergency room. He vaguely remembers flashing lights, a bunch of beeping machines, his clothes cut from his body and then being jetted off to another part of the hospital.

He heard her voice, or someone who sounded like her. What would she be doing here? Sometimes he felt warm, and then cold and then warm again. Right now, he's cold and his body feels like he's been dragged under a train. Can't open his mouth or eyes. Definitely alive. Were those fuckwits wearing steel-toed boots? Last time he tries to help someone. Next time…he can't gather his thoughts… next time…there won't be a next time.

A metallic vibrato echoes around him. His brain gives a command and his body applies the middle finger. Maybe he's a god-damned vegetable, a lemonhead. But that's a fruit. Still, the death card isn't completely off the table.

Shermeto cracks open his eyes—a sliver of sharp light slashes his retinas—and slams them shut.

He groans.

"You're awake." A statement. Not a question.

He opens his eyes slower this time and twists to the left: walls the colour of curdled milk, a white curtain with a strip the colour of dried blood at the top dangles from a track in the ceiling. Tubes hang from a bag of clear fluid and disappear under the blanket. He lifts the corner and inspects the spot where they feed into his arm. *Son of a nutfucker.*

Shermeto cranks his head to the right and winces. "I can't see you." The words scrape out. His throat feels like he gargled a handful of thumbtacks.

A flutter of movement. A hand reaches forward. Female. Short, evenly cut fingernails. Clean hands. A shoulder. A neck. A face. His stomach lurches. She's the same. Mostly. Brown curls sweep around her cheeks. Light spills through the half-open blinds, creating disjointed patterns across her skin.

"You got fat," he says.

She leans over him. Eyes narrow into questions. He's got no answers.

"Nice to see you, too. Do you need some water?" She hands him a Styrofoam cup, holds the straw to his mouth.

He slurps at the straw, not taking his eyes off her. Kendra looks so much like her mother he wants to yack.

"It's warm." He spits water onto the blanket.

"It's wet."

He pushes her hand away.

The plastic chair creaks as she sits. "You're lucky you're not dead," she says.

"The jury's still out on that one."

She fills his cup again.

He drinks the water. Colder this time. "You can leave now."

"Jesus, Dad. What happened to you?"

He shrugs, sending a stab of pain down his side. Kendra rolls her bottom lip between her teeth, just like her mother used to do.

"What do you want from me? Go away."

"Been here all night. Not going anywhere. An explanation would be nice."

"Don't owe you nothing. If I want help, I'll bloody well ask. Bug off."

Her body stiffens. "Lily is worried. We're all worried."

He chokes out a grunt. "Bullshit." He flings the blanket off his legs and tries to sit up. Pain tears through his side, forcing him back into the bed.

Kendra sighs and leans back in the chair. "Really, Dad. The streets?"

Shermeto wiggles his toes. At least he isn't paralyzed. That would be inconvenient. "What do you care?"

"You could have phoned. Anytime. I'd come get you," she says. "Were you drinking again?"

"For the love of Christ, Kendra, cut me some slack. Haven't had a drop in months." Technically true. Though not from lack of trying. He's an opportunistic drunk. "Where's the damn doctor? I want out of here."

"You're in no shape to go anywhere."

"I need to piss. Gonna stop me from doing that?"

"I'll get the nurse."

"I can do it myself." He tries again to sit up, but the pain is too much.

"Let me help."

She's trying to conceal a smirk, he thinks. Of course. Why wouldn't she be enjoying this? Aloud, "Don't tell me what I can and can't do. I can whiz when I want to."

Her eyes narrow and widen again. He wants to slap those stupid question marks off her face. All right. Yes. He's a terrible father. Not like he's been hiding it.

"I don't need your pity."

"There's a difference between pity and wanting to help. Whatever you need. You want a place to stay, I can do that. I've always been willing to do that. You want to take a piss, I can help you get your sorry ass out of bed. You only need to tell me what the hell you want."

Her eyes turn glossy and her face reddens.

Don't fucking cry. He hates criers. Why do girls always cry? Happy, sad. Angry, frustrated. Not getting what they want, turn on the guilt drops.

He closes his eyes. Wishes her away. Without words, of course, because he's a pathetic pansy who would fall for the guilt. He'd let her get the better of him, and then he'd let them down. Again. Not this time.

She's what? Thirty-something? He tries to do the math. If he's pushing sixty, and she was born—Jesus—when was she born? Forget it. He'll go with thirty.

"I bought you some things." She points to a cupboard tucked into the corner near the foot of the bed. "Not much. Some clothes. Toiletries."

"Where's the stuff I came in with?"

"The incinerator by now." Kendra closes her eyes, pinches the bridge of her nose between her fingers. For a long time, she doesn't look at him. *Can't blame her. He's not exactly the shining image of a father.*

"James left me."

"Always thought you could do better."

She looks at him but says nothing. Finally, she stands, "Where is that doctor?" She turns and leaves. The curtain divider rattles in its track.

The bleachy smell of the room is giving him a headache. And he wants a smoke. "You're kind of a dick to her, don't you think?"

Who the fuck? The curtain moves again, and a gray head appears. A man in the same hospital get-up as Shermeto. *Another prisoner in this antiseptic box.* The man pulls the curtain back and slides over a chair. He folds his arms over his chest and waits.

"She's only trying to help."

"I don't know you," Shermeto says. He counts the lights flush with the ceiling. One. Two. Three.

"I'm Walter. Looks like you took quite a beating. But you'll live."

That's what Shermeto's afraid of.

"You gonna tell me your name?" Walter says a moment later.

"No."

"Very well. It's going to be that kind of conversation, is it?"

Four. Five. There're cracks in the ceiling. Long and jagged. Scars.

"You're the first roomie I've had in weeks."

Probably talked them all to death. There's a water stain in the corner.

"You married? I was married. Fifty-six years. Lordy. Can't believe I kept my dick in my pants the whole time. One woman. Half a century. That's got to be some kind of record, don't you think?"

Shermeto yawns. His chest tightens.

"The kids stopped coming a long time ago. Moved myself into a retirement home. For the company."

Shermeto yawns again.

"You're tired."

The man is a rocket scientist.

"That home's a joke. Rules. Be in your room by this time, lights off. They dim automatically at eleven every night. What if I want to stay up with David Letterman?"

Not a very good one.

"Why are you here?" Shermeto asks.

"Bum ticker." Walter pats his chest. "It's ok. Had a good run. I'm ready." He looks hard at Shermeto. "What do you do?"

Kendra returns, followed closely by a doctor with a clipboard tucked under his arm. He's a matchstick of a man, with less hair than Shermeto and a carefully groomed mustache and beard. He's wearing blue jeans and a blue shirt under a white coat. The doctor lingers at the foot of the bed, arms at hip level, clutching the clipboard in his hands.

Walter pushes himself up from the chair and climbs back to his bed. Kendra pulls the curtain closed.

"Dad, this is Dr. Caskin."

Shermeto stares at the doctor. The doctor stares at him. *Is the bastard mocking him?*

"Delmore Edwin Shermeto?" The doctor says.

Shermeto cringes at the sound of his name. The last person who called him Delmore got kicked in the shin and given a wedgie. That was third grade. Since then everyone called him Del. That was until he changed his living arrangements.

"How are you feeling?"

"Like I got run over by a Zamboni."

The doctor laughs. Not a real laugh, a chuckle. A cluck.

"I imagine that's exactly how it would feel. You took quite a knock to the head. Some swelling, broken ribs, but you'll be all right. Looks worse than it is."

"When can I get out of here?"

"Not just yet." The doctor glances at Kendra then back at Shermeto. "The police said you did a brave thing."

Kendra's face freezes. Her head snaps toward him.

Shermeto snorts. "Stupid is more like it."

"Regardless, someone out there thinks you're a hero." The doctor glances at the chart. "Do you have someplace to go when you're released? Says here no fixed address. Is that correct?"

Shermeto nods.

"I can't discharge you until I know you have some place to go," the doctor says. "A shelter?"

Shermeto shakes his head. "No way. All thieves and bible bashers."

That isn't the only reason. The shelters are full of the desperate, the undernourished, the oversexed. Who wants to share a small cramped space with two or three others where you are as likely to get raped with a tube of toothpaste as get a hot meal? No, thanks. He'll take his chances outdoors. Make his own rules.

"He can stay with me," Kendra pipes up.

Can she not just shut up? Don't need her help. Not then. Not now.

"Is that a possibility?" the doctor asks.

He waits for Shermeto to say something but he's got nothing to say. Shermeto glares at Kendra.

"I'll take care of everything," Kendra says to the doctor then she leans over Shermeto, lowers her face to his ear and whispers, "If you want out of here, go along with it." Kendra turns back to the doctor, "When do you expect he can go?"

"A couple of days. Maybe tomorrow."

Kendra nods. "He'll stay with me."

Shermeto nods, forces a smile.

The doctor seems satisfied.

Kendra folds her arms over her chest.

"Could I have a moment alone with your father?" The doctor turns towards Kendra. "There's a cafeteria downstairs. Food's not so good, but the coffee is the best you'll find anywhere else."

"Of course." Kendra swings her bag over her shoulder. "I'll be back later."

When Kendra leaves the doctor checks the monitor and grabs a light from the wall behind him. He presses Shermeto's eyes apart. The light stabs his eyeball, straight through to his brain.

"It hurts."

The doctor nods. "I'll send a nurse in shortly." Chair legs scrape the floor as he pulls a seat up to the bed. "Right now, we need to talk." His jaw tightens—square, rigid—chewing carefully on his next words. "We had to run some tests. Standard procedure when someone comes in with possible head trauma or internal injuries. We drained the fluid from your knee cap. I am surprised you were even able to walk." He pauses, checks the chart, the monitor. "While not all the tests are back yet, we found some cause for concern. I think you may already be aware of this..." The doctor pulls out a blue folder. Shermeto's seen that folder before.

"I believe you know Dr. Davidson over at the cancer centre?"

Too well. Shermeto nods.

"He wants to see you. He'll be by tomorrow."

Ain't that special. A reunion.

"I've heard the spiel. I know the prognosis. I'm going to die."

In fact, he thought it would have already happened, but three years later and he's still standing. How's that for fucking statistics?

"What stage am I now?"

"I can't say. Dr. Davidson is reviewing the results." He taps the pages in front of him. "Liver cancer. I suspect you already knew that."

"I'm aware." Shermeto presses his eyelids closed and wishes for everyone to leave him alone.

"You could have received treatment. What happened?"

"I'd like to be alone now," Shermeto says.

The doctor nods and stands. "Get some rest. We'll talk tomorrow. I'll send a nurse in to give you something for the pain."

Shermeto has no intention of hanging around.

KENDRA

This is a good thing, Kendra thinks as she climbs back into the car. She digs her phone from her purse. One missed call from James, a dozen texts from Gary. She reads through the texts and smiles. Considers calling him then drops the phone on the seat beside her. This is what she's been waiting for and now she has things to do. The last time she felt this focused…well, hell, she can't remember.

The parking lot is packed. *How can there be so many sick people?* Water drops cling to her windshield. At least it's stopped raining for a bit. She scrolls through the texts: Gary asking for an update, does she want to get lunch or dinner later.

It's too easy, she thinks. Her father never agreed to anything this quickly. And if she can't make him listen this time, when will there be a next time? Should there be a next time? Kendra squeezes her eyelids tight. *This is ridiculous.* She thrusts the car into gear and backs out of the parking spot.

The phone rings.

It's James.

"What?" she says. A car horn blares and she slams on the brakes.

"You around? Will come get my stuff."

"It's not a good time." She pulls back into the parking spot. "I'm at the hospital."

James is silent for a long time. "Are you okay?" he asks.

"It's not me," she says. "Dad."

"Oh. What happened?" James asks.

"Do you actually care?"

"I'm not a total asshole, despite what you may think."

"I'm sorry." The fight begins to slip away from her. "You always kept my head on straight. I don't know how to do this without you."

"You'll be fine. You always are."

"I'll be home in about an hour."

"See you soon."

***

Tired, aching trees, trampled by an excessively soggy summer, line the streets and shoot up between century homes. Aged, weather-beaten, they still sell for more pennies than she'll ever see. Not that it matters. Kendra prefers the suburbs where people walk their dogs three times a day, greet you with a smile and nod. She'll take that any day over these close, cramped streets. The one ways, no ways.

She takes the on-ramp to Memorial Drive, running parallel to the river. A smooth shot home—or not—up ahead, bumper-kissing traffic.

"Goddammit." She rolls down the window, fans her face with her hand. A warm breeze floats up off the river, bringing the smell of wood rot and decay. Inch by slow inch, she moves forward. Taillights blinking on and off in front of her.

Along the pathway to her right a man pushes a shopping cart over-filled with black garbage bags, among the runners doing laps around Prince's Island Park, and the casual walkers out enjoying the break from the rain. The bags are piled so high he can't see where he's going. Is that what Dad's been doing, living like this? Desperation clinging to the soles of his boots, dragged behind him like a piece of toilet paper. Why? He doesn't have to; he has a place to go.

A car honks. Kendra glances up. Two car lengths spread between her and the vehicle ahead. Steam coils up from the damp road. The air even tastes wet. The river lies between her and the city, sweeping frantically along its path. Spring runoff now bearing down on the city, bringing seasons of debris. She saw the mayor on the news the other day, warning those in flood zones to be ready, followed by images of people building sandbag walls to protect their expensive homes along the Elbow.

The river looks agitated, the water edging up to meet the bottoms of pedestrian bridges. *Still a ways to go*, she thinks. *People worry too much.*

Up ahead a firetruck blocks the right lane. Police cars nose up to the bank. An ambulance. Emergency responders cluster together on the ridge where yellow tape wraps around trees. Kendra cranes to see what's going on as she inches the car along. Four men in medic uniforms roll a sheet-covered stretcher down the short bank.

***

Up and down her street are ranchers, bungalows, split levels, all with carefully manicured lawns. Her own lawn is a disaster. She cuts the engine in the driveway and stares out at the grass, at least four inches longer than all the rest. No flowers, no landscaping, no curb appeal. No metaphorical white picket fence. No two and a half kids.

Baby Spice greets her at the door, purring, then flops on her side and stretches to expose her white belly.

"At least someone is happy to see me."

Kendra smiles and rubs the cat until Baby Spice nips at her hand. She lifts her into her arms and wanders into the kitchen. Dishes from this morning still scatter the counter. An empty food dish next to the fridge. Baby Spice jumps to the floor and mews as Kendra fills her water and scoops kibble into the bowl.

"Don't be greedy. You had breakfast."

Baby Spice turns her rear to Kendra and stalks from the room. When Kendra is home alone, she wanders around shutting off lights, turning them back on. She talks to herself more than she wants to admit. Answers herself sometimes too. She has her work, but everyone else's happiness is beginning to crush her. She considered giving up the weddings for portraits or baby photography. Newborns, not maternity photos. Her father loved nature, but that didn't pay as well.

Look for and capture the meaning in the random. Because life is random. It's not posed the way you want it to be. It doesn't have the right light all the time, nor the right texture. You have to find it. Create it. That's where the real power is. See beyond what's in front of you.

Words from her father she hadn't thought about in years. He'd been so smart; she'd admired him.

James will be here soon. He can't see her like this. She splashes water on her face and heads outside. The lawnmower is next to the shed. Kendra leans over the machine checking the gas level. It's full.

She grabs the pull cord. Nothing. She pulls again. Still nothing. The third time there's a small sputter but the machine gives up before it starts.

"Come on." She screams and yanks the cord again. Three times in quick succession, the way she'd seen her father do it.

Back when they were all together: Mom, Dad, her, Lily and little Steven. In the summer she followed her father behind the lawnmower barefoot until her toes turned green, then they would all roll in the grass clippings. That was until Lily broke out in a serious rash over her whole body and couldn't stop itching for weeks. Mom had slathered butter all over her body and they'd joked she could go outside and baste.

Kendra's shoulder hurts and sweat gathers on her forehead but the machine finally roars awake and she stands back, gasping. "Finally."

The backyard isn't really a yard but a paved patio flush with the ground with rarely used patio furniture and an enclosed fire pit. The pit had been her idea, imagining family gatherings around the BBQ. Turns out one needs a family to start with.

She and James had argued over it in the store. He thought it wasn't practical and would never get used, and she promised it would.

"You just wait and see," she'd said. She hated it when he was right. Too tired after work, she'd be busy processing photos, not caring if she ever saw another breathing human. If he wasn't reviewing briefs and writing contracts, James would plunk himself in front of the television or stare for hours at his phone. It hadn't always been that way. They bought the house before they married. The perfect first home. They painted the walls together, James laid laminate flooring, she decorated the baby's room.

The lawnmower carves a path from the back to the front, around and around. Her feet are soaked after the first pass. She scans the street for James. The front yard isn't huge. Four passes are all it should take, but on the third time around the lawnmower sputters and dies. Grass sticks to her shoes and the hem of her pants.

A huge pickup truck she's never seen before pulls into the driveway. James hops from the cab, sunglasses perched on his nose.

"Nice job." He nods at the lawn.

His hair is shorter, and he might have a tan.

"It stopped working."

"Grass is too wet."

She glances past him to the truck, thankful he at least came alone.

"Here. Let me help." James lays the lawnmower on its side. "See."

Large clumps of wet grass have clogged the blades. He drops it back over and with one tug of the cord, the machine roars back to life. While James finishes the lawn, Kendra returns to the house and pours two glasses of iced tea. When the machine silences, she meets James in the back.

"You'll probably want to rake up the clippings," he says.

Kendra nods and hands him one of the glasses.

"Is there much left?"

"A few boxes."

He takes a drink then sets the glass on top of the BBQ. "Thanks."

Kendra follows James into the shed. He pulls boxes from a metal cabinet and separates them.

"Aren't those yours?" Kendra asks.

"No. Think that's your dad's things."

She'd forgotten about those. The few boxes that remained after Dad's roommate sold off anything of value to cover his share of the rent. Camera. Computer. Lights. Reflectors. Only two boxes. She'd brought them home and tucked them in the cabinet, unopened.

"I'll go through them later."

James grabs a box and heads out the door. She grabs another one and follows.

"You don't need to do that."

"I want to." Kendra sets the box on the ground and leans against the truck. "How are you doing?" she asks.

James shrugs, drops the boxes into the back of the truck.

"So when's the wedding?"

James snaps around. "What are you doing?"

"Conversation. Something wrong with that?"

"Think we're past the small talk, don't you?"

His words sting more than she wants to admit. He heads back. Kendra doesn't follow. It's like him to turn it all around on her. He gave up first. So really, what does she expect him to say? Admit he's terrible and can't live without her? That he made a mistake and wants to come home? That he wants to help? Yes. A part of her wishes for that. But it wouldn't change anything. She runs her hands through her hair. James returns with a couple more boxes, plunks them on the ground.

"Think that's it," he says. "Do you need anything else?"

Stay, she wants to say. *Come inside.* The words form in her mind, but stick hard to her tongue. She shakes her head. James climbs in the cab.

The sun seems higher. Hotter.

"What happened to us?" The question more rhetorical, nostalgic.

James leans out the window. "You'll be fine. It's better this way."

There's a sadness in his eyes. Is that regret? He does miss her, but even she knows it's too late.

He reaches beside him and hands her an envelope.

"Everything's in order. You just need to sign."

Her throat begins to constrict, her vision blurs. She knew it was coming but why now? Why today?

James backs out of the driveway and she waits for him to fade into nothing at the end of the street before running back into the house. She slams the door and locks it, tosses the envelope onto the table and sinks into a chair, tears streaming down her cheeks.

***

They married in the spring. An outdoor wedding in his parents' backyard. A small affair. His parents, her father and sister, a couple of friends and the fetus growing inside her. No one knew except James. They planned to wait until after the wedding to tell anyone. Neither wanted to be those people who only got married because of a baby. His parents already didn't think she was good enough for their son. A pregnancy would only complicate it more. But in truth, they loved each other, were already planning on getting married, the date only moved up a little bit.

A few weeks later, while on a photoshoot in Fish Creek Park, she fell to her knees clutching her stomach, the pain unbearable. The couple, bless them, rushed her to the nearest hospital. James arrived a short time later. Clearly, he already knew, or expected the worst.

"At least you're okay."

He laid his head on her stomach, kissed her gently on the forehead. But she didn't feel okay. She'd failed him and suddenly she worried that maybe he didn't really love her, and this was the only thing holding them together.

"We'll try again," he said.

***

Kendra pulls herself together, tucks the envelope into a drawer and sends Gary a quick text before slipping out to the shed. It's raining again, and the garage is cold. Water drips through the seams in the roof, leaving small puddles on the floor. The boxes are where James left them. She considers dumping it all in the garbage. *Can't really be anything worth keeping in there.*

Kendra opens the first box.

"Holy crap."

It's like she's been slapped by the stench of raw meat and fermented apples. A couple of sweaters lay on the top. Kendra pulls them out and tosses them on the floor.

Loose papers, past due bills, disconnection notices from the house they lived in as kids, mismatched socks, one shoe, safety pins and an old electric razor with so much hair caught in the teeth she doubts it works. All garbage.

On the bottom of the box an apple carcass has withered and dried, its stain soaked into a brown envelope. She plucks the apple off the envelope and tosses it with the rest of the garbage. A stack of photos falls out of the envelope into her lap. Mostly black and whites, 8x10 and 5x7 images of her family. How it used to be.

Stevie at six years old, a gap-toothed smile and an ice cream cone. Her mother, lying on a blanket, hand shading her eyes, peers coyly up at the camera, her sunhat propped on her stomach. All three kids, organized by size, are sitting in the shade of a tree. She doesn't remember when the photo was taken, but she thinks Stevie's about eight. Right before the accident.

She lingers longer than she should on the photo. So much would have been different if he hadn't died. Her mother might still be here. Her father too. The whole family, close and connected.

Kendra shakes the thought away and stuffs the pictures back in the envelope. She sticks them in the keep pile. The next box has more papers. Contracts from photo shoots, more bills, and a blue folder with 'Shermeto, D' printed on the tab. She flips through the sheets: a series of test results. A radiation and chemo schedule. Appointments most definitely missed. She checks the dates again. Three years.

***

Folder in hand, she scrambles back to the house, grabs her purse and keys just as the doorbell rings.

"Not now," she mutters and opens the door.

Gary is standing there, rain glistening off his coat, hair plastered to his head, and a giant grin on his face. He holds up a bag of Chinese food.

"Thought you might be hungry," he says.

"Shit." Kendra freezes. "Forgot you were coming."

"Should I laugh or be hurt?"

She smiles. "Something's come up."

"Nothing can be so important that you can't eat first." He waves the bag in front of her. "It's Chinese." He grins.

She thinks about the folder, about getting to her father, but Gary's right. Nothing's going to change whether she gets back to the hospital now or later. And he'll likely deny it, even with proof in her hands.

She hesitates. She shouldn't bring Gary into this, she thinks. It's not his problem. But the way he stands there, head cocked slightly to one side, the shit-eating, up-to-no-good grin spread across his face, how can she resist?

Gary drops the bag on the kitchen table and rummages through the cupboards for plates. "What's that?"

Kendra slides her jacket over the folder. "Nothing important."

"You were rushing out the door, clutching that in your hand. It's definitely something."

She stares at the folder. All her father's betrayal stuffed inside. Did he really think no one would ever find out? What was he thinking? Why wouldn't he say anything? Too proud. Too stubborn. But she's almost the only family he has left.

Gary opens the containers and sits down, making himself at home. Too comfortable for her liking but he doesn't seem like he's going anywhere.

"So?"

He kicks out the chair next to him. She sits down.

***

"I've been telling everyone he's dead." Kendra shakes her head. "Who does that?"

"Did you believe it?" Gary spoons rice into his mouth.

Kendra shrugs. It wasn't a stretch. And if she hadn't answered the phone, he could have stayed dead.

"What happened?"

"I don't know."

"I don't believe that."

Kendra studies Gary's face, the sincerity behind his eyes. "What did I do to piss off the world?"

"Stop making this about you."

He isn't being mean, but the words sting nonetheless.

Baby Spice saunters into the kitchen, gazes up at Kendra and lets out a desperate mewl.

"Hungry, again?" Kendra grabs a can of wet cat food. The cat curls around her feet.

"Spoiled brat."

The empty can *thuds* to the bottom of the garbage. She leans against the counter and watches the cat devour the food. Gary's back is to her.

"I haven't seen him in a couple years," she finally says. "He showed up here, drunk and dirty. His roommate had kicked him out and he moaned about how it wasn't his fault."

***

He'd barreled in, sweating beer and piss, like he owned the place. The stench made Kendra gag as they sat around the kitchen table. A mix of BO and musty, sour rot seeping from his insides.

"When's the last time you showered?"

James had no problem being brutally honest. Direct. He felt that's what her father needed because god forbid Kendra ever told him how it really was. Her father ignored him.

"Archie's being an asswipe. Can't stand being around that guy no more. It's his way or no way."

"It is his house; he has that right," Kendra said.

Her father rolled his eyes. "Whose side you on anyway?"

"Not taking sides," she said.

She set a bowl of homemade macaroni and cheese on the table in front of him.

"I don't know what you expect me to say." She searched James's face for support but got nothing. He just scooped food into his mouth and chewed quietly.

After dinner she made up the couch for him to crash.

"You need to get your shit together."

"I know." Her father hung his head.

"What you're doing isn't working and we can't keep helping you."

"Never asked for your help."

James appeared in the hall. "You don't ask for help, you demand it by coming around when it suits you. Only when you need something."

"Who asked you?"

Her father stood stone still, searching for more words but none ever came. James slammed the bedroom door. Kendra stood in the hallway a moment longer then followed James. There was nothing more to say.

By morning he was gone. No note. Nothing. She wondered where he'd gone off to but didn't even bother to find out. A couple weeks passed before she finally tried to visit but Archie hadn't seen him in weeks, so Kendra had gathered his belongings and brought them home, a big part of her relieved that she didn't have to choose any longer.

***

"What could you have done?"

Gary's elbows press into the table, taking in every word.

"I could have tried harder."

Deep down she knows this isn't true. She'd done everything she possibly could. He'd been taking everything from her since her mother died and she let him.

Gary leans back in the chair. "This isn't your fault."

Kendra wishes she could believe him. "I don't know what to do."

Gary stands suddenly. "First of all, let's get that room ready. If he's coming home now, he'll need a place to sleep."

Kendra picks at the edges of the folder.

"That file's not going anywhere. Get him home first."

Kendra leads Gary to the basement.

"Nice set up," he says as they pass through her office. A series of framed photos of the downtown skyline hang from the walls. "You've got a great eye."

"Another lifetime."

The spare room is full of boxes piled in the corner, clothes meant for the donation bin, old blankets, scattered across the bed. Extra camera equipment: tripods, reflectors, backdrops tucked in a corner, mostly forgotten.

Gary drags the gear into her office and then together they move everything else into the laundry room. Bags of clothes and old blankets get stuffed into bags and Gary immediately takes them upstairs.

"We'll take them to the drop-in centre."

"Good idea," Kendra says.

She strips and changes the bed, scrubs the window ledge and baseboards then stands in the middle of the room. "Something's missing," she says. Then it hits her. She runs outside and brings in some of the envelopes full of photos and spreads them out on a table.

"Whoa," Gary says. "Are these yours too?"

Kendra shakes her head.

"Damn, these are great." Gary picks up a picture of a young boy. "Who's this?"

"My brother."

"I didn't know you had a brother." He studies the photo.

"And a sister." She pauses. "He's gone."

Gary raises an eyebrow.

"Died a long time ago."

"I'm sorry." He drops the photo. "And your sister?"

"Toronto."

"Are you close?"

"We were once."

"You never talk about your mother."

"Nothing to talk about. She's dead."

She expects Gary to turn and bolt from the house. Who wants to be around that much baggage?

"That sucks. Was she sick?"

"She was sad."

He nods. "The worst that's happened to me is when my mom ran over my dad's foot with the lawnmower. He still won't let her forget it."

SHERMETO

The nurse rolls into the room behind a cart full of bandages, oint-
ments and a little paper cup. Her name tag reads Bonnie. *Bonnie
with purple hair and nostrils as thin as chewed straws. It's a wonder
she can even breathe.* Her lips rest in an emotionless smirk, eyes
dead as owl pellets.

Without a word she begins to remove bandages from his face,
ripping off and tossing the old bloody and yellow gauze onto the
cart.

Shermeto winces as she presses new pads into place, stretches
tape across his bruised skin.

"Any pain?" she asks.

"What do you think?"

She hands him a small paper cup holding two round pills along
with a cup of water. He swallows the pills down dry.

"Do you need anything else?" she asks.

"Need to take a leak and you got any food around this place?"

Bonnie checks her watch. "Dinner will be around shortly. Can
you stand?"

Shermeto shakes his head. If he could he'd have been gone ages
ago.

"You need to get up." Curt. Precise. "Not going to get any better
just lying there."

Bonnie reaches her arm around his shoulder and guides him to
sitting. He strains and groans; he can't remember ever being in this

much pain. Knives slashing at his sides, needles stabbing his face. He lies back again.

Visibly annoyed, Bonnie presses a button and the head of the bed begins to rise until he's sitting upright.

"The sooner you're on your feet, the sooner you can get out of here. It's no difference to me. But you will need to walk out of here." She refills his water jug. "I'll get you a wheelchair."

"I'll do it on my own."

Bonnie stands at the end of the bed, arms folded. Smug. Shermeto grits his teeth and dangles his feet over the edge of the bed. He lowers himself to the floor. One step and then another, dragging the IV pole along with him. Hurts like a motherfucker, but he isn't about to tell her that.

The curtains around Walter's bed are pulled tight but Shermeto can hear the man wheezing. Maybe Walter's worse off than he let on.

The bathroom light flickers and brightens. Bonnie tries to enter the bathroom behind him but Shermeto slams the door, hopefully smashing that smug look right off her face.

Bad light, he notes, passing the mirror. Jaundiced. He can't tell what exists under the purple bruises bulging from his skin.

He straddles the toilet, bracing with one hand against the wall. With the other, he digs under the hospital gown, finds his junk and aims.

A shower is tucked into the corner of the bathroom, curtain draped over the front. He sniffs under his arms. When was the last time he showered?

Shermeto strips off the hospital gown and pokes his head into the shower. Big and shiny and white. Clean. Unstained. His heart shudders a moment, a glimpse of a memory he doesn't want.

Water spits from the shower head, falling in a steady stream. He touches the tender red boil under his arm, the infection spreading towards his armpit then yanks out the IV, ignoring the blood drops, and climbs into the shower.

The new bandages on his face become soaked. *Bonnie's not going to be happy about that.* He peels them off, dropping them on the floor outside the shower. *Those assholes really did a number on him.* There're bruises in places he didn't even know existed.

Shermeto closes his eyes. So how bad is it now? Three years, and he's still kicking. Cancer is supposed to attack and destroy, like it did his mother. Only three weeks from diagnosis to finding her slumped in her chair. She was only supposed to be taking a nap.

"We found a mass on your liver," the doctor had said.

He couldn't silence the buzzing in his head as he sat across the desk from Dr. D. With hair pulled back in a ponytail, he didn't look like a doctor. Too young. He should have had a guitar strapped to his back and been passing around a hash pipe. This guy, no older than his son would be right now.

"Sounds bad," Shermeto said.

Dr. D studied the file folder in front of him.

Shermeto imagined the doctor struggling over paint samples. This brown, or maybe this one. Then the painters come and carefully cover the office walls with the colour of creamed coffee. There're worse browns he could've chosen.

Diplomas and certificates hung evenly apart, supposed proof that the man across the table knew what he was talking about. *Listen to this man. He'll save your life.* But maybe he didn't want to be saved. Did they ever think of that?

"Stage One. We caught it early."

Behind the doctor stood shelves of books, titles only the doctor could understand. Medical texts. Lymphomas and carcinomas. On the top, peering down like it was ready to spit pins from its mouth, was a wooden Indian mask. Maybe Incan or Mayan. Voodooish for sure.

"From gout to cancer. Feels like a radical jump."

Kendra had made him go to the hospital because of the unrelenting gout knee. A series of tests and there he sat.

"Will I die?"

"Likely not for a long time. We have options. Surgery. Chemotherapy. Radiation."

"How long?" Shermeto asked.

"Sorry?"

"Until I die."

"Stay away from alcohol. So far it's only in your liver. I'd like to surgically remove the mass then begin a course of radiation."

"If we did none of that, how long until it's over?"

The doctor stared hard at Shermeto. "Depends on a lot of factors. Without treatment it will spread. Five years. Maybe more, maybe less." He laid his pen down on the desk and folded his hands in front of him. "I don't think you understand. It's early. We go this course and those numbers look far better. Maybe even double."

"You can't know that."

"You're right. I don't know how aggressive it is, but I'd like to try." He paused. "Do you have a support system at home? Family? Friends?"

Shermeto picked at a callous on his palm. "No surgery."

"You should tell them. Let them know what's going on. It's a big decision."

"Thanks, Doc. Is that all?" Shermeto stood, his knee throbbing worse than ever before. "Can I get a copy of that?" He nods to the file on the doctor's desk. "Would be easier to explain to the family."

The doctor had relented, but Shermeto never told anyone.

Now, he shuts off the shower and grabs a towel. On the other side of the door, voices erupt in laughter. Bonnie is with Walter and there's a hint of gravy lingering in the air. He follows the smell back to his bed. A covered tray sits on the table.

"Sly old man," Bonnie says.

"Kid you not," Walter says.

"Can I get you anything else? A coffee? An extra bun?"

"No need to give this old coot any special treatment." Walter laughs.

Shermeto climbs back into bed. The sheets are cold but soft. Bonnie appears at the foot of the bed.

"So, you're walking all right?" she asks. She rolls a machine up to the bed and straps a cuff around his arm, her face pinching in disapproval as she inspects the spot where the IV used to be while inflating the cup around his arm.

Shermeto lifts the lid off the tray. The cuff fills with air and squeezes his arm. Meat slathered in gravy and onions and a plop of mashed potatoes that looks like that sludge in the gutters after a hard rain. He doesn't care. Today he eats like a king. He tears the bun apart and dips it in the potatoes.

"Your heartrate is elevated." She tears off the cuff and makes some notes on his chart.

"No kidding. Walked a marathon to get to the crapper."

"And don't you feel better?" She replaces the bandages on his face and the IV.

"Could I get an extra bun?" Shermeto stuffs the ball of dough in his mouth.

"That's all there is." She turns on her heal and leaves the room.

The meat is tough, doesn't even look real. Gravy drips down his chin into his freshly cleansed beard. He'd give his left nut for a razor. Maybe the right one too.

The mashed potatoes are gritty, the fruit cup too sweet, the syrup stings his lips and the coffee is no longer hot. Yet he swallows every bit and wishes for more.

Walter calls from behind the curtain. "You want my bun?"

***

Shermeto spends the next hour wishing he hadn't taken the bun as his stomach roils and screams back at him. The conversation is relentless, the only relief being that Walter didn't seem bothered by the one-sidedness. It gives Shermeto plenty of time to concoct a plan. Finally, after the sun has gone down, Walter grows tired of his own voice and begins to snore. Shermeto closes his eyes and waits for the whispers in the hall to fade. Kendra flashes in his mind. And then Grace. Too many memories coming at him all at once, he can't take it. The quiet is too loud. He rips out the new IV. The floor is cold against his feet, his ass hanging out of the gown. He makes his way, slowly but upright, to the cupboard in the corner.

There's a backpack on the shelf, a pair of hiking boots beside it, soles intact, the newness of which he knows will blister his feet within seconds. He pulls the backpack down and dumps the contents onto the bed. A stick of deodorant, socks, underwear, a t-shirt, pants, a new hoody with a Canadian flag on the front and a small Nikon digital camera. *What's he supposed to do with this?* he thinks. Does Kendra believe this is the answer to all his problems? He drops the camera back in the bag.

In the outside pocket of the pack he finds his wallet. The same wallet he'd unwrapped many Christmases ago, a gift from Penny, though she was too young at the time to have chosen it herself. From the colour of the leather, the number of slots for cards and money, and the leaves punched into the front, it was more Lily's style. It's faded along the edges and molded to the shape of his back pocket, but it's his. Everything appears intact, along with a few new bills that Kendra must have tucked in there. He drops the wallet on the bed and strips off the hospital gown, struggles into the hoodie until the fleece falls soft against his scrubbed skin. The pants are way too big. He cinches the waist tight with the also-new belt. He tucks the wallet into his back pocket.

It'll take days to break in the boots, but his only other choice is to go barefoot and that's never a good idea. He stuffs his feet inside and leaves the laces undone for no other reason than when he tries to bend to tie them, his stomach muscles pinch, or a rib threatens to stab his lungs. His jean jacket drapes over the arm of the chair, dark blood stains on the front and down the arms. His blood. That can stay.

He slings the pack over his shoulder and checks up and down the hall. The floor is empty, the lights dimmed. There's an emergency exit right next to him, but that means stairs. On the other hand, to get to the elevator he'll have to pass the desk, and if Bonnie's there he won't make it far. He considers his options. One not more favourable than the other. A clock juts out from the wall, about six inches from the ceiling. 23:43 in glowing red numbers.

He pushes open the emergency exit. No alarms sound.

Fortunately, according to the big white "3" painted on the wall in the stairwell, he doesn't have far to go. He makes his way down the concrete shaft, hanging tight to the handrail, each step like a swift kick to the gut, pain radiating from his kneecaps.

The main floor hallway is empty, a straight shot to the front door. No one at the information desk would know he's going AWOL. And would they even care? *Just act natural.*

He straightens his shoulders and marches down the hallway. The desk is empty, and he easily slips outside just as his legs are about to buckle. He grabs onto a planter and catches his breath. The wind picks up. The stars, if they're up there, are covered by thick clouds. He smells the rain, teetering on the cusp of another drenching day. He shrugs back into the jacket, rolls the long sleeves up to his wrists and limps across the parking lot.

There's a bus stop down the street, but he only has the few bills Kendra gave him. Bus drivers don't make change and he outright refuses to waste money on an over-priced ride by some turban-wearing immigrant. The walk will take him all night and it will hurt, but it's not like he's got anywhere else to be. Nothing else to do.

A wave of dizziness catches him off guard and he stops, waits for the nausea to pass. For a moment, Shermeto considers stumbling back inside, but what good would it do? No one can heal him, no one can make it all go away.

He makes his way through the parking lot, around the herd of grazing cars to the street. There are no ambulances hurrying to save a precious life, no panic-stricken parents, no woman about to launch a baby out her twat. Only clouds, patiently waiting for the right moment to open and let it all pour out.

He thinks about death a lot, his death. Will he simply slip away, like falling into a deep sleep, with no notice or will he be ripped apart by it? He'd even considered all the ways to suicide. He doesn't do drugs, never could handle the hallucinations or the dry mouth. The alcohol might have done it, but lack of funds and…Harlow. Fuck he misses Harlow. Can still see his blue lips, his eyes frozen open, dull. He shakes the image from his mind and focuses on the dark houses where people sleep innocently, arrogantly unaware of what goes on in the night.

Gravel kicks out under his feet, the steady *shush shush* of his boots scrapes the ground, fractures the night. Something moves in the bushes. Shermeto freezes. A critter ambles into the road, black with a long white stripe down its back, tail raised. It offers a curious glance then slinks away. Indifferent. No threat to one another.

The skunk knows.

Shermeto knows.

The skunk nuzzles through a garbage bag propped up on some old tires. The bag drops, and the skunk's fear fills the air. Shermeto gags, his eyes begin to water. His fear smells nothing like that.

A few houses down, the smell dissipates. Shermeto stops and lifts the lid of a garbage can. Nothing but paper and cardboard. No bottles. No cans. He slams the lid down.

He emerges from the alley and crosses the street, standing on the hillside overlooking a highway. A pedestrian bridge spans the width of the road, cars whip back and forth underneath. Stairs dip down the hillside, buried under overgrown weeds, decrepit arms reaching out to cut off his path. He studies the traffic below: headlights, tail-lights, steadily back and forth. He stares at the road. *It's not the fall that'll kill you, it's the sudden stop at the bottom*, he thinks. *Suicide by splat. Knowing his luck, he'd crush a toe, break a leg.*

The ramp descends behind a soundproof wall and he is once again enclosed in the back pocket of more row houses. A dog barks. A cat perches on a fence watching bats dart around in the blackness, and the closer he gets to the city centre, the older the homes become. There are old cars up on blocks, parked against faded and broken fences.

Once he tried to poison himself with wild mushrooms but instead spent most of the night in the bushes, squatting over dead brush, pissing out his asshole.

A cab rolls past him, pulling into a darkened gas station. The engine silences, the headlights go out. The driver gets out and disappears around the opposite side of the building. A couple minutes later he returns, zipping his pants as he hurries back to the car. He doesn't get back inside, but instead leans against the car door, lights a cigarette and flips through his smartphone. Shermeto steps forward. Kicks a rock across the parking lot. The man turns, eyes wide. He moves to extinguish the cigarette but seems to think twice about. He reaches into his pocket and pulls out the pack. He places it on the hood of the car and gives it a shove. The cardboard slides down the back window and lands on the trunk. Shermeto snatches it and pulls one out then tries to hand it back. The driver shakes his head.

"Keep it."

Shermeto nods and tucks the pack into his pocket.

"Need a light?"

"Please."

The man lights the cigarette for Shermeto.

"Quiet night," the cab driver says.

"Never quiet enough."

They smoke in silence until fat raindrops get fatter, breaking apart on the windshield. The cab driver crushes out his cigarette.

"You need a ride somewhere?" the cab driver asks. "It's gonna be another wet one. Never seen rain like this in a long time."

He's obviously not from around here, Shermeto thinks. "I'm fine. Not far to go now."

"Have a good night then."

The car pulls out of the parking lot, brake lights flaring red, blinking through the steady sheet of rain now coming down. The canopy is hammered by the downpour. The gas station won't open for several more hours. He can stay here and wait it out.

He won't admit it aloud, but it was nice to see Kendra; he only wishes it was under better circumstances. She would have done anything for him. Her way of making it right. Not that she needs to. None of this is her fault though he knows she carries that burden and he's never done a lick to convince her otherwise.

She's going to be pissed that he took off.

***

The Peace Bridge stretches its web across the river, one of many connections between the outskirts and an energy-hungry city. He studies the lines, the way the moon reflects off the glass, the red dancing off the surface of the water. Lights flicker on and off in the office towers high overhead. Shermeto remembers the city long ago, when the world was slower; more peaceful. The early hours of the morning are the only time of the day where he can almost recapture that bliss. Soon the Car2Gos will start going. The SUV's, delivery vans, transit grumbling. All honking unappreciative demands, weaving through the streets in a high-priced, oil slick line-dance. Don't they know the bottom will eventually fall out? It always does.

Shermeto's home is on the banks of the river in an overgrown shroud of trees, where the leaves and shrubs are higher than his kneecaps. The perfect spot to forget and be forgotten. In the spring and summer his camp goes unnoticed except by those who know where to look, or river enthusiasts and fishermen. In the winter, when the leaves shed, it's a little less private but the brambles are still thick enough to offer him ample privacy. Sometimes he spots teen lovers desperate for some kink, a stoner looking for a quiet place to get high. It's safe here. As safe as one can be living rough.

Shermeto pulls his hood up over his head and finds his footing down the bank. The rain makes his movements unsteady. He carefully tests each slippery step, so he won't land ass over tea kettle in the brambles and stinging nettle. It happened once, over two years ago. Granted he'd shared a bottle of the cheapest whiskey with Gerard and then stumbled home. Harlow found him the next morning face down in the spongy muck. Spent the next week in unbearable pain trying to rub away the nettle. He doesn't want to go through that again.

He reaches the ground below, lets out a sigh of relief and then picks his way through the brush. The camp is empty. A tarp drapes from a branch, lashed to a thick trunk with frayed rope. A layer of mesh netting is stretched haphazardly over the tarp, hanging low to the ground to keep out anything with wings. Not much he can do about the crawlers. They always find a way in, park their mite-sized torsos where they want, lay eggs in his beard. He tries not to think about that.

There's a sleeping bag, a couple of blankets, a can opener, odd clothes fished from the donation bin at the Sally Anne. Nail clippers, pliers, empty soup cans, full ones too; a fork, a spoon and a knife. Home sweet home. People pay exorbitant amounts for riverside living. All this was his for the great low price of zero.

He sits on his milk crate and watches the water. Harlow sat in this exact spot, waiting for him to sober. It was over a year ago now. Shermeto'd never met anyone like him. Being out here was like a permanent camping trip. He knew the knots, could make a fire from two sticks of wood, knew what berries and shrubs could be eaten and which would give you the shits or worse—kill you. And he could read the river like no other. He would know why the water was not calm but not flailing either, would know if they should be worried at the way it lapped up the beach, closer than usual, nipping at the rocks, gobbling up the sand. The river spoke to him, but it doesn't speak to Shermeto, no matter how many times he asks.

Harlow believed when people died they returned to nature. "One day, I'll come back as the trees, or the clouds or the river." Harlow skipped a stone across the surface.

"I'll be that rock that just sank to the bottom," Shermeto retorted.

"You'll be more than that. I see you in the sun or the rain."

Shermeto laid back, clamping his hands behind his head. "Ha, yes. I'll piss all over everyone."

The water is edging up the bank, higher than yesterday. He reaches out and dips his hand in then pulls it away quickly. *What would Harlow think?* Move his stuff inland a bit more, that's what he might say. That the river is unforgiving, demands respect. Only right now he can barely keep his eyes open. He'll catch a bit of shut eye. Deal with it in the morning.

***

What do you dream about?

I don't dream.

Everyone dreams. Come on. What do you dream about?

Shermeto is sitting on a stump, the base of which is on fire, but the flames don't reach him. Each fiery tongue has a distorted face on it. And someone is speaking.

What do you dream about?

The voice is female, barely a whisper.

I don't dream, he says again, searching the flames and the darkness. Slowly bodies materialize around him. Jagger, Gerard, Scissor, Joe and Marie are there, and Kendra and Lily. Reuben sits cross-legged in a grocery cart, stroking his long beard. A boy, his back to him, gently rocks the cart. Is that Stevie? Is that his boy? Shermeto reaches for him, but when he gets close, the boy dissolves. Shermeto sits back among the flames and the boy reappears. Reuben chuckles and bounces up and down in the cart.

But who's speaking? There are other human shapes, some squatting, some standing up straight, just shadows without any real form. And Shermeto is in the middle of it all. How did he get there? He's not strapped down; he could get up and walk away. No fear, only impatience.

Who is there? he finally asks.

You don't remember me. Such a shame.

The whisper is in the trees, in the dark, in the earth, in the moon and sky. All around him. He's in a vacuum alone with the voice. His vision becomes ruddy, his friends begin to dissolve and morph into the darkness. Jagger is sucked into the ground. And one by one, the others turn to ash or dirt or mist. As if they never existed. Shermeto tries to call out but there is no sound, no words. His arms are heavy, glued to his knees. The flames grow higher and then one by one, they flicker and go out. Snap. Snap. Snap.

He is alone.

On the stump.

***

"Shermeto? Shermeto you in there? Shermeto! Dude, get up."

Thunder clouds smash against one another. Shermeto bolts awake. Jagger is standing over top of him.

"What the fuck?"

"Come on. We gotta go."

"What time is it?" Shermeto stretches.

"Who cares? You're gonna drown." Jagger's features are drowned in the downpour; water runs off the brim of his hat.

It's still dark. He couldn't have been asleep for long. Rain pummels the tarp, water spilling onto the ground and rushing away to meet the river. The sky and the earth as one. Shermeto is soaked, the ground covered with water.

He wipes away the sleep. Jagger seems so much taller now, offers a hand to help him up.

"Let me go. I can get up on my own."

Jagger takes a step back. "Not much time. The river is going apeshit."

Shermeto peeks outside the tarp. His milk crate is gone. Washed away. A few utensils not where he left them. The tarp sags desperately under the weight of the rain, the wind testing the frayed knots, and the river is in his bedroom. He scrambles out from under the sopping blanket, kicking away the dead weight. His feet sink into the mud.

"Grab what you need."

"Where are we going?"

The rain pounds Shermeto's head, plastering his hair to his face, long trails sweeping down his cheeks. There's anger in the current, ripping along the banks, taking everything not tacked down. White caps peak on the surface of the water; a milky, gray foam.

"I know a place."

Lightning slashes Jagger's face. He cringes as thunder smashes directly overhead.

Shermeto throws a few cans of tuna and a can opener into his pack and heaves it onto his back, then he wades through ankle deep water. The earth sucks at his feet. They climb the bank and follow the pathway. No one is out yet. No joggers, no bikers, no walkers taking advantage of the pathways and nature. Only Shermeto and Jagger and the storm.

"Where you been?" Jagger asks. They make their way back into the park and curl under a rotting wooden bridge, a monument, decoration. Something photographers use to capture an engagement shot. He once crammed a whole wedding party under the arch.

"Got into a scrap. Nothing serious." They watch each other in the dark.

"Good thing I found you."

That's up for debate. The uncertainty makes his head ache.

Why not end it all? That question pokes at him all the time. *Why this? Why here?* A useless wad taking up space. *What's the point?* Give up. Get on with it. But it takes courage to end one's own life. Maybe the suffering is his glue.

Jagger tugs on his arm. "Come on. It's not far."

"Not going to no shelter."

"It's not a shelter. You'll see. Trust me."

Shermeto grunts, but what other choice does he have?

"How long we known each other?" Shermeto asks.

"Dunno. It was winter. February."

Around the same time Harlow died. Not long at all. "Four months, give or take."

Jagger shrugs. "What's it matter?"

"It doesn't. More of an observation." Shermeto pulls his soaked jacket around him and follows Jagger.

***

The second coldest day in February, only days after Harlow died, Shermeto stumbled along, his grief blurring the streets into a slithering mess of grays and blacks. He'd shared a nip with others in the community, something he hadn't done in a long time, but Harlow wasn't there anymore, and he could do whatever the fuck he wanted. He felt every last warm drop reeling through his body. Light and dark became one. Headlights, streetlights. He couldn't tell the difference and it didn't matter. He'd darted out of the way of an oncoming streetlight and fell on his ass, his head smacking the curb. He lay there a few moments at the opening of an alley, then he heard a moan behind him, the scratch of movement along pavement. He found Jagger cowering in the corner, hugging the shadows, arms wrapped tight around his knees. Shermeto stared down at the man, dark hair sprouting out from under a toque, a purple eye, blood crusted to his lips.

"You get run over or something?" Shermeto asked.

Jagger shook, teeth clattering.

"Jesus, man. You okay?"

"Leave me alone," Jagger moaned again.

"Easy there. Trying to help. Should I get an ambulance?"

"Don't need help."

"I strongly disagree." Shermeto leaned in close, too close—he fell over into the man.

"Get the fuck off me." Jagger's arms flailed, a knee connected with Shermeto's upper lip.

For a second Shermeto thought he'd lost a tooth. He spit blood onto the ground then rolled onto his back.

"Guess I deserved that." Cold seeped through his jacket, edging out the booze for some dank form of clarity.

Jagger's eyes narrowed, studying Shermeto for so long he began to feel exposed.

"Got a staring problem or something?"

"No, I have a bleeding lip." Shermeto gathered himself off the ground. "Come on, before you freeze to death."

Jagger's face went slack and then he too pushed himself up, using the wall for support. They staggered back to The Flats and huddled around the fires. Jagger pulled out a flask and took a sip, then handed it to Shermeto.

"A little more can't hurt."

It could hurt a lot.

And that started a week-long bender. Shermeto hated Jagger for it. Hated himself more.

***

The sun is punching its way through the clouds and failing miserably. An ominous gray haze hangs over everything. Fog but not fog. Sheets of rain thick as canvas pour off awnings, and form snaking trails through the streets. Shermeto presses into a shop doorway while Jagger tries to see through the downpour. All the dirt and rot and heat residue, slugging along, dropping into the dark sewers. Jagger seems to be counting, tracing a path. His shoulders are straight, and he's shivering. Then suddenly he turns and nudges Shermeto, nodding across the street. Before Shermeto can react— pull him back, argue—Jagger dashes across the street. He stops and yells back to Shermeto, but the rain gobbles his words. Jagger waves his hands, the rain flattening his hair to his head.

Soon the locals will roll out of bed and spill from their homes, filling the streets, pressing him into the shadows. They'll bitch and complain about the rain, ooh and ahh over the rising river and go about their day, dry and at ease. Jagger starts back across the street. Shermeto steps out and meets him and together they cross a parking lot to a gravel driveway. Jagger stops at a gate and waits for Shermeto to catch up.

"No time to sleep, old man."

Shermeto laughs and follows Jagger through the gate. They are in the backyard of an old house. Trees drape their knotted arms out overhead, scratching and clawing at the air. Fat raindrops drip, drip, drip. Weeds grow up along the fence amidst chip bags, beer cans, sandwich wrappers, a used condom.

"What is this place?" Shermeto asks.

They climb the stairs to a deck.

"Careful. The wood is rotting," Jagger says, placing his hand gently on a wooden rail that sways under his touch. Shermeto nods. Jagger slides the glass door open and slips inside.

They're in a kitchen, or at least the bones of what was once a kitchen. Brown rings outline where a fridge and stove once stood. Cupboard doors hang by hinges or are missing altogether. The house smells damp and the corners are full of mouse droppings.

Newspapers and old magazines scatter the floor. Graffiti covers the walls, obscenities, who loves who and who wants to bang who and with what.

Shermeto catches a whiff of what might be gasoline, or kerosene. Jagger disappears into the next room, leaving Shermeto to linger in front of the word CRAVE in fluorescent green and yellow and red paint. He contemplates the shape and curve of each fat letter. Bubble letters—that's what the kids used to call them. His life is in these lines, clearly marked, defined by a single word and it seems so obvious in the moment.

Dust billows out under Jagger's feet as he shuffles across the floor. He hands Shermeto a blanket. It's heavy wool, an army blanket, dirty and unrelenting. Smells like blood and mothballs.

"Where'd that come from?" Shermeto wraps it around his shoulders, trying to eke every ounce of heat from its fibres.

"Just say thank you."

"Thanks," he says and follows Jagger through the house to what might have been the living room. A black sheet and plastic cover a big window. The walls are peeling or gouged, revealing exposed wires, insulation and rotting 2 x 4s. Jagger sits, his back against a wall. Shermeto spots a wooden crate and flips it over.

"What is this place?" Shermeto asks again.

"A priest used to live here. Or so I heard." Jagger chews on his thumbnail and spits the pieces on the floor. "It's been condemned for months."

The blanket isn't helping. His clothes are so wet, the cold claws deep into his bones.

"Do you believe what they're saying?" Jagger asks.

"About?"

"The river. It's getting wicked high."

"Nothing to worry about," Shermeto says.

"That's not what the newspaper's saying." The ceiling groans overhead.

"You believe everything you read?" Shermeto says, ears cocked to the sounds of the house that seem out of place.

"Maybe you're right."

"Usually."

Another uncomfortable silence passes between them before Jagger speaks again. "One of these days you may not be so lucky."

There's a hardness in his voice that wasn't there before.

"Sounds like a threat."

Jagger shrugs.

"I'll take my chances," Shermeto says.

"Your bruises are healing."

"They do that."

"And you're looking kind of yellow. You feeling all right?"

"Full of piss and vinegar."

The sarcasm doesn't seem to register with Jagger or he chooses to ignore it.

"Need to get out of these clothes. Does this place have running water?" Shermeto drops the blanket on the floor and pulls off his jacket, hangs it on a doorknob and settles back on the stool.

"Not a drop. But at least it's dry."

Shermeto can't disagree with that. He never thought it might feel so good to have an actual roof over his head. Today he will make an exception.

Jagger rolls a joint, licking the edges of the paper, tuned into the task in front of him. The tip of his tongue creeps from the corner of his mouth, touching the tip of the scar on his lip. He pops the joint into his mouth and pats his pockets.

"Got a light?"

Shermeto hands over his lighter. Jagger inhales deeply. A skunky smell wafts through the room. Jagger holds his breath and offers the joint to Shermeto.

"What the hell. Dying anyway."

"It's good for the pain." Jagger smiles, crooked.

It's been years since Shermeto took a hit of anything other than whiskey. Unless you count smokes. He doesn't. Life is shit. You have a smoke. Life is still shit. But the drink. That's something. Puts the mind at ease.

The smoke burns, curling around his lungs in a gentle embrace. He holds it in, one, two, passes the joint back to Jagger, three, four, five, and exhales a plume thicker and wider than a skunk's tail. He smiles and waits for the weed to work. And it doesn't take long.

His hands pulse and tighten, pulse and tighten. The fog seeps into the narrow slits his eyes have become and settles, soft. Like an old friend come for a visit. He can hear every creak of the old house, and the rain rattling against the roof.

Shermeto closes his eyes and imagines himself floating above the river. Above the house. Above the city. Down below, nothing matters.

"What's in this shit?" he asks.

"Good, eh?" Jagger studies his hands, turns them over as if he's never seen them before today. "Not the deep vein high, but it'll do."

Shermeto kicks at a piece of newsprint under his feet. He wants to take off his boots but thinks better of it. Who knows what's lingering in the cracks of this place. Not anything he wants in his cracks, that's for sure.

"What's upstairs?" Shermeto asks, standing.

"Nothing much."

"Show me."

"There's nothing to show. Not so much as a mattress or pillow case. Not a square of butt wipe."

Shermeto sits back down. He doesn't really want to go up there anyway. "Do you live here?"

"Sometimes."

"Tell me the truth. No one else comes here?"

"You got me." Jagger holds up his hands in defense and smiles. "Can't keep anything from you."

"How long?"

"How long what?"

"You been here."

"Not long. You hungry? I'm starving."

Shermeto nods. His stomach is about to eat itself.

"The church is serving up grub this afternoon."

They still aren't very dry, but Shermeto has been through worse. Winter is especially brutal, but he manages, always finding a place to hunker down. He wonders how long Jagger has been coming here and why only now he lets Shermeto in on his secret. All those nights out in the cold, this place could have changed them. Could have saved Harlow.

"Hear that?" Jagger says.

"What?" Shermeto's eyes are too heavy.

"The rain. It's stopped."

DAY THREE

THE RIVER

No Loitering.

The sign presses into the wall, white and accusatory. It's meant for them and school-aged kids. Leave your backpacks at the door. What they really mean, don't hang out in front of the store, you'll offend the paying customers.

Read between the lines.

A man in a black coat leans over his shopping cart. White hair runs wild, hangs past his shoulders. A couple of teenagers exit the coffee shop.

"You smell that?" The teenagers laugh, holding their noses for effect. "You piss yourself?"

"Not recently," the man mutters back and continues to dig through his stash while the teenagers skip past, forgetting him the instant they're out of sight.

The man calculates his collection, his treasures.

To most it's useless garbage. Buggered wheels, skipping and re-sisting over cracks in the pavement. A metal prong protrudes from the side of the cart.

The delicate veer in wide circles around him, plucking at their phones. Oblivious. Anxious. None of them wonder about the person who sits in the shadows all day long, desperately longing for a little kindness, a second to be noticed. Why do they have to be like that?

The parking lot is packed tight with people with no place to go.

They race by, cupping gold-plated lattes and shitty coffee. Filipino nannies with screeching toddlers in tow, out for a stroll in the blazing sunshine, but not before grabbing a Venti Caramel Macchiato and carrying on in a caffeine haze. The old man checks his pocket, finds nothing but a bottle cap and two useless pennies. He pushes his cart down the sidewalk, dragging his shadow behind him.

The sky opens, driving darts into the surface of the river, shards of glass striking and cutting, reaching underneath to the agitated slurry below. Thunder, lightning splashes the faces of those along the banks, umbrellas, raincoats, ponchos, admiring the ferocity of the waves, muttering to one another. They lean over balconies, in awe of the sheer force. Magical. Godlike. No sign of stopping. And then suddenly it ceases, dries up. Puddles, the only proof of existence, gather in pockets along the twisted pathways through the park, reflecting the clouds above. And the people, they twist back inside to the comfort of their iPhones and Netflix.

For the rest, when the rain comes, they scatter, find cover, and only when it ends do they pick their way back. Feet shuffle and scrape along the wet pavement. Grass sparkles in the re-emerging sunlight. Water drips down the sides of buildings, off awnings. And they emerge from the trees into the wide open, skin exposed, embracing the sun, the heat, huddled on wooden benches, tainting the air, soggy and unkempt. A man urinates in the bushes.

Murmurs. Chattering teeth. Crass statements against the weather jumbled with the groans and growls burbling inside them. Patiently they construct their next move: the five w's. When will they eat? Where will they go? What will become of them? Who will remember? Why bother?

Robins peck at the ground, snagging their own meals, keeping it for themselves, or to regurgitate back at the nest. Warm and dry. Safe.

Most travel alone, some move in pairs, a select few have a group they can rely on. They huddle together on the cold nights. Share stories around a fire, laugh and sing, a nip here, a toke there. Around the circle, do-si-do. It's not all cynical and dirty. They have names, had a life, and for whatever reason have been forced to follow a different path.

A couple sits on a bench, nuzzling up to one another. Their energy burns, scorches. One in particular thinks it's not right. While others suffer, these two have each other. It's not fun out here. It's not a vacation. It's hell. Pure and simple. The man stands under a streetlight, hands shoved deep into his pockets, watching the couple. Husband and wife.

The husband's head dips down to his chest. The light catches his face and he sinks into sleep. The wife is dozy too, but smiles when approached, hesitant yet welcoming.

"Let's walk." His voice is kind, convincing.

Concern feathers across her cheeks as she glances back at her husband, his shoulders slump in contentment.

"Shh. It's okay. We won't be long."

"Can't go without him," she whispers.

"Very well then." A swift kick to the shin does the trick and the man jolts awake. He rubs his eyes. Sees his wife being led away and follows.

"Where are we going?" she asks.

"I want to show you something."

KENDRA

Visiting hours don't start for another hour. Kendra sits in the car wondering what to say to him. What could she possibly say that he would hear? Last night she had it all figured out. Stomp in there, drag him home no matter the size of the fight. But by the time she woke up, she'd lost her nerve and now she's unsure: does she tiptoe in and try to reason with him or go with plan A?

Gary listened where James turned away. Gary heard while James pored through brief after brief, nodding, pretending. There wasn't an edge of judgement, only simple, quiet enthusiasm. Like he *really* wanted to know everything. Every last sordid detail. James always seemed bored.

One thing for sure, nothing's going to happen if she stays here. She pulls up the hood of her raincoat and dashes across the parking lot, in through the main entrance. Water pools at her feet as the elevator takes her up. Up and up. The numbers slide by too slowly. Her stomach clenches, knots and releases, clenches again. Until yesterday she had been doing a fine job not thinking about her father, about any family matters. His leaving was a blessing of sorts. Until it wasn't. Until James up and left anyway.

A nurse barks orders into the phone, while another is huddled, whispering with the doctor. Orderlies pushing patients in wheelchairs. There's energy on this floor that didn't exist yesterday. Hyper. Enthusiastic. Anxious.

Kendra gathers herself and starts down the hall towards her father's room.

"Ma'am."

Kendra swings around and is met with steely eyes.

"Can I help you?" The woman asks. A nurse with her hair pinned up tight on the top of her head.

"I don't think so." Kendra says. "I'm here to see my father, Del Shermeto."

The nurse glances at the doctor who is now staring at Kendra. He steps forward, gently brushing her shoulder. "Let's go in here."

"What's going on?" Kendra looks over her shoulder to the room where her father is resting. Waiting. She stalks down the hall and bursts through the door. Walter glances up at her. The other bed is empty. A wave of nausea pulses through her.

A gentle hand on her shoulder.

"Kendra, right? Come with me."

She shrugs his hand away and follows the doctor back down the hall into an unmarked room with a sofa and table full of neatly stacked magazines.

"Did he die? Why didn't anyone call me?"

"Please sit."

"I don't want to sit. What's happening? Where's my father?"

A lump settles in Kendra's throat. She can't breathe.

"He's not here."

She swallows hard, pushing the lump deeper into her stomach. "You lost him?"

"I wouldn't say that."

Kendra stands. The fluorescent lights buzz overhead.

"You let him leave." She sinks into the sofa, leans her head back and closes her eyes. A headache presses at her skull. "He couldn't have gotten far. Maybe he's hiding somewhere."

"We can't hold anyone against their will."

"What you're saying is you didn't even bother looking?"

"Sorry. It's out of our hands now."

"That's bullshit and you know it. He's a homeless man and you don't give a shit whether he lives or dies."

"We did all we could, all we are legally obligated to, given the circumstances." He pauses. "I'm really sorry."

Kendra nods, but not in agreement; she doesn't believe a thing he's saying. They don't want to deal with him. Some part of her gets it. But if they're not going to do anything, then who will?

***

Kendra stands outside the glass doors of the police station, her reflection staring back at her with a lop-sided featureless expression. Her father was right. She's getting fat. At least ten pounds since James left. Doesn't even look like her. Distorted. Disfigured. Does she really look this terrible? Her reflection doesn't answer. Why would it when it's meant to toy and tease and judge?

Kendra opens the door.

Her experience with police stations is limited, the last being when she was a kid just after her mother died. Or was it Stevie? She can't remember. There wasn't anything suspicious about her mother's death.

Suicide. Doesn't get more open and shut than that.

Kendra expects the steady bustle of bodies darting back and forth, phones ringing, the innocent until proven guilty being booked, but the station is empty. The waiting area smells like shoe polish. Shouldn't there always be someone at the front?

She scans the countertop. No bell. But she doesn't have a chance to consider this for too long. A door on the other side of the room opens and an officer appears. He glances up and casually saunters around the cluster of desks in the middle of the room. He drops some files on one of the desks and then leans over the counter. He doesn't smile.

"How can I help you?" His voice flat. Bored.

Is this part of the training or is he naturally an asshole? A tanned, dark-haired asshole. His name, according to his tag, Constable T. Napier. What does the T stand for? Thomas. Tim. Tony. Tyson. Theo. Ted. Theodore. None seem to fit.

"I want, I mean—I need—"

The officer stares at her. He's reading her. Judging her.

She swallows her nerves. "I need to report a missing person."

"A child?"

Kendra shakes her head.

The officer pulls a sheet of paper out from under the counter and slides it towards her. "Fill this out."

Kendra takes the paper and scans it then glances up at the officer. His cheeks are narrow, with hard lines, a square jaw. He doesn't even know how to crack a smile. She nods at the officer then sits in a chair. Blue upholstery against yellow walls. The chairs are welded together. *Is it possible that someone would try to steal a chair out from under their shiny noses?* She pulls a pen out of her bag and begins to fill out the form. Her name. Address. Relationship to the missing person. How long have they been missing? *That's a loaded question.*

The officer is standing by a photocopier slowly feeding sheets of paper into the machine and waiting for it spit out the duplicates.

"Excuse me?"

The officer doesn't look up.

"Excuse me?"

He holds up his hand. Kendra taps the counter with her pen. *This is stupid. She doesn't belong here. They can't help her.*

The officer shakes out his copies, grabs the original with more indifference than a sleeping cat, makes his way back to the counter.

"Finished?"

"No. It's my father."

The man waits for her to continue. Expressionless.

"He's downtown somewhere. I need to find him."

"Then he's not missing."

"He lives on the streets. The river—you know?"

"He's likely been evacuated. They're shutting it all down."

"Where would they take them?"

He turns his back to her and rummages through some papers on his desk. He slides a sheet of paper across the counter. She reads it quickly. All the evacuation sites. Must be twenty of them.

"Thank you."

"Do you still want to file it?"

***

What now? She sits in the car, the radio tuned to the local news. Homes in low-lying areas along the river are being put on evacuation alert. A long list of neighbourhoods but Kendra only pays attention to one. The downtown core at immediate risk. The zoo, businesses, condos, transit would have been shut down, the homeless shelters evacuated, just as the officer mentioned. She doesn't know where to start. He could be anywhere.

Her head becomes a flurry of thoughts, she can't focus on only one. Her chest tightens, her breath comes in rapid gasps. A buzzing behind her ears like a million mosquitos searching for a place to settle.

***

Right after James moved out she started therapy. Her mind was a tangle of nightmares and although she had no thoughts of suicide— she had begun to wonder the point of it all. Wake up, eat, breathe, work, come home, and repeat. She tried talking to the cat, but in this case, she needed someone to talk back to her. Wash. Rinse. Repeat.

So she swallowed her fear of what people would think, cracked open the Google and made calls until she found Melanie. Or Mel as she liked to be called.

Walking in the first day wasn't much different than walking in now. Even the air in the room put a person at ease. Mel holds the sessions in her home. A nice, older style bungalow in a community just north of the city centre. The streets are narrow, cozy, trees pillaring upward like sentries keeping watch.

She rings the doorbell and waits, folding her hands in front of her, behind her, letting them dangle at her side. A cyclist zips by on the street. Kendra presses the doorbell again. Finally, she catches a flutter of movement behind the curtain and the door opens.

The smell of cinnamon and cloves sails out the door and catches her by surprise. As does the man standing in the doorway. *Shit, does she have the wrong house?*

"Can I help you?"

The man is clean shaven, hair pulled back in a long gray pony tail, small round glasses perched on his nose.

Kendra glances at the house number to be sure.

"I'm looking for Mel."

The man smiles. "She's with a client right now but I think she's almost done. Come in?" He stands aside and waits. "I'm Richard."

Kendra nods and sits on the chair by the front window.

"I don't have an appointment."

Richard nods and sits at the island dividing the kitchen from the living area.

"I made muffins. Would you like one?"

Kendra shakes her head.

"No, thanks. But they smell wonderful."

There's a new picture on the wall since the last time she visited. The Golden Gate bridge, swallowed by fog and the rough bay beneath it.

"She shouldn't be much longer."

Richard offers her a glass of water which she takes for no other reason than she needs something to do with her hands.

"That's fine. I'll wait."

A few minutes later Mel appears with a woman at her side.

"It'll get better," she says, placing a hand on the woman's shoulder. She gives a cursory nod to Richard, who silently motions to Kendra.

"Do we have an appointment?" Mel checks her watch.

"No, sorry. I just really needed to see you."

"Sure. I have a few minutes."

Mel's office is more of a lounge than an actual office. No desk. Only a couple of plush chairs and a sofa around a small coffee table. Pictures. Books. A big leafy plant by the window.

"Can I get you a drink?" Mel asks.

"I'm good." Kendra sits at one end of the couch, Mel on the other end.

"What can I do for you today?"

"I'm spinning."

"James again?"

There's judgement in her tone.

"No. Not this time. Though he served me with papers."

"How did that make you feel?"

"I don't know. Surprised, I guess. But it's fine."

Her eyebrows lift. "How so?"

"My father."

The gap between them feels thick, muggy. Mel seems to consider her next words, searching her memory for any mention of a father. Kendra hasn't mentioned him much, even though he's always been a part of the bigger problem. Maybe, *the problem.*

"You've mentioned him briefly. Refresh my memory."

"We used to be close, but now. I don't know. He's not the man I thought he was."

"Does he have to be a certain way?"

Kendra thinks about this. She's seen many fathers of her friends and often wished hers could have been like them. But circumstances are different. She knows this. Kendra clasps her hands together, her nails digging into her knuckles.

"I've been a terrible daughter."

"Guilt is normal in these situations."

"It's more than that. I didn't see the signs. Or chose to ignore them. Is that normal?"

Mel pinches her lips together. Her eyes narrow.

"And now it's too late." Kendra sneezes.

"Is he dead?" Mel pushes a box of tissues across the table.

"No." Not yet. At least she doesn't think so. God, she hopes not.

"Then it's not too late."

"I don't know where to start."

The words spill out then. He's homeless. He's sick. He's a drunk. Doesn't want to see her. Pushes her away all the time and maybe she brought that on herself, but maybe it's him and she needs to keep pushing back. But he's out there somewhere and the river is rising and if he's downtown somewhere, maybe it is too late. She's confused, scared.

"It's too much."

"He sounds like he's had a lot of problems, but you know what those are. You've been there. Lived it. You know what you need to do. You feel it deep in your gut. Take your fear and press through it. I think you'll be pleasantly surprised at what comes out on the other side."

Mel stands. "I really wish I could speak with you longer but I have another appointment. Why don't you come back next week? I can pencil you in."

Kendra nods and stands.

"You're stronger than you realize."

On the way out, Richard hands her a muffin wrapped in plastic.

"For the road," he says.

SHERMETO

Shermeto and Jagger step outside. The sun peeks from around the clouds, creating large squares of orange light across the dead grass in the backyard. He stands in the sun-square, the heat washing through him, if only for a moment. His clothes cling to his body like a soggy second skin.

They crawl slowly along the river path. The sky is clear. So blue; in contrast to the brown murkiness passive-aggressively stripping away layer upon thin layer, eroding, widening.

"Got a smoke?" Shermeto asks then remembers the pack the cabbie gave him. Probably squished by now.

Jagger shakes his head. "Fresh out."

"Ah, never mind. I got some." He fishes one out and offers another to Jagger.

Shermeto's legs are sore, the muscles pinched, seizing with each step. His feet feel raw, his heels rubbing at the back of the new boots.

"What's wrong?" Jagger stops to light his smoke then offers the lighter over.

"Nothing to worry about."

Shermeto finds a spot on a park bench and removes his shoes. There are fresh socks in the backpack. He peels off the wet ones and rubs his feet. His nails are yellow and twisted, the bottom of his feet red and wrinkled. Foot rot. Like they used to get in the trenches. Seems like a thing of history, but it's more real than anyone knows.

Jagger sits beside him. "What would you do without me?" He

pulls out the dry socks. Shermeto doesn't mind. They've been in this together for so long.

"Ever think it's too much?" Shermeto asks.

"You're talking gibberish, old man."

Shermeto takes the socks and slides them onto his feet. "Not kidding. This is no life. Not really."

"It's the best we got."

"Maybe you're right."

He slaps Shermeto on the back and glances up at the sky. "That's the spirit."

Shermeto grunts and slips his boots back onto his feet. "Let's scrape up some grub."

A man in pressed khakis and a vest enters the park from the city side, an umbrella arched over him. A couple walks hand in hand. A bird screeches from a tree and a dog barks.

Music drifts towards him. A familiar song, sung to the simple finger-strumming of a guitar. Shermeto scans the park for the source. A woman, sitting cross-legged on a blanket, her back pressed against a storefront window, cradling a guitar in her arms. Fingers stretch around the neck, moving easily over the chords. In a low, grungy rasp, Bonnie Tyler style, she sings, *Have You Ever Seen the Rain?*

All the time, he thinks.

Buskers are a breed of their own. Beggars, bums like him, but with a home to crawl back to at the end of the day. Four walls. Windows. They spend their days in the crowded urban sprawl, for what? A few bucks that'll hardly pay the rent. He doesn't miss that kind of responsibility. Only they offer something he doesn't and have a permit to do so. Socially acceptable begging. Yet, they too are often misunderstood. If you're not working a nine-to-five in a cubicle in one of the big-ass towers, you are not worthy of even a glance.

A crowd gathers around her. The girl can't be more than twenty. A baby. Tattoos reach up and around her neck. The open case in front of her goes mostly ignored. Hands are stuffed deeper into pockets protecting pocket lint, loose change. Shermeto stops to listen while Jagger carries on ahead. Orange light creeps across her face from the split in the clouds overhead, the patterns of sunlight moving with her lips. Perfect, even light. Part of her face remains obscured in shadow, the rest lit, angelic. She sings with her eyes closed, lips moving easily over the words.

Shermeto tried begging once. Sitting on the street corner holding a Tim Horton's cup he'd fished from the trash. But he got more insults than a standup comic could dish out and not nearly as funny, and that's only from those who didn't avert their eyes, pretending not to see. *Not having a home isn't contagious*, he wanted to shout. Not some incurable virus spreading through the body. Not a cancer. He wasn't a fucking cancer. Know what he was? A series of circumstances, stacked one on top of another, smothering him, chasing him to this place where he went without a fight.

Shermeto doesn't know good music from bad, but he likes what he hears. It doesn't make his head throb.

"Jagger. Hold up."

Jagger stops and glances back. Shermeto leans against a street light, elbows stretched behind him, listening. Watching. She doesn't care if no one pays attention. She's lost in a private world, bringing joy to herself and maybe a select few. Making the world a little less messy for a moment.

The song ends. Listeners drop coins into her case and carry on down the street.

"You're real good," Shermeto says.

"Thanks." Her voice is soft, not gravelly like he expected.

"Beautiful morning."

"I like the mornings. Get out here first thing. Get the best spots."

"Even in this?" Shermeto nods to the sky.

"Doesn't much matter."

Shermeto thinks he understands.

The girl squints up at him. Glances at Jagger. Then back at Shermeto. She's looking at him. Like really looking. He turns away.

"It looks worse than it is."

She smiles. "What's your name?"

"They call me Shermeto."

"Your parents name you that?"

"It is what it is."

"My mother named me Sky. Guess that's weird, too."

"What do names mean anyway?"

"I think names say a lot about a person."

"Jibber jabber," Jagger comes and stands beside Shermeto. "You can tell a lot from the kind of ginch they wear too, the size of the crack stain, but I'm not gonna show you that."

Sky considers Jagger for a moment then turns her attention back to Shermeto. His stomach starts to cramp, stabs of pain radiate up and down his sides.

"I should dart. Places to go. Things to see. You know," Shermeto says.

"Here."

Sky pulls a pencil case-sized bag from behind her back and hands him a twenty.

"What's that for?"

She shrugs. "Get a coffee. Or whatever."

Shermeto pockets the bill as Sky begins a new song that he doesn't recognize. The rasp gone. When he glances back, her eyes are closed again. Part of the music. She won't remember him in an hour, but he will remember her.

"How do you do that?" Jagger asks.

"What?"

"Be so nice to some people."

There's always a teaching moment. Shermeto waves the twenty in the air.

"We're homeless, not assholes."

Shermeto pulls a can of tuna from the bottom of the backpack. The can opener is rusted and only works some of the time, he has to get the tooth just right and press the handles tight, but his fingers resist. He gets most of the can open and bends back the lid the rest of the way. He drains the water on the ground under the bench and pinches the bland fish between his fingers. Kind of like chewing tobacco the way he tucks it into his cheeks until he has an ample enough mouthful to chew down. The longer he chews, the fuller he feels. A trick his mother taught him. Don't scarf down the food. He tried the same thing with his own kids, but it never seemed to stick. He offers the can to Jagger, who shakes his head.

A couple of city workers dressed in bright orange ponchos cross the platform, offering a polite nod in their general direction and study the river.

"Wonder what's going on?" Jagger says.

Shermeto scoots to the other end of the bench to try and catch bits of the conversation. One of the men pulls out a walkie talkie and begins speaking.

"At least a metre," the man says.

A garbled voice on the other end. Shermeto can make out only a few words between the static.

"Flood." Static. Static. "Bridge out." Static.

"We'll keep you posted," he says back.

Shermeto stares out over the water. It's fast. It's high. But there's been worse. *Nothing to get the panties knotted over*, Harlow would say. It's different now. The surface seems leathery, writhing. The distinct smell of sewage chokes the air.

KENDRA

Kendra gets back to the car just as her phone rings. She stares at the display. It's her sister. What's wrong? Something must be wrong if she's phoning. She answers on the third ring.

"What's up?"

Silence and then a scratchy cough.

"Lily? Everything okay? You sound sick."

"It's nothing."

"How are you?" Kendra asks.

"Pregnant. I'm pregnant. Can you believe it?"

Kendra lets the words sink in until she wants to spit them out. She loves her sister, is happy for her, but it always stings a little bit. Kendra got the crap end of the ovary function, broken uterus.

"You there?" Lily asks.

"Of course, I'm here. Sorry. Just getting in the car."

"Don't talk and drive."

The car feels muggy. Sweat instantly beads on her forehead and it's hard to breathe. She rolls down the window, inviting cool air to wash through the car.

"Yeah, yeah. So how did this happen? How far along? Have you told Penny?"

"Slow down. Do I really have to explain how this happened?" Lily laughs. "Christ you're older than I am."

When Lily laughs it's like a burst of bubbles. Kendra smiles.

"I miss you."

"Me too. I wish you were here. It's not going to be the same this time."

True. Kendra was there every step when Lily was pregnant with Penny. Kyle fucked off when he found out about the baby. Their father was there too. As much as he could be.

"So how far along?"

"Thirteen weeks. Wanted to wait until we were out of the danger zone, you know, and Penny is thrilled. Can't wait to be a big sister."

"I'm really happy for you. This is amazing." The clouds part. Blue sky opens. "When are you due?"

"December 25, can you believe it?"

"The kid is going to hate that."

An elderly man pushes a woman in a wheelchair down the sidewalk, holding an umbrella over her head. He reaches down and pats the woman's shoulder. The woman tilts her head back and smiles at the man. *That's what happy looks like*, Kendra thinks.

"Are you okay?" Lily asks.

"What?"

The man helps his wife out of the wheelchair and into the car.

"You're so quiet. What's going on?"

"Nothing."

"Don't lie to me. I know you better than that."

"You've got enough going on."

"Don't do that."

"Do what?"

Kendra shuts off the heat.

"Get all controlling and think you know what's best. If something is wrong, you better tell me."

"It's Dad."

"Oh."

Kendra relays what she knows so far. "I don't know what to do."

"Well, you know what I think, but I know you and you won't rest until you find him. I can't believe you even need to ask."

"I have no idea where to start."

"You'll figure it out. You always do."

***

An unexpectedly warm April morning. Kendra had helped Lily plan a Disney Princess party at her house. James spent all morning blowing up balloons, hanging streamers and banners. *Happy Birthday, Penny*, scrawled across a chocolate cake with pink icing. The heads of all the princesses on edible paper placed delicately on the top. Friends from school arrived right on time. Parents eager to dart off, a couple hours free of brats. It seemed like a good idea at the time. How hard could it be to handle fifteen kids for a couple of hours? They darted around the house, hanging from bannister rails, sliding down the stairs on their knobby behinds, laughing and making noises Kendra thought only a dog should be able to hear. Wished only a dog could hear.

Lily eyed her across the kitchen, concern spreading across her face then she mouthed, *Dad*?

Kendra shook her head. "Haven't heard from him." She checked her phone then to make sure she hadn't missed a call.

"He should be here by now. It's not like him. He's never missed Penny's birthday," Lily said.

But Kendra knew. Their father had become more distant in recent months. Wouldn't take any of her calls, didn't come over for dinner. The drinking had become worse. He'd always been a drinker. It intensified after Steven died and later after their mom, but he still never missed any of the important things. Something changed. He'd respond with a growl and distorted grimace when Kendra asked.

They assembled the children for an energetic game of pin the tail on the donkey, James in charge of spinning the sugar-infected kids. Kendra hung back, picturing vomit infused into her hardwood floors. She glanced out the window every few minutes.

Shortly after the third kid pinned another tail off the end of the donkey's nose their father stumbled through the front door. His hair, at odd angles, he looked like he hadn't slept in a week, and he smelled even worse. He laughed and pushed his way into the living room. Faces turned, mouths dropped. The kids looked terrified.

"Don't let me interrupt the game," he slurred. "Pretend I'm not even here." He fell into the coffee table. Kendra reached out to grab the wobbling lamp before it crashed to the floor.

"Dad!" She ushered him into the kitchen and sat him at the table. "What the hell are you doing?"

"Coming to wish my Penny-Loo a happy birthday, what do you think?" He turned in the seat. "Penny! Come here kiddo."

Penny popped her head up and slinked into the kitchen. She stood by the counter, refusing to come any closer. Back and forth, her head moved from Kendra to her grandfather, silent questions, confusion.

"Come on." He patted his lap and reached for Penny.

Penny backed up. Lily knelt beside her and whispered something in her ear. Penny smiled and returned to her friends.

"Thankless brat," Shermeto said.

"Excuse me?" Lily faced him. "You walk in here, gooned out of your mind and she's the thankless one? Fuck you. Get out of here."

"Figures." Shermeto didn't move. He looked at Kendra. "You gonna let her talk to your old man like that?"

"You better go," Kendra said.

"Jesus Christ. After everything I did for you. This is the thanks I get?"

"Come back when you're sober."

"Fuck you. Fuck you all to hell." Shermeto kicked the chair as he stood, sending it backward.

"Come on, Dad." Kendra led him to the front door.

"You have no idea. You're killing me inside. A little bit at a time."

She knew that wasn't true, but it carved a fissure between them. *How would she ever fix it?*

***

Kendra thrusts the car into drive and heads north. She doesn't want to go home but doesn't know what else to do. She flies up the highway, takes an off ramp and winds through residential areas, pulling into the parking lot of a popular green space. She grabs her camera off the backseat and follows the paved path to the top of the hill where she has an unobstructed view of the city.

An obtrusive blemish on the prairies, a different planet. How does he survive in that chaos? And how will she find him with so many places to hide? What can he be doing down there? What does he get out of being there instead of with his family, people who love him and can help him?

She can't remember the last time her father seemed truly happy. Kendra steps around a puddle of rust-coloured water.

Red water.

She sees her mother's face in that puddle. Distorted by the passage of time. A memory. She'd pretty much forgotten the curve of her mother's cheek, the love in the crook of her arm. She can't see her eyes, the colour had been lost long before that day. And she remembers that day. Every detail from her mother's limp arm hanging over the edge of the tub to the gurgle of the water as it slipped away, taking her mother's life with it. Her father cradling the body, sounds of grief crackling the metallic air. All this takes up that space in her brain reserved for the good times. Like the road trips to Drumheller, skinned knees dowsed with as much love as rubbing alcohol. Bandages, stitches, broken bones.

Red water.

It took her father, too.

"What's wrong?" Her sister entered the bedroom. Kendra backed out of the bathroom and shut the door. A barrier between truth and fiction. Blurred lines. A trick of her imagination.

"Let's go play dolls." Kendra steered Lily into the hallway.

"You never play with me," Lily squinted up at Kendra.

"Well, I want to play now."

Lily glanced across the hall to their parent's bedroom, arms folded across her chest, then finally gave up and gathered her dolls into a circle on the floor. Kendra sat across from her, eyes focused forward, one ear tuned to the guttural moans leaking from the bathroom door.

They played ballroom, dressing the dolls in bright gowns, dancing, drinking Earl Grey tea and eating hors d'oeuvres: caviar, finger sandwiches, skewered olives.

Her father emerged from the bathroom and paused in the doorway, his face slack, confused. Kendra heard muffled words uttered into the phone and then the handset crashing to the floor.

"Stay here," she said.

He crumbled to the floor, back against the wall, knees pulled up to his chest. She'd never heard him sob like that. He crumbled a single sheet of paper in his fist.

When she tried to peel the letter from his hands, he held it tighter, tearing the edge of the paper. She never read her mother's last words, didn't have an explanation for any of it. Her father stole that from her.

**

Kendra gazes down at the city. From here it's like a dream she can't shake. He's down there somewhere and a part of her doesn't care. She hates him for what he took from her. The chance to grieve her mother, her childhood. Everything goes back to that moment. She tried to be a good daughter. Help as much as possible. Take care of Lily. All the things her mother used to do. She tried her best, but it wasn't enough. This is how he repaid her.

Kendra catches movement off to her left. A black and white dog bounds up the hill, its tags jingling as it tries to keep up with its own paws, a leash dragging between its legs. The dog slows and barks.

"Hey doggie." She holds out her hand. "Where's your owner?" The dog pauses, inches closer then stops, glances back the way it came and then barks again.

Kendra expects a head to appear any moment or a voice to call out, but no one comes. The dog jumps a couple of times and barks again then darts back down the hill. It stops and glances back at her. Barks. Waits. Barks. Waits.

Finally, Kendra follows the dog. Tall grass scratches at her pants as she navigates along the worn trail. The dog stops. Kendra inches closer. A man is lying on his back on the ground. Late sixties, maybe. Gray creased pants and a green golf shirt. He's wearing brown loafers and isn't moving. The dog circles the body then props its head on the man's stomach.

Shit. Please don't be dead. Not today.

Kendra approaches slowly.

"Hey mister? Are you okay?"

The man doesn't answer. She kneels beside him. The dog lets out a low growl, square-chested between her and his owner. The man's chest is rising and falling. Barely. But still. She lets out a sigh and grabs her phone.

"He's not dead," she tells the operator after explaining where she is.

"Stay with him. Someone will be there soon." The woman's voice is soft, reassuring, with an edge of compassion. "Is he breathing?"

"His chest is moving."

"Good. How fast are the breaths?"

"Slow." She tries to touch him, but the dog snarls and snaps at her.

"Slow and shallow or slow and deep?"

"I don't know what you mean?"

"Does it sound like he's snoring? Any noise at all?"

"No noise."

"Is he on his back or stomach?"

"Back.

"Is there any blood?"

Good grief. Don't let there be blood.

"Not that I can see." Kendra hears sirens in the distance. "I can hear them."

"Ok."

The sirens get louder and then fall silent.

"How will they get up here? There's no roads."

"Can you see them?"

"No."

"Make yourself visible so they can find you."

Kendra climbs back up the path to the top of the hill. A firetruck pulls into the parking lot, followed by an ambulance and police cars. She waves her arms back and forth. The firetruck drives through an opening Kendra didn't think was big enough for a small vehicle and bounces up the hill along the paved path. The others follow.

"Are they there?" the dispatcher asks.

"Yes."

"Ok. I'll let you go now."

"Thank you," Kendra says and ends the call.

A fireman jumps out of the truck.

"Are you okay?"

"It's not me. Down there."

She can't take her eyes off him.

"There's a dog," Kendra says.

The man smiles and starts down the hill with another fireman. The dog barks frantically and lunges at the fireman. A police officer races down the hill and secures the dog. Kendra starts after them.

"You should stay here." The other police officer is more serious. "Let them work."

Kendra nods. This guy has a permanent snarl on his face.

"Do you know the man?"

Kendra shakes her head.

"Can you tell me what happened?"

She tells him everything she knows while the medics finally make their way down the hill. She can't see what's going on.

"Guess you didn't expect this today," the officer says.

"Guess not." Kendra glances out at the skyline.

"Pretty amazing isn't it?" the officer says, following her gaze.

Kendra nods. "How can you find someone down there?"

"What do mean?"

"If you were lost—on the streets—how would someone find you?"

"Homeless, you mean?"

Kendra nods.

"They wouldn't."

SHERMETO

A couple months ago Jagger showed up on a bike, his hair slick with oil. He wasn't so much riding the bike as propelling it forward with his feet.

"Where'd you get that?" Shermeto asked.

"This old thing?"

Shermeto didn't expect a straight answer from Jagger. He probably stole it from a backyard, though it wasn't in great shape, bent wheels, missing a pedal.

Jagger tilted his head and smiled. A toothy, creepy-as-fuck grin on his face that made Shermeto's skin crawl.

"Where you going?" Jagger asked. "I'll come along."

"Nowhere special."

"I'm headed there too."

Jagger pushed forward, the front tire awkwardly accepting the balance corrections. Black paint flaked along the bars showing gray metal underneath, the chain rusted and dangling loose. A couple of the spokes were missing, and the front tire was so badly bent the rubber scraped against the frame. Not unusual to see lots of bikes, easy and inexpensive way to get around. Jagger overcorrected and fell into the grass on the edge of the path. He grumbled under his breath but picked himself back up and climbed back on.

"No one ever teach you to ride?" Shermeto asked.

"Sure." His knuckles white against the handles, arms taut.

"Your balance is all wrong."

"It's the bike. A total piece of shit."

"Try gliding."

"That's what I've been doing."

"Do you want help or not?"

"Not."

It was far easier to teach three kids to ride. They stayed close to the path, the river glimpsed through the occasional break in the trees and brush. Some areas so thick and overgrown you wouldn't know what might be hiding inside. People lounged on benches or lay in the grass, reading newspapers or books, sipping coffee from paper cups.

"Try pedaling now," Shermeto said.

Jagger stopped, placed his foot on one pedal and pushed off, instantly losing his balance and falling into the grass again.

"This is stupid." Jagger kicked the back tire. "I told you it's the bike."

"Practice. You'll get it."

Shermeto repeated the words again in his mind. The familiar shadow crept through him, a darkness that had hovered on the periphery for years, darting in and out of him at unknown times. Intervals. Little things. Bubbling to the surface. Reminding him. He hated to remember.

"Where you going?"

Shermeto didn't realize he'd gone several paces ahead, but once he did, he didn't stop. He couldn't.

"Thought you were going to help?"

"Can't help you."

Jagger ran after him, pushing the bike.

"Come on. I'll keep trying. It's fun. See?"

Jagger jumped back on the bike and pedaled. Forward. One. Two. Three. "I'm doing it." Jagger let out a holler, an excited yahoo for anyone who would listen.

"Watch out for—"

Shermeto's words cut off as Jagger ran headlong into a tree. Blood dripped down his arm, his ego badly bruised.

***

Jagger is not the same person he was back then. None of them are. Jagger has his own way.

"Whatever happened to your bike?" Shermeto asks.

"That old piece of shit? I dumped it by the bird sanctuary. Chain snapped." Jagger moves with a swagger, haughty, an energy that creeps under Shermeto's skin like a parasite. But then there's things like yesterday, saving him from being swallowed by the river.

They pass under a bridge, feeling the steady swoosh clank overhead as cars rumble back and forth. The river dangerously close to the pathway, claws pulling itself farther up the bank.

Swoosh clank.

Someone is whistling. His eyes dart and focus, searching for any movement. And then he sees it, or rather *him*, coming across the grass, pushing an overloaded grocery cart.

Swoosh clank.

Shermeto nudges Jagger and points.

"There goes my buzz," Jagger says. "Let's get out of here before he sees us." Jagger tugs on Shermeto's shoulder. "Come on."

Too late.

"Lord love a duck. Shermeto? Is that you? I thought that was you? Who's that with you?"

Jagger mutters something under his breath and stands behind Shermeto. Shermeto waves. "Reuben." Shermeto approaches the man. "Let me help you with that."

Reuben's cart overflows. Black garbage bags stuffed on top of black garbage bags and pressed down. A shoe is pressed up against the inside grate of the cart, the match may be under there somewhere, but Shermeto thinks it's unlikely. Reuben tends to grab anything, useless or otherwise. Like the kite protruding from the top, the body bending in the wind, the tail trailing behind.

Shermeto helps Reuben pull the cart under the bridge; the wheels scrape the dirt. Reuben studies Jagger who is busy rolling another joint, then turns to Shermeto.

"Whoa. Hope you got a few licks in yourself."

White hair juts out from under the toque pressed over Reuben's head. His nose flares and settles with each breath. There's craters in the old man's face, along with numerous scars. Reuben's been out here longer than anyone Shermeto knows.

The old man makes a space to sit, ignoring Jagger.

Under the weary lines, soft eyes peer out, gauging everything around him.

"What happened to the beard?" Shermeto asks.

"Bugs. They were getting up my nose. Nuisance."

Shermeto nods. "Don't think I've seen you like this. Good look."

"What's in the bag?" Reuben nods towards Shermeto's pack.

Jagger shakes his head and sets the newly rolled joint on his lips. Shermeto grabs his pack and stuffs it behind him. If it's not nailed down, Reuben'll swipe anything. Don't matter if it's claimed or not. Finders keepers to the nth degree. By his own rules.

"Not much," Shermeto says.

Reuben gazes out at the water. "Buckle up, we're in for a wild ride."

"I don't follow." Jagger blows smoke in Reuben's face.

"You likely wouldn't." Reuben stands and digs through his cart. A moment later he pulls out a rolled-up newspaper and lays it flat between them. He places his finger in the middle of the front page on the left eye of the mayor.

"Turning the city into a frenzy. People packing and hoarding. Fearing for their lives. Bozos. The lot of them."

Shermeto scans the headline, gets the gist of the article without having to read it. The city is on high flood alert.

"Worried for nothing. Even the last time. Barely a bump in my day. Oh, lookie, water up to my ankles." Reuben folds the paper and tucks it back in the cart. "Nothing came of it then, nothing will come of it now. And they call us the crazy ones."

"Nothing like one million anxious socialites." Jagger wafts in his own fog.

"Ah. The jagged one speaks. He's not wrong."

"You two know each other?" Shermeto asks.

"Crossed paths a time or two. Ain't that right, jagged one?" Reuben pats Jagger's foot. Jagger pulls away and gives Shermeto a look that he doesn't feel like deciphering. "So what are you and the jagged one up to today?"

"About to grab a bite somewhere," Shermeto says.

Jagger shakes his head, eyes wide.

"Care to join us?" Shermeto asks Reuben.

"I suppose I might. Scarfed down some toast over at the drop in, but the nitwits were out of eggs. How do they expect a man to survive without his daily dose of protein? Got cash?"

Reuben eyes Shermeto's pack again. Shermeto shakes his head.

"Well, that old Eye-talian church serves up a bum lunch every day."

Reuben clenches and unclenches a hairy, liver-spotted fist. Fingernails caked in black crud. He tucks his hands into his armpits. Of all the people Shermeto knows, Reuben he knows the least. A friend of Harlow's but a grubber. A moocher. A thief. Shermeto checks his own hands. The shredded knuckles, scabbed over. Nicotine-yellowed fingers. The shower couldn't even get that out.

"That's where we're headed," Shermeto says, hefting his pack up to his shoulder. "You can come along if you want."

Jagger coughs.

"Lend an old guy a hand?" Shermeto helps him up. His breath smells like that sweaty spot at the top of the ass crack. "Coming jagged one?"

"Suddenly lost my appetite," Jagger says to Shermeto.

"Suit yourself." They leave Jagger under the bridge, Shermeto pushing Reuben's cart. Every few steps, his feet get tangled in the kite tail. "What's the kite for?"

"Never know when something might come in handy." Reuben keeps walking. His pant legs are frayed, the gray cotton scraping pavement.

"Everyone's got the crabs," Reuben says.

He doesn't stop, doesn't turn to explain. The wheel on the cart darts back and forth and suddenly catches in a rut. The cart comes to an abrupt stop.

"Goddammit." Shermeto swallows back a series of other obscenities as a mother and littler girl with pigtails, dressed in a pink shirt and jean shorts passes by them.

The wheel is jammed tight. Reuben stops and turns but doesn't come back to help.

"Over at the drop-in. Crabs. Lice. Making the rounds again. Should see them all, slurping their noodles and scratching their pricks. Disgusting."

The woman grabs the girl by the hand and pulls her along, picking up speed. Reuben laughs.

Shermeto gets the cart back on the pathway and they carry on. A dog darts from the trees, latches onto a rolling ball and returns it to the owner. Shermeto's never liked dogs, or any pets for that matter. Didn't make sense. But sometimes, the mutts are the only pals some of them have out here. He'd rather be alone than have to worry about another mouth to feed.

"Why you let that jagged one bum along with you? He's got something going not right up in the head."

"He's alright. An acquired taste," Shermeto says.

"Don't trust him."

"He doesn't relate well to other people. I helped him out once. He returned the favour."

"Don't fall for it. That guy is no good. Really. No good."

They reach the church. A line of homeless stand on the sidewalk waiting for the doors to open.

"I write things down. When I see stuff. People. Things going on."

"Yeah?" They cross the street.

"Them deaths are weird, don't you think?"

"Weird, how?" Of course, Shermeto has been thinking the same thing.

Reuben tilts his head and scowls.

The crowd shudders into the church. Anxious. Pushing against one another.

"What do you want me to do with this thing?" Shermeto nods

to the cart.

Reuben points to a low hedge beside the church. "In there. Don't want no one getting their meat hooks into it."

Shermeto parks Reuben's cart then glances up at the sky. So much day remains. They climb the stairs to the smiling face of a clean-shaven man Shermeto's never seen before.

"Good afternoon. Welcome." The man points to the staircase inside the foyer. "Follow the stairs."

The smell of boiling tomatoes and spices reaches up the stairs. A hint of something flowery. The room is enormous. White-walls splashed with rows of plastic tables placed end to end and metal folding chairs set around them. Shermeto imagines the corners sprinkled with holy water to keep out the bad juju. His feet should burn as he walks across the floor.

The line up at the kitchen is long and the tables are filling fast. Many dark, grisly heads are already lowered over bowls, devouring soup and tearing at bread. Reuben makes straight for the line. Shermeto hangs back, admires the splatters of artwork tacked to the wall. Traced hands with smiling faces on the thumbs, finger-painted splotches of colour, a scene of presumably a mother and father and child in front of a lopsided house and broken tree, the sun imposing itself with big smiling rays. And in the same picture, angry clouds spitting droplets of blue rain. Stick figure families with stick figure pets. He imagines the average person's heart may swell with warmth, but the images make him sad. Somewhere between tear-tugging and slit your wrists.

"Hello."

The pastor or preacher or reverend, Shermeto doesn't know which or whether it even makes a difference, pulls up beside him, his hands folded behind his back. Up close he's a bit older than Shermeto first realized. Yet no dark lines under his eyes, no scars etched in his face, not even a pock mark. His fingernails clean and trimmed.

The man places a hand on Shermeto's shoulder. "The Sunday school kids are very talented."

Shermeto studies the images. For five-year-olds, they're a masterpiece, possibly some of the best work they'll ever produce.

"Are you an artist?"

"Depends on your definition."

"Anything that requires abstract thinking. Creates emotion."

"That's too general."

The man assesses the room. "Are you hungry? Better get in now."

Shermeto nods. He's starving. Across the room, Rueben leans over the kitchen pass through, animated limbs, women in hairnets laughing, blushing at the fabricated flattery.

"I'm Father Brian."

Father. Right, he forgot about that one. Shermeto nods but doesn't return the introduction. The last thing he needs is someone tracking his movement. That's why he hates the drop-in centre so much, having to register every time. The whole point is to stay invisible.

Father Brian leads Shermeto to the kitchen.

"Please help yourself. As much as you want." The father turns his attention to the continuous flow of bodies filing into the basement. "Not sure we'll have enough food." He beelines for the kitchen.

Shermeto surveys the tables. He doesn't recognize a single face except Reuben who has finally seated himself. A woman with a hairnet smiles up at him. "Tomato soup and ham sandwiches."

She slides the plate and bowl across the counter.

Shermeto nods. "Thank you."

"Saved you a seat." Orange soup dribbles down Reuben's chin. "It's good," Reuben says. "Eat."

The soup is buttery thick and burns the roof of his mouth. He gobbles it down quickly then takes a bite of the sandwich, chewing slowly. His jaw aches. Another thing to add to his long list of problems. And then the nausea begins to curl in his gut, the burn of acid-reflux writhing its way back up.

"You gonna eat that?" Reuben eyed the remaining sandwich.

Shermeto pushes the plate toward him. "Knock yourself out."

There must be almost a hundred people pressed into the room.

Eating, talking, laughing, as if reminiscing about an old friend freshly departed, a corpse in a box, a pile of gray ashes. Some hang their heads, refuse to make eye contact, while others challenge each other for a spot in the line, negotiating over an article of clothing, or simply arguing over who got there first. Voices rise.

A man in black jeans and a squashed face pushes another. Doesn't take much to get them started. *Is that what happened to Gerard? He said the wrong thing to the wrong person?*

Shermeto studies the room, landing carefully on each face, wondering if one of these people, his people, could have done such a terrible thing. There's no gesture he can read, no flashing neon over their heads, an arrow pointing downward. What happened yesterday or last week or forty years ago, locked up tight. The secrets dying with them. A roar and a thud of a fist landing in an eye socket. The squashed-faced man drops to the floor, arms pulled tight around his head. Father Brian rushes between them, but the fight is over before it really begins.

Father Brian escorts them both up the stairs. There's now barely enough room to stand, let alone form a proper line. The Father is taking a long time to return.

"We need to talk." Reuben has licked his bowl clean, not even a crumb left on either of the plates. "There's something I've been wanting to tell you."

"Sounds serious."

"Not here."

A scuttle of movement by the door and a woman and kid enter the room. A quick search and then they squeeze to the wall. Her skirt is bright orange and yellow zigzags, and it reaches past her feet. Shermeto can't catch his breath. A white cardigan, at least two-sizes too big, hangs from her shoulders. She whispers something in the kid's ear, dark ribbons of hair falling around her face. He nods, and zig zags his way to the kitchen, darting through legs to the front of the line. When the kid passes by the table, Shermeto chokes on a mouthful of air, falls into a fit of hacks and lung spasms. *It's him.* But it's not him. The same sandy hair, light eyes. Shermeto's chest hurts.

Everything hurts. Someone is pounding on his back.

"Jesus, man, you okay?" Reuben leans close to his face. "Are you crying?"

The kid is staring at him, the resemblance created by his imagination. Same height. Same build. Same hole in the knee of his pants. Stevie had more skinned knees and grass stains than Shermeto could count.

Had his boy come back to him? It's a dream. All in his head. Snap out of it for fuck sakes. It's not real.

"Talk to me. Shit. Is he having a stroke?"

"Should we call an ambulance?"

Shermeto coughs into the back of his hand, battling each breath until they slow.

"Not having a stroke." He shoos Reuben's hand away.

The kid turns, his gaze drifting past Shermeto, searching for the woman in the corner. He finds her and relaxes. She's trying to disappear into the corner.

No one minds that the kid butted ahead. He's balancing a tray with two soups and two sandwiches. He doesn't have any spoons.

"Hey, kid," Shermeto calls out and the kid pauses. Shermeto grabs a couple of spoons from the metal container and sets them on the tray. "Hard to eat soup with your hands."

Shermeto offers what he hopes is a smile.

"Thanks," he says, his voice no more than a whisper.

Plates and bowls wiped clean, chairs scrape the floor. Burps, pats on the stomach and the room begins to empty. The kid makes it back to the corner. Relief settles over the woman's face.

"Are you listening to me?" Reuben pokes Shermeto's arm.

"What?!" Angrier than he intends.

"Don't have to be dick." Reuben picks crumbs off the plates with the tip of his finger. "You almost died. Want to get out of here? I need to tell you something." He licks his finger.

Father Brian leads the woman and kid to an empty table. They exchange words. There's a familiarity between them. Has she been here before? Why hasn't he seen them? These two he would remember.

"You coming?" Reuben pushes back, knocking the chair behind him. His elbow connects with skull.

"Watch it." A man erupts from the table, fists ready. *Here it comes.* Edging on a fight. Shermeto would place bets on the other guy, wide biceps and a tattoo of a skull on his forearm.

"Sorry. Didn't mean nothing by it." Reuben holds up his hands in surrender and backs away. He turns to Shermeto and whispers, "Got any money?"

Shermeto nods and instantly regrets it.

"Well, lord love a duck." Reuben pushes away from the table and stares down at Shermeto. "You coming?"

"Give me a minute. Stomach's all knotted. Need to take a shit."

"Glad I got guts of steel. Meet you outside."

The bathroom is small and smells like mildew. He locks the door and leans against it. The image of the woman and kid are stuck in his mind. What's their story? Not often there're kids on the streets. The police or child services snatch them up like nobodies business. Which tells him they haven't been there long. He recognizes the fear behind the woman's eyes, the way she's folded in on herself.

He balances his backpack on the edge of the sink and digs in the outside pocket for his wallet, pulls out the cash, slips a couple of bills into his pocket and folds the rest into his sock. The picture is tucked in a slot behind his long-expired driver's license. He pulls it out and studies it. Grace and all three kids. Grace is shading her eyes from the sun. Lily and Kendra are hugging Stevie between them, his face smushed into Kendra's stomach. He can't be more than three. On the backside of the photo, in faded blue ink, Kendra's phone number. *He could call her, let her know he's okay.* Tell her to stop worrying, he's got this. Promise to come for Thanksgiving. But that won't take away the pain. It won't heal him. He'll have to admit so much that he's not yet willing to. He folds the picture back in the wallet and drops it back in the pocket. Then he remembers the camera. He digs it out from the bottom of the bag and studies it. There's even a memory card in the slot and batteries. What did

Kendra think he was going to do with this? Put a camera back in his hands and it would make everything ok? She's confused and desperate.

But he likes the feel of it in his hand. It's not his fancy Canon, doesn't have all the lenses, but it would work in a pinch. Great for a newbie photographer. He turns the camera on and peers at the digital display, at the focus on the door, on his feet, at his boot laying on its side next to the toilet. Unintentionally he snaps a photo and something triggers in him as he studies the image. Is this what it has all amounted to? He shuts off the camera, sighs and drops it into his pocket.

The woman and kid are gone. The plates and bowls have been cleared. Father Brian stands by the exit personally wishing everyone well. There's no way to avoid it. Shermeto cringes under the touch.

"Thank you for coming. I hope you got enough to eat."

"Thank you."

It's the right thing to say.

"Come back anytime."

Shermeto starts to pull away then hesitates. "Do you know the woman that was sitting over there? The one with the kid?"

"So many come and go; it's hard to keep track of them all."

"Of course." Shermeto inches up the stairs. "You spoke to her."

"Yes. I know who you mean. Do you know them?"

"No. She reminds me of someone, is all. Do you know where they went?"

Father Brian shakes his head. "Sorry. No. But they just left. Couldn't have gotten far."

Shermeto shuffles up the stairs and outside. The sky has cleared. The sun is blistering, giving off the kind of muggy heat that will further leather his skin. He scans the sidewalk up and down, both sides of the street, but he doesn't see them. Reuben digs through his cart, intent on finding something in the bottom. The garbage bags are spread across the sidewalk and he's muttering under his breath.

"What's the matter?" Rueben says, his hand buried inside a flat boot. He pulls out a pillow case.

"Be right back." Shermeto hurries to the end of the block. Cars rush back and forth. Which way? *Think. Which way would he go?* The crossing light changes and he's thrust along with the other pedestrians to the other side of the street; past a Chinese restaurant where garlic and ginger burps good afternoon to the passersby. A Chinese couple volley unintelligible words back and forth between them. The woman points to the roof and stutters out whiney screeches. The man looks up. Shermeto looks up. All he can see is weathered brick.

Farther down the street a man shakes out a floor mat, then sweeps the sidewalk. He glances up and offers Shermeto a short nod. Another block down he spots the woman's skirt disappearing around the corner. Pressing his legs harder, he tries to pick up speed, but each step crunches at his knees. When he reaches the spot where the woman disappeared, they're gone.

Shermeto returns to the church, deflated and relieved. What would he even have done had he found them? There're no words to explain, nothing that makes any real sense. Reuben has replaced everything back into the cart. Jagger is with him, adjusting the kite tail.

"Not like that," Reuben says, snapping the tail away. He lays it out so that it dangles over the handle bar on the cart, then wraps it around a couple of times so the tip kisses the ground. "There you are." Reuben thrusts a notebook inside his jacket. "Let's go get that drink." He shoots Jagger a menacing glare and pulls the cart from his grasp.

"What was that all about?" Shermeto says to Jagger.

"That guy is nuts. Thought I was stealing his stuff."

"He doesn't trust you."

Jagger shrugs. "Do you?"

"They don't know you like I do."

Jagger nods and smiles. He's lost another tooth since this morning and he's discarded the bike somewhere.

"We're going to get drunk. You coming?" Shermeto asks.

"I'll pass."

"All right. Find me later."

"You can count on it."

Jagger's smile doesn't match the rage behind his eyes.

Reuben rattles his cart. ""Come on. Not getting any younger."

***

The guy behind the liquor counter has a curly mustache and a curlier smile.

"Need a bag?" he asks.

Shermeto shakes his head.

The bottles hit the bottom of his backpack with a satisfying *thunk*.

***

"It's here. All here," Reuben says.

"Ridiculous." Shermeto grumbles a few steps behind. Reuben's hair looks yellow in the sun.

"I've been keeping notes. I'll show you. It's all there. Since the beginning of the year."

"Doesn't make any sense. Why would anyone target us specifically?"

"Why wouldn't they?" Reuben reads over his own scrawled handwriting. "When did you get so naïve? Why do you think that pig farmer over in BC targeted hookers?"

The old man is talking gibberish, Shermeto thinks. *One of those conspiracy nuts who thinks they're all out to get them. Best not to play into his fantasy.*

"No one cares. Prostitutes. Homeless. We're not so different. Fishbowl scum."

The hem of Reuben's pants is shredded, threads catch under his boots.

"Could have been an accident," Shermeto says.

"Not that many. No way."

This isn't new chatter. Killers, thugs, other homeless, supernatural phenomenon, the coming of Christ. Bullshit, as far as Shermeto is concerned. Accidents, pure and simple. The one thing they do all seem to agree on, however, is that no one should be out alone after dark. In the shadows anything can linger. Anything can jump out and devour them. Fear hangs over them like a fog. But that's old news. It's a chance you take when you step into this world. "Things changed after Harlow died," Shermeto says, breaking the seal on one of his bottles.

They huddle under a tree. Reuben lays out a notebook in front of him and jabs the page.

Shermeto takes a swig from the bottle. The burn seems to bypass his liver and beeline straight for the blood stream. He passes the bottle to Reuben. Soothing. Numb. Comfortably numb? Lyrics twist through his mind. The same painful lull of the raging river. He can't see it from where he's sitting, but he feels it. The current rushing through him, trying to tell him something. But what?

"Hello?" Fingers snap in front of his face. Shermeto swings around.

"Fuck man, where you keep going?" Reuben asks.

Shermeto grunts and takes another slug off the bottle. Rueben doesn't really care what's going on with him or anyone else; he's obviously got nothing better to do. But Shermeto, he's got a bottle to polish.

"People die out here all the time. How is this any different?" The alcohol is beginning to coat his brain, like a soft blanket being pulled snug around him.

Shermeto leans his head against the tree.

"There's a pattern."

"You've lost it, old man."

"Stop saying that. You sound like that greasy prick that keeps following you around. What you got with him anyway?" Rueben thrusts the notebook onto Shermeto's lap. "He knew Harlow, you know."

Shermeto looks at the page, at the names, the dates, causes of death. Some unknowns in terms of names, causes ranging from exposure to dehydration, malnutrition, 'beaten to a pulp'. Nothing out of the ordinary. Nothing to get all twisted about. Except for the recent names. In the last month, six names, all familiar to Shermeto.

"How'd you get all this?"

"Research." Reuben points at his forehead. "I watch. Listen. Should try it some time."

Shermeto shakes his head and continues to read. Arthur. Blunt object to the head. Scratches up and down his chest.

"How do I know you didn't do this? Some of these are pretty detailed."

"Ha. Do I look like I could do something like this? What possible reason would I have?"

Shermeto can think of several reasons. Reuben is a thief. Everyone knows it. Always keep one eye open around Old Reuben or he'll steal your underwear. Many of the things in that cart of his could have belonged to any one of these people. What's in the bags? Not that knowing will do any good. Reuben takes a swig of the bottle and passes it over.

"You wanted to tell me something?" Shermeto skims the pages, working his way backward.

"Not important." Reuben seems nervous, jittery. Probably the alcohol.

Shermeto finds what he's looking for. His finger presses hard to the page.

***

Harlow's frozen, dead face comes to mind. It had been a cruel winter. The lineups at the shelters longer than the stays themselves. Harlow wanted to wait anyway.

"Not sleeping here," Shermeto said.

"You'll freeze out there."

"Take my chances."

Harlow, obviously torn, wanted to get warm, but didn't want to leave Shermeto out on his own. He blew warm air into his hands. *They'd find a place.* And they did. Shermeto stole a blanket and a couple of hats from a shopping cart and set off down the river. In a parking lot they stopped and huddled under a semi-trailer, pushed as far back under the tires as they could get, the gentle shush of the river only a few yards away. They wrapped themselves together under the blanket, pulled their hats down over their faces and that's where they stayed. Too cold to even talk.

"This is stupid," Harlow muttered.

Shermeto ignored him. "Go to sleep."

"You fucking owe me."

Sometime in the middle of the night Shermeto woke to dogs barking, the screech of sirens several blocks away. He rolled over. No feeling in his fingers, his face numb. Ice crystals glistened on the underbelly of the trailer. Shermeto nudged Harlow, he didn't stir. Harlow's fingers balled in fists. The blanket lay at his feet, a hat pulled over his face. Harlow's skin had turned bluish-gray, and ice hardened his lips.

"Come on. Wake up."

Shermeto punched his friend in the shoulder, in the stomach, slapped him across the face, waited for the sting of pink to spread across his cheeks, but nothing.

Shermeto sat back against a tire. Too cold to cry, afraid his eyelids might freeze shut. "I'm sorry," Shermeto said.

***

Shermeto closes his eyes and listens to the soft hush of the river, the calls of birds darting overhead. Voices drift towards him. Closer.

"You ever wonder if it's worth it?" Reuben asks.

Shermeto doesn't answer.

"I've been out here a long time. Seen a lot of things. A lot of people, coming and going. It's different here than anywhere else."

"How so?"

"Colder for one. In the winter. Shit. Can't tell you how many times my nads almost froze off."

Shermeto nods, sinks deeper into his warm fuzzy place.

"If you're gonna be homeless, go someplace warm. That's my advice. Not here. That's asking for a death sentence." Reuben burps.

"What you do before this?"

Shermeto's eyes snap open. He tilts his head at Reuben, studies his face, his eyes.

"Does it matter?"

No one except Harlow and Jagger ever asked him about his life before, in fact, he's not even sure if Jagger ever bothered.

Reuben shrugs. "That's always the question, isn't it?"

"Or the answer."

"Gotta take a leak." Reuben pushes himself up from the ground and limps across the grass then disappears into a tangle of trees along the bank.

Shermeto closes his eyes again. *He's not like all the others,* he thinks. He came of his own accord. Gave up everything. Walked out on life. Does that make him better than the rest? He thinks so. He can leave anytime he wants, that's the difference between them and him.

Reuben returns and drops back to the ground beside him.

"Spot me a swig." He nods towards Shermeto's pack. They suck back the last of the bottle. Alcohol dribbles down Reuben's chin. He swipes it with his hand and then licks his palm.

"Good to the last drop," he says and settles into the grass. "What happened to Harlow's body?"

"I tossed it in the river," Shermeto says.

"No, you didn't."

"Sure did."

He's not lying. A bitch of a task, in fact. Dragged the body across the parking lot to the river bank with the intention of rolling him in the water, only to find a thick layer of ice. He tugged and pulled across the snow and ice until he heard a hint of a crackle. He sat back and waited for the ice to give way and take his friend along its frozen path down the centre of the river. Shermeto slunk back to the bank and watched the body bob and sink, then bob up again. Someone would find him.

A couple lies in the grass on the other side of the path, their faces partially hidden in shade. Their gaze darts between one another, nattering back and forth. One points to the river below. Reuben begins to snore softly beside him. He wishes he could sleep. His exhaustion has turned a rusty yellow orange; smoldering coals, dust curling away with the currents.

What if Reuben's right? What if there is something to these deaths? The notebook lies open on the grass. Harlow's name written at the top of the page, circled several times. Is that where it started? Thousands of notes. Jotted in tired handwriting. Months of scribblings. And if it does have something to do with him, then no one around him is safe.

Shermeto flips back to the recent names again. It isn't unusual for someone to be there one minute and gone the next, but these are people who he knew in more than passing. Arthur. Shermeto worked a few jobs with him. The most recent a few months back. They had stood in silence on the corner, waiting for someone to come along. The thing with the corner, you could stand out there for a whole day and have no one come along except a few cops checking up. Once a news van pulled up, the reporter getting out to ask a few questions. They stood on the street, gripping their carts for fear someone would steal the remains of their lives, uncover their secrets. The memories would usually kill you before anything else.

The day with Arthur they didn't have to wait long. Shermeto and Arthur shared a smoke between them as a pickup pulled up to the curb. A man rolled down the passenger window and leaned over.

"You two looking for something to do?"

"Sure thing."

"Hop in," the man said and unlocked the door.

Shermeto sat in the middle.

"What kind of job?" Arthur asked.

"Moving day. The wife and I are leaving the city. Boxes and furniture."

"Where you off to?" Arthur kept the conversation going.

"Back to BC."

"Sounds like you'd rather be anywhere else," Shermeto said.

"All for the marriage."

"Happy wife. Happy life." Arthur laughed.

The man drummed his fingers on the steering wheel.

"Name's Don."

They introduced themselves.

Don took them deep into the outskirts of the city. Nice estate homes piled up around them. Castles. This was where the people with too much money congregated. They wound into a subdivision along curved, perfectly manicured streets and lanes. Not a shrub out of place. Then through to a more average neighbourhood with older style homes where trees grew in gnarled knots, and fences and gates needed repair, not so different from his previous life. They pulled into a back lane and Don stopped the truck.

"Don't worry about the wife. She's a tad cranky today."

Around the front of the house a U-Haul stood empty, waiting, boxes piled on the front porch. The house could use a paint job, lattice work along the bottom of the porch was broken so small animals could easily move in and out. Arthur grabbed a box and hauled it to the truck.

"I'll bring the boxes out and you load them into the truck."

Through the large front window, Don was talking to a woman. She kept pointing outside at them. When she brought more boxes out, she refused to make eye contact.

"Thanks for the work, ma'am," Shermeto said.

The woman offered an almost imperceptible nod and went back into the house. Don came outside with more boxes.

"Don't worry about her."

"She's not happy we're here," Shermeto said.

"Between you and me, she's not happy about much."

By mid-afternoon, sweat dripping down their foreheads, Don brought out a tray of sandwiches and a jug of water with glasses, then went back inside. The pair gulped back the water and ate the sandwiches with nothing but the sound of chewing and swallowing between them. A magpie squawked in the lightly fluttering trees. A shimmer of breeze, barely perceptible, did nothing to relieve the heat. Shermeto pulled off his hoodie and dropped it in the grass at the bottom of the steps.

The woman suddenly let out a screech.

"Don! They stole my plates. I told you not to let them in here."

Don set down the box he was carrying and went to his boiling wife. Shermeto could practically see the veins in her neck throbbing, the red in her cheeks.

"They were right there and now they're gone."

Don put his arm on his wife's shoulder and pushed her back into the house.

"I'm calling the police if they don't return them right now."

Shermeto and Arthur glanced at one another, the question on both of their minds. *Did you take it?* Shermeto knew he hadn't. What would he do with a bunch of plates? And where would he put them? Arthur had been with him the whole time. No way he could have taken them.Don came out of the house, shaking his head.

"Sorry. She's gone and snapped."

"We didn't take nothing," Arthur said.

"I know. Don't worry about it. They'll turn up."

And they did, of course. Already packed in the back of the U-Haul.

According to Reuben's book, Arthur turned up dead out in Bowness a month ago. Unknown cause of death.

Joe and Marie are next on Reuben's list. A funny couple. Met on the streets and inseparable. Shermeto shared stories with them on several occasions, the last of which was in the park right after a rain storm. Must be going on six weeks ago now. They came out of the trees and lumbered around the cenotaph. He hadn't seen them since.

The afternoon slips away before he knows it and soon the sun begins to sink. He closes the book and peels off his shoes and socks. The cool air paws his skin. His eyes are heavy, determined to shut before night falls. The woman and kid flicker to his mind. The way she held the kid close, watching every move, like if she blinked, he'd be gone.

He dozes and dreams. Abstract patterns. Flattened squares.

Stretched circles. His fear. His failure. Hovering beyond his grasp. Frozen in the seat of a car the colour of anger, ripe edges turning to fire, the smoke peeling around him, diving and swerving with the shapes, through the open car windows, tweaking inches from his nose. He can't move. Groping fingers singe his skin. His mouth opens to scream and suddenly fills with water. A metallic garden of icy waves surges around him, through him, nothing more than paper fibres weaving together. His skin unravels, floating beside him and then begins to reconstruct, taking on the thinly veiled shape of his regret, before suddenly disintegrating into miniscule drops.

Shermeto coughs himself awake. Cold. Alone. Relieved. Shapes are just shapes, no distorted patterns to interpret. A car alarm blares. No one notices. The sun sinks over the mountains, pinks and oranges speckling the water.

Where are the woman and kid now? Are they safe? Warm? He's not supposed to care so much, but the kid can't be much older than Stevie. So long ago he strains to remember the angles of his face, the curve of his smile. The memories are warped, like an action shot caught with the wrong shutter speed.

"You're awake," Reuben sits up.

"Lucky me."

"Got any more booze?"

Shermeto shakes his head. He does but he wants to save that for himself.

"Probably shouldn't hang around here too long. It's getting dark." Reuben glances at his wrist where no watch is strapped. "Got a smoke?"

Shermeto has a few left from the cabby. He pulls them out of his shirt and hands one to Reuben, and pops one in his own mouth.

"Forgot how good these things taste."

Reuben takes a long pull off the cigarette. Shermeto can hardly see his face anymore. The cherry flares and dissolves, then flares again with each inhale.

Shermeto nods. "Have you ever wanted to get out? Go back. You know?"

"I got nothing to go back to."

"But if you did?"

"I'm a lifer. I'll die out here."

Shermeto glances towards the river, which is invisible except for the constant rumble and gurgle. It's getting closer. He catches movement in the dense brush. A person? Animal? Is he still drunk? He closes his eyes and opens them again. Definitely something there. He can feel its steely eyes. His stomach tightens. A buzz edges through him. He reaches for Reuben and whispers, "Do you see that?"

"Told you. It's out there. Waiting. Don't go to sleep."

The air turns soupy. Shermeto can't breathe. Reuben grunts.

"What is it?"

Shermeto's voice is hoarse, the words disintegrating before they can bridge the gap between them. He glances at Reuben. His eyes wide, a glint of white. When he turns back to the trees, there is nothing but darkness and the river alive, angry. Air rips around them, icy claws grazing his skin.

Reuben begins to snore beside him. Shermeto watches the river-bank, the brush. There is something there, he's sure of it, can feel it. And then he sees movement and a figure emerges from the brush. Shermeto blinks and stares. It's not possible. He pushes to his feet and follows slowly along the path. Definitely a person, familiar in the way he moves, a secure swagger he's only ever seen on one other person, but it's impossible. Harlow went into the river. Shermeto put him there himself.

Shermeto searches for the words but they're so incredible he can't force them past his lips. The man walks along at a clip and crawls down another bank to a beach of rocks. He stands at the rivers edge, and for a moment the moon catches his eyes and Shermeto knows.

The man turns and a thin smile stretches across his face. Shermeto takes a step forward but stops as the man walks into the river and dissolves back into the darkness.

KENDRA

When Kendra returns Gary is perched on her front step. Wide-eyed. Curious. He holds up a bag of groceries.

"Breakfast for dinner," he says.

As he cracks eggs into a frying pan, turning sausages in another, she tells him what happened in the park.

"Good thing you were there," he says.

Gary's back is to her. He has a nice back. Long, narrow, shoulders of a linebacker.

"You saved someone today," Gary says, swinging around with a fork in his hand.

"I guess I did," she says. She doesn't want to imagine what might have happened to the man, or the dog, had she not been there.

"Any word on your dad?"

Kendra shakes her head. "Don't even know where to start."

"Street by street?" Gary suggests.

"There's a lot of streets."

"You don't have to do it alone. I'll help."

"Nice of you to offer, but really, this is my problem, not yours." She grabs a pen and notepad from a kitchen drawer.

"You don't like to ask for help, do you?"

"Never." Kendra smiles and sits back at the table and quickly jots down all the possible places her father could be hiding. When she rereads the list, she shakes her head and sighs. "It's all so cliché."

"What do you mean?" Gary turns back to the stove.

"Under bridges. Behind dumpsters in back alleys. They don't really live like this do they? It's make-believe, what we see on TV."

Gary shrugs. "Anywhere they can get out of the elements. It's not so crazy. A shelter is a shelter."

"Maybe."

"What about an actual shelter?"

"If he won't stay in the hospital, why would he go to a shelter?"

· "Someone might at least know him and where to find him." Gary scrapes eggs onto the plates and adds sausage links. He sets the plates on the table. He stands back proud, hands on hips. "I'll call around and see if anyone knows him."

Kendra can't help but smile. She can't—or rather won't—call it love, but she strongly likes this guy. "You really want to help?"

"Wouldn't be here if I didn't."

Kendra believes him.

"What happened to your brother?" Gary asks.

***

Kendra's tenth birthday and misplaced childhood jealousy started the horrible ball rolling. Screams lit the air. Water sprung from the sprinkler, slowly arcing back and forth as the kids ran through it. Water up their noses, in their eyes, rolling around on the wet grass.

Her mother was inside making iced tea from real lemons the way Kendra liked it. The steady tinkle of the spoon against the container reached her, but she couldn't see her dad anywhere. Not since he laid out and staked down the Slip n' Slide.

Stevie sat on top of the sprinkler.

"Get off there." Lily pushed him out of the way. He fell, and his bottom lip began to quiver. *Not today. Stupid baby.*

Mom came out on the porch and set the iced tea on the table.

"Where's Dad?" Kendra asked.

Mom shaded her eyes and searched the yard, then shook her head and continued to pour the tea. "Do you want ice cream with your cake?" she asked.

"Yesss." Kendra jumped off the porch to join her friends and was instantly in a shower of water. "Steven. Stop it." She yelled but Stevie only angled the water more in her direction. Everyone laughed.

Then her dad appeared, coming out of the shed. His smile reached out like a soft hand on the shoulder, wrapping around her, holding tight. She smiled back. He ran towards them, grabbed the sprinkler from her brother and a chase around the yard began. More screaming, doubling over in gut-splitting, pee-your-pants laughter. They tried to get the water from Dad, but he was tall, so much stronger than the rest of them.

Kendra crouched low to the ground. When he wasn't watching, she pounced, latching onto his leg.

"Noooo," he cried out. "She's got me."

Kendra laughed. Her dad reached down and scooped her into his arms and ran around the yard. Now she was the princess and the centre of all the attention. Children scattered, laughing, hiding behind bushes and on the porch where her mother sat, sunhat covering her eyes but not her smile. Father and daughter fell to the ground.

"I'm getting too old for this stuff," he said, shading his eyes from the sun.

"You're not old," Kendra said.

"Wait and see. One day." He tweaked her chin.

"Daddy. Daddy. Watch me." Steven stood at the start of the Slip n' Slide.

"Go for it, buddy."

Stevie ran at the slide and flew onto his stomach, letting the water carry him to the end. But he didn't stop. He hit the grass and somersaulted once, landing hard on his side. The air filled with a blood-clotting shriek. Dad leaped from the ground, Mom flew off the porch. All her friends fell silent. Stevie curled on his side, tears spilling down his face, clutching his arm that resembled a wet noodle.

"It hurts." Stevie screamed louder and louder.

"I'll take him. You stay here." Mom nodded, while Dad whisked Stevie into the backseat of the car.

Kendra's shoulders slumped. All her friends gathered around the car. Her birthday ruined.

***

"He died from a broken arm?"

Kendra stifles a laugh. It's not supposed to be funny. "No. Of course, not."

But that incident led to the next.

SHERMETO

It had to be the alcohol, there's no other way to explain it. A whisper nips through the trees as the branches overhead come into focus, the river is rough, carving over the rocks. He rubs at his face and slowly makes his way back to Reuben. But Reuben is gone and so is Shermeto's backpack. "Jesus, fucking Christ." The cart is gone, too.

"Goddammit. You better hope I don't find you," Shermeto screams. "Rip your eyeballs out through your asshole." His lips crack, fresh blood seeps into his mouth.

Shermeto knows full well if Reuben doesn't want to be found, he won't. *Damnit. He knows better.* He kicks a can along the sidewalk, catches up then crunches it under his foot. Could be weeks, even months until they cross paths again. Harlow loved the old coot but was always just as happy to see him go. They'd rumble together for a few weeks and then without notice, Reuben would be gone. No one worried. It's who he is.

"Where does he go?" Shermeto had asked once.

Harlow shrugged. "No one knows."

"Do you trust him?"

"As much as anyone else." Harlow grew silent, thoughtful. "He knows stuff though. Don't discount what he says. His delivery may be off, but there's something to it. He sees and knows more about life out here than anyone else."

Shermeto had brushed it off at the time. Now he thought maybe Harlow had been grossly mistaken.

At least he didn't get his sock money. Shermeto crosses the street and makes his way toward the railroad overpass. He stops, glances behind him. Windows are boarded up, businesses long since forgotten. He can't see into the dark cracks but knows someone is watching. He feels it like the itch in his groin, every ache and pain.

Creeping along the streets at this hour, he usually feels safe. No judgmental stares. He passes under the railroad tracks and climbs up the hillside. He pauses at the top to catch his breath and watches cars blaze past, completely unaware of his little blip in this god forsaken universe. He plunks himself down on a rock. Between the darkness and the overpass behind him, he's impressively invisible. All he's ever wanted, he found here. In the darkest holes of a city he used to love but couldn't fit into. The only place he was finally able to silence the screams.

A semi-truck leans on its horn, cutting the dark in half. He studies the city lights, a sprinkle of colour, stars blinking. The Calgary Tower is illuminated in a bright blue tonight.

A police car rips by, siren muted, lights flashing, but with the usual intention. His back wrenches when he twists, and he folds over, gasping for breath. Sweat beads on his forehead, in his armpits, down his back. Is this it? He's dying now. And it's going to hurt. He vomits in the dirt. Pukes himself to tears, until there's nothing left but dry heaves. Cold and alone, he desperately wants to punch something.

The tears come harder. He knows it doesn't have to be like this. He misses Harlow. And Kendra and Lily and Stevie and especially Grace. It stings too much to think about his Grace. Shermeto blows his nose on his sleeve, wipes his eyes. What a loathsome mess he has become.

"Hey mister?" A voice from behind him. Shermeto snaps around. Standing in the dirt a few feet away is the kid from the church. Where'd he come from and where's his mother?

"Little late for a kid to be out," he says.

"Why are you crying?" There's a wariness on the kid's face. He's ready to bolt at any moment.

"Not crying."

"Yes, you are. I saw you."

"Where's your mother?"

"Back there." He points behind him.

"You should go back then. Not safe out here."

"I'm not scared." The kid takes a tentative step closer.

That makes one of them. Shermeto is fucking terrified.

"What's your name?" Shermeto asks.

"Not supposed to talk to strangers."

"You started it."

The kid squints at him. "My name is Reese."

"Like the peanut butter cups."

Reese squeezes his face. "Gross. I hate peanut butter."

"Who hates peanut butter?"

"Allergic. Makes my face blow up like a bloated fish. That's why I have this."

The kid pulls an EpiPen from his pocket and holds it up like a magic wand.

"That must be scary."

"Lots of things scarier."

Shermeto can't disagree there. "Saw you and your mother at the church this afternoon."

The kid kicks at the gravel. "I remember. What happened to your face?"

"A scuffle. Nothing too serious."

"Does it hurt?"

"Hardly notice it anymore."

"I had a black eye once. Lots of bruises."

"Makes you tough."

"They hurt a lot."

"Did you at least get your own licks in?"

"Not strong enough. When I grow up, I'm going to be really strong. Lift weights, like a wrestler. Then no one can ever hurt me again."

Shermeto reads the sadness on the kids's face and realizes he's learned too much. It's not his place, but he feels a surge, a need to protect this kid. Then quickly, *what makes him think he can protect anyone when he can't even take care of himself?*

"Mom worries a lot. I should go." The kid takes a few steps back, then stops. "You coming?"

"Where?"

"There's fires to keep warm and tents and stuff."

The Flats. It's possible that's where Reuben went.

Shermeto lumbers behind the kid who stops every few steps to let him catch up. They don't speak as they wind through tall grass, behind abandoned buildings, making their way to The Flats. The place is named because it's exactly that…flat and tucked neatly into an abandoned section of the old rail yard. Police know it's here, but don't bother coming around much. The community keeps to themselves, except for the occasional graffiti splatter on the side of parked railcars, or the boards along the chain link fence separating the old from the new.

Laughter and music mingle with the campfire smoke, a hint of weed and a lot of cigarettes. Young and old huddle in clusters, under blankets or lean against the fence, firelight catching a glint in their eyes. Around random firepits, flasks are passed back and forth, shadowed faces sitting in circles, stretched out, smoking and drinking in front of their tents, reclining over bed rolls.

A gentleness settles over Shermeto as he feels he is at home, with his people. These are the ones who took him in, gave a place to just be, to dwell in his misery and forget about it for a little while. Only he never forgets.

He searches for anyone he knows, a glance of recognition, a smile. Except the occasional nod of curiosity, most keep their heads down. He doesn't recognize the faces like he once did. The kid leads him across The Flats to a far back corner, where beyond the tents and chain link, the river scrapes the banks. There're a dozen around this fire. He spots the woman first sitting on a tire rim, her knees tucked up to her chin. The conversation stops as all the faces turn to them.

"Well, Jesus Murphy. Look what the cat dragged in."

It's Duncan. Shermeto'd thought he got out a year back.

"Where you been hiding?" Duncan asks, lurching to his feet. He grabs Shermeto by the arm, leading him into the circle. "Skootch over," he says to a woman with a black eye and blacker hair.

The boy's mother scowls at the kid.

"Get over here right now. You can't be going off on your own. I told you that. What if someone sees you?" She pulls him down beside her.

"Sorry." The kid tucks his head under his mother's arm.

"You know better." Her face softens. "Don't know what I would do if I lost you."

"Where you been at?" Duncan digs inside a cooler and holds out a sweaty bottle of beer. "It's a twist off."

Shermeto wipes the bottle on his pants before opening it. "Here and there. You see Old Reuben recently?"

"That old bugger. Nah. Ain't seen him in a coon's age." Duncan takes a swig of his own bottle. "What you want with him?"

"Got something of mine. I want it back."

"Saucy fucker. Still scooping what ain't nailed down." Duncan clears his throat. "You know everyone? That there's Danielle. She's with me." He nods to the woman with the shiner. "Ginny's with Rocky. The old fart curled up sucking his thumb is Dave, they call him Doughnut sometimes, but still haven't figured out why. Sharon. Rick. Mouse. And the little one's Tessa. She's not as young as she looks. Reese and his mama bear, Rose. Hey all, this is Shermeto." Duncan slaps him on the back. "We go way back."

Duncan turns to Danielle, "Get my man something to eat, woman."

Danielle scowls and reaches into a cooler beside her. She pulls out a sandwich and hands it over.

"Thanks." He's not really that hungry. The beer is filling any holes that he might have had and doesn't settle in his gut like everything else.

"That fancy sausage shop down the way. They just throw out

their old stuff. Made a deal with one of the bakers. We can have the leftovers, but we have to put it all together ourselves."

"I does all the work and these buggers eat it." Danielle gives Duncan a soft punch on the arm. "Ain't that right, lover?" Her voice reduces to a condescending sneer.

"You're a good woman." Duncan pulls out an enormous Ziploc bag full of cigarettes and pops one his mouth. He offers the bag to Shermeto. "Take two," he says.

"Where you get all those?" He takes a couple.

"Connections." Duncan smiles. No more explanation than that. No more is needed. Take in all the information you can, reveal only what's necessary. Rose is rolling up one of the kid's sleeves, smoothing down the his hair.

Dave sits up, groggy, nodding from one to another. He stops on Shermeto.

"Hey, I know you." He points a gloved finger at Shermeto.

Is that an accusation?

"Makes one of us," Shermeto says.

"You and Harlow used to go about."

Rose's head snaps up.

"It'll come to me." He taps his forehead. "Got into a fight with that bastard, what was his name? Stealing all the bikes and kiddy pools from backyards. Damn. Don't remember his name. Busted up his lip real good."

Shermeto knows exactly who he's talking about. Last year, during a string of burglaries the city was blaming on the homeless, Harlow took it on himself to find the guy and put a stop to it. Didn't go so well for the other guy. Found all the items back in a thicket by the bird sanctuary.

Rose leaned forward, listening carefully.

"What happened to him?" she asks.

"No clue. Haven't seen him in ages." Dave shifts uncomfortably, twisting his body and straightening his legs. He lets out a soft groan.

Duncan flicks his cigarette butt in the fire and passes out more beers.

"Coppers busted me again the other night. Threw me in the clink. Loitering. Can they even do that? Arrest someone for just being in a certain place at a certain time? Bullshit city. Bullshit cops."

Shermeto thinks this one is Rocky. Dark hair, maybe a scab or mole on his cheek. Either he's slouching or he's significantly shorter than the others.

"They snatched my gin right out of my hand. Worked hard for that bottle and they take it like it's nothing. Doubt it made it back to the station."

This one might be Sharon. She's soft-spoken, yet with an underlying tone of *don't mess with me or I'll fuck you up*. Shermeto has no intention of messing with anyone.

A murmur of agreement bubbles through the group.

Duncan turns to Shermeto. "You had any run-ins with the cops?"

Shermeto shakes his head. "Not lately." It's true. He mostly keeps to himself. No need to make trouble where it's not necessary.

"Lucky bastard," Dave says.

Another murmur turns to a grumble.

Shermeto casts his eyes on Rose. She's leaning forward, almost hypnotized by the flames, worrying threads free from the cuff of her sweater. She's anywhere but here. She's wearing the same clothes as earlier. Reese is watching Shermeto. He smiles and hides his head. Shermeto studies the group but no one seems to be paying any attention. He snubs out his cigarette and tosses it into the fire then guzzles the rest of his beer.

"I got kicked out of the Salvation Army. Zero tolerance policies and all. Wasn't even my fault. That Crazy Al with the wonky eyeballs, he brought the goods. Nothing happened to him. What with all this rain, been trying to find a dry bunk. But tonight, we're under the stars."

A fight breaks out behind them. Rose's eyes widen, she pulls the kid closer to her while the pair spits insults at each other. A shove. A slap. Hair pulling. And as quickly as the fight begins, it stops.

"Happens all the time," Duncan says. It doesn't set Rose at ease. She nods and gives a thin smile.

Duncan turns to Shermeto. "Why you looking for Reuben?"

"Bad judgement call," Shermeto says.

Duncan nods but doesn't press.

"Lots of that going around these days," Duncan says.

From the shadows Jagger appears. Straight-faced. He scans the group, pauses when he sees Shermeto. "There you are." He pushes in between Shermeto and Duncan.

"You know this guy?" Duncan asks.

Shermeto nods.

Rose is staring at them, her gaze peeling away layer after layer. Shermeto can't bear to feel what may be underneath. Her lips purse like she wants to say something. He shifts uncomfortably in his jacket and turns his attention to Jagger.

"What happened to Reuben?" Jagger asks.

"Don't want to talk about it."

"Yapping again, the old bugger. Don't believe any of his conspiracy theories," Jagger says.

Fire crackles between them, their faces illuminated in orange light. A bottle of JD changes hands while sparks shoot up, fireworks dissolving in the night air. An ember lands near Shermeto's foot. He crushes it with the heel of his boot.

"Jesus, fuck." Duncan shoots up off the ground, swatting at his pants.

Ginny stares into the flames, hands folded on her lap. A smile lightly cracks her lip.

"Not funny, bitch." Duncan sits back down.

"Who's laughing?" Ginny flicks her lighter and shoves the flame near his face.

"Back off." He snatches it from her hand.

"Give that back."

"You want it, come get it." Duncan sticks it down his pants.

"Not going near your dirty pecker."

"Not what you said last night." Without warning, Duncan cuffs Ginny in the back of the head. Ginny lunges, knocking him backward. Straddling his chest, she slaps him repeatedly across the face.

What the hell? Shermeto stares across the flames. Jagger seems mildly amused by the display.

"Foreplay," Tessa whispers. "They do this all the time." She glances sideways at Jagger, her head slightly cocked. Coy.

Shermeto nods. Makes perfect sense. Or not really. The brawl turns into a kind of tug o' war and then they are rolling in the dirt. Laughing. Lunging. Laughing some more. Finally, Duncan thrusts Ginny off him and sits up. "Well, we're out." He grabs her hand and leads her to a tent in the corner.

Shermeto feels as though that should be his cue, but he has nowhere to go. No good searching for Reuben tonight.

"Stop picking your nose." Rose swats Reese's hand away from his face. "People don't want to see your snot." The slap isn't hard, only enough to explain herself. Reese sits on his hands.

"I'm hot." His hair falls over his face, keeping all his secrets covered.

Rose sighs. "Take off your sweater then."

Reese pulls the green fleece over his head and wads it into a ball. Rose stuffs it into her canvas pull cart, and glances over her shoulder again. Fear, misery, confusion spread from cheekbone to cheekbone. Always watching.

Harlow had that look many times. When the police slowed to a crawl, searchlights glaring at them, he knew at any minute he could be hauled out of there and forced to take responsibility for his past. *Never let your guard down.* It's a simple mantra that gets forgotten. Rose passes that same trepidation and insecurity to her son.

"Is he coming? Do you see him?" The kid searches the shadows and huddles closer to his mother. Rose offers a weak smile and ruffles the kid's hair.

"Hungry?" she asks. She hands him a plastic bottle of water, sticky where the label used to be. "Drink." She glances at the cooler.

Shermeto nudges Danielle and points at the cooler and over at Rose and Reese. Danielle scowls but pulls out a sandwich.

"They can share."

There's a bite to her voice.

"Thank you," Rose says so quietly she reminds him of a scolded puppy, backed into a corner. She unwraps the sandwich and tears it in half, the bigger part goes to the kid. Even scolded puppies will attack back. Rose bares no teeth. Her shoulders relax, and she nudges the kid playfully.

"Where you two from?"

Firelight flickers in Jagger's eyes. He scoots forward. Rose's shoulders harden, but Jagger's oblivious.

"Leave them alone." Shermeto moves and parks himself as a buffer between Jagger and the nervous pair. "They just want to eat."

Jagger tosses another log on the fire. The wood snaps and sparks shoot into the sky and the fire catches and blasts waves of heat.

"There's this moment, first thing in the morning, they call it the golden hour, when the light is perfect." Shermeto doesn't know why he's talking about this, but it's the first thing that comes to mind.

"Who's they?" Rose leans forward slightly.

"It's a photography reference."

"You take pictures or something?" Rose speaks in barely a whisper.

"Used to."

"What happened?"

"Life. I guess."

"Do you miss it?" Rose takes the bottle of water from Reese and takes a sip.

"Sometimes."

Capturing light through a lens. The smell of chemicals filling a darkroom. An image slowly emerging from a blank page. Felt like magic to him. In this digital age of photos, people don't know what they're missing. Lazy clods. Now anyone can pick up a camera and claim themselves a photographer. And maybe a select few will show some signs of talent. But mostly, they're bum shots and selfies.

"Seems like something no one would ever want to give up."

Jagger stands and pisses into the fire. The coals sizzle and smoke then fall silent. Jagger's hat hangs from his back pocket.

"So now what?" He zips his pants and sinks down next to Tessa.

They nuzzle each for a moment and then Jagger turns to him. "You gonna stay here all night?"

Shermeto shrugs. "I might." Not even a twinkle of a star can be seen. Lightning flashes in the distance. A low, faraway grumble follows. "Here we go again."

Jagger's lips turn upward in a greedy smile. "Can't be any rain left to fall." He laughs then sits back down.

"There's always more rain." Rose wraps her hands around the bottle.

"That's optimistic." Jagger practically spits the words. When no one responds he keeps going. "Had a good day today," Jagger says. Now all eyes turn to him. "Was sitting down at the park and out of nowhere this woman, she comes out of nowhere and asks if I need something to eat. Then hands me a bag of food. Just like that."

"Awful nice," Shermeto says.

"I thought so."

Tessa buries her face into Jagger's neck. They start to laugh. Tessa unzips Jagger's pants and her hand disappears.

"Jesus Christ. Do that somewhere else. There's a kid here."

Tessa snaps her head around and practically hisses, "Mind your own business, old man." Jagger says something that only she can hear. "Fine." She takes back her hand and the pair stand. "I'm out of here. You know where to find me. And I'll keep an eye out for that fucknut."

Jagger pulls his hat from his pocket and locks it onto his head. "What did he take from you anyway?"

"Want my wallet back is all. Don't much care about the rest," Shermeto says.

Jagger nods. "Gotcha. Well, you know where to find me." The pair staggers away.

"You have someplace to go?" Shermeto turns to Rose.

"We manage."

"We have a tent. Over there." The kid points, almost too enthusiastic. It hasn't occurred to Shermeto that these two had been staying here. How long?

"Can't be easy." Shermeto glances at the kid, taking tiny bites of his sandwich, pulling the crust free and tossing it in the dirt. This is no place for a kid.

"Stop wasting food," Rose says. "Don't know when we'll eat again." Rose lets out a sigh. "Constantly checking over my shoulder. If it's not one thing, it's another."

Shermeto nods. He thinks he understands, but maybe he's completely off his nut. Rose snatches the rest of the sandwich from the kid and rewraps it in the plastic. She tucks it inside the cart. "Bedtime."

"I don't wanna."

"Not open for discussion. Go."

The kid lifts his eyes to Shermeto. "Will you be here when I wake up?"

Shermeto shrugs. Anything is possible.

KENDRA

Kendra drinks a bottle of wine to Gary's one glass. Her head swirls, becoming opaque.

"You okay?" Gary asks.

They haven't spoken for at least half a bottle. Comfortable silence. Kendra misses that. In fact, she didn't realize how much until that very moment. "I'm really good." She knows her words are slurring, but she doesn't care. His glass is empty. "Refill?"

"One's enough for me. Not much of a wine drinker."

"Do you want beer or something?"

He smiles and shakes his head. "Not much of drinker at all."

Great. Now she must seem like a lush. "Is there a story there?" She runs her finger around the rim, eyes the bottle.

"Not really. Just don't like the way it makes me feel. Can't stand hangovers."

Kendra pushes her glass away. Is he judging her? Shit. She hardly knows this guy. Of course, he's judging. Tallying each glass. "Sorry. I don't usually drink like this."

"I don't mind other people drinking. I think you may have needed it." He moves closer. "You're cute when you're nervous."

He leans in. Their lips touch. It's not the first time, but for some reason it feels like the first time. That heart-quickening first touch. A glance. A whispery touch. Is it the alcohol thinking? Well, let it think. She lets herself fall into him. Presses back with her lips, her hands moving through his hair. His hand around the back of her neck, pulling her closer.

Gary takes her hand and leads her into the bedroom. Kendra's face burns—from the wine or something else—the imprint of his lips still on hers. They fall gently onto the bed, his hand warm on her belly, reaching slowly up and underneath her bra. She tenses, unintentional, but he catches it.

"You okay?" Gary whispers, taking back his hand.

"Yes," she gasps. He pulls his shirt off then moves his head to her stomach, kisses her skin, traces light circles under her breasts with his fingertips. The thought of James flashes behind her eyes, but she quickly pushes him away.

DAY FOUR

THE RIVER

When did they start to hurt one another? The river moves in circles. Riling. Wondering.

Bubbles snap at oars, crashing, cutting through its skin. A boat rides the waves, bouncing. The occupants squeal and roar in lubricated laughter. The river arches and the hull rises, tilting awkwardly starboard side. The fun drains from their faces as they find themselves in the drink, the fools swallowed by the waves. The river doesn't want to hurt anyone. Only make them see.

They gasp and snort. The river lifts them towards the bank, leaves them to scramble through mud and over slippery rocks, falling into the grass to catch their breaths. Such a ride. They hoot and holler. High-fiving one another as their vessel crashes along the surface and hangs in the beams of a bridge downstream.

Defiant. Satisfied. The river has more power than these people could ever dream. In just one moment it can rip out everything that was precious, important, and leave them holding their hats in their hands, a single bag.

There's a reason for its existence, besides the obvious.

The river has come to help.

To save them.

KENDRA

Kendra wakes in a fog of sex. She feels hungover. Gary snores beside her, the blankets tangled between his legs. She peels herself from the bed and staggers to the bathroom, Gary's smell on her, in her. She turns on the shower and climbs under the gentle water. It almost feels sinful to scrub him away. Technically she's still married. How can wrong feel so right? But is it wrong? She didn't choose to end the marriage. She didn't choose any of this.

***

Six months ago, she hadn't seen it coming. Or maybe she had and didn't want to admit it.

James sat her down at the kitchen table.

"I can't do this anymore."

"What are you talking about?"

"This. Us. It's not supposed to be so hard. You walk around angry, passive aggressive. And I can't help you." Was he really putting the blame on her?

"You made it pretty clear you didn't want to help. You've imagined this perfect little family, where you can do no wrong and when it gets tough, you disappear," James said.

"Is it so wrong?"

"The fact that you even need to ask is the problem."

"So, it's my fault."

So typical of him to twist her words like that. She was tired of arguing. "Do what you want."

Kendra had left James sitting at the table and went to her office. She knew what he was doing, even though he hadn't admitted as much. That piece of trash woman from his office. Cliché as fuck. Well, let him have his cliché. She wasn't going to stop him.

***

The water turns cold. How can she bring Gary into this mess? It's not fair to him. Would she push him away before he had a chance to get that close? She hopes not, but she doesn't see any other way. Her father is *her* problem. Not his.

Kendra dries off and throws on sweatpants and a t-shirt and slips into the living room. She turns on the TV, volume muted, and brews a pot of coffee. The river is top news. Warnings. A ribbon across the bottom of the screen. Emergency Alert. State of Emergency: Alberta Floods 2013. The images are unbelievable. Houses washed away, gaping gravel holes where roads should be. Kendra turns up the volume and stands, arms folded across her chest.

A flooding crisis is unfolding in many Southern Alberta communities. Thousands in Calgary are under mandatory evacuation orders. Parts of Okotoks are under water. The army has been called in to High River. Most residents of that town have been told to leave. Roads in Bragg Creek are being chewed away by the river. Much more on the emergency and what the weather will bring us next. Stay tuned.

Her cell phone rings. Unknown caller. She snatches it up, because maybe, just maybe.

"Hello?"

Only breathing. Not heavy dirty breathing, but there is definitely someone on the other end. Listening.

"Dad. Is that you?" The words come out a dull whisper.

Silence.

Kendra slips out the back door and stands on the patio. The rain taps the roof, impatient. "Come home. This is silly. There's a room ready for you."

She waits. Still nothing.

"Why didn't you tell me you are dying? We could have helped. You need to come home. Tell me where you are. I'll come get you."

The line goes dead.

"Shit." Kendra throws the phone on the counter and pours herself a cup of coffee, then slowly pads back to the bedroom. She stands in the doorway watching Gary sleep. Curled up and warm. Too comfortable. He doesn't deserve any this. It's going to be James all over again and she doesn't want that either.

The phone rings again and she rushes back to the kitchen.

"Where are you?" Her voice is calm, even. *Don't press him too hard.*

This time a voice comes back, no more than a whisper and not her father. "6th Ave Parkade."

"Who is this?"

The line goes dead again.

Kendra grabs her coat and races out the door.

In the car she flips on the radio, listening to the warnings. The river is expected to crest this afternoon. Most of the areas along the river have already been evacuated. So many more on alert. She can see the water as she weaves into downtown. Higher than she's ever seen it, but still not breaching the banks. It's wild. Raging. Large swells sweep up, she imagines thousands of roiling serpents, plunging down and tearing the surface as they come up for air.

The streetlights open her path, illuminating everything in a murky yellow haze. Along the sidewalks, people rush for their vehicles, pulling suitcases, arms laden with boxes. All their precious belongings. Who knows when they will return?

A woman cuts across the street in front of Kendra, ignoring the flashing red light. She slams on the brakes. The woman turns, eyes wild. Panicked.

Cars pull into the street from their underground parking. Trucks, cars, SUVS. A man weaves between the lanes of traffic on a scooter, bags piled behind him. There is a steady string of red taillights in front of her. This will take forever. Firemen set up barricades on the cross streets. Sandbags are stacked high in front of store doors and windows.

She tries to ignore her fleeting thought: what if she can't find him? And then what if she does find him? What if he's already dead?

***

After her mother died, she thought she'd lost her father on more than one occasion. Pulling him out of bars, blistering drunk. Bringing him home to sleep it off but then the next day more of the same. When he finally stopped going out, she thought she'd won. At least he was bringing it home with him, content to drink alone in the shed.

On more than one occasion, she found him slumped in the corner. She really thought he was dead. Photos lay spread across the floor or on his lap. Images of her brother, of her mother, of her mother and brother together.

Kendra gathered up the pictures and set them on his workbench. The familiar smell of developer long since drowned out by the stench of old beer and sweat. He'd set up a sleeping bag and pillow on the floor. Empty beer bottles lined the tables, a cooler in the corner with a thin layer of lukewarm water.

She'd sat beside her father, leaned her head on his chest. A soft gasp, a slight flutter of movement. He wasn't dead.

***

This is ridiculous. Traffic is stalled in and out of the city. Kendra pulls over to the curb and jumps out. She hurries down the sidewalk, across the street and down a block. She falls into a throng of evacuees spilling from their high rises to the street, valuables in hand. There's a clog of vehicles trying to turn into the street from their underground parking. A few blocks from the parkade, she breaks into a jog, passes emergency crews setting up barricades, diverting traffic.

"Good morning," she says, when one of them spots her. Her heart pounds in her chest as she rushes to catch her breath.

He nods, eyes weary. Afraid. "You need to hurry."

You have no idea.

***

The closer she gets to the parkade, the more the dread wells inside her. An image of her father flashes across her mind, something she hasn't thought of in a long time. Fifteen years, in fact. Despite his destitution after her mother died there was a brief period where he cleaned himself up. It wasn't enough. All the years picking up his drunk ass, shuttling him home, begging him to dry out, she decided she couldn't do it anymore. There'd been a fight. He'd thrown a plastic candle at her head and accused her of being an ungrateful child. In her own tantrum, she packed anything that would fit in a suitcase and moved in with a friend.

Her father didn't talk to her for weeks. Then a couple months later, at the beginning of her second year of photography school, she walked into her first *Location Photography and Lighting* class and found her father standing at the front of the room. Clean, bright-eyed, he'd even got a haircut. An older version of the man she missed and wanted back the whole time.

"Isn't that your dad?" Her friend, Carl, raised a thick eyebrow.

She slunk in her chair for the full fifty minutes of the class, figuring out how she could transfer out. Her father pulled her aside before she could flee, insisting they talk.

"You look good," she said, later over a coffee.

"I'm clean."

She did the math. It wasn't long enough for it to matter.

"Two months." A smile spread across his face, filled right up to the eyeballs.

"I'm happy for you." The coffee was too hot and tasted like tar. "Why now?"

"I can't keep hurting everyone around me. I haven't been there for you or Lily in a long time, and it hasn't been fair. I'm going to AA meetings twice a week, sometimes more, and I've been seeing a therapist." A cheer erupted from the other side of the restaurant. "And the school hired me back. Isn't that great?"

"It is. It's really good."

This stretch of goodness lasted half a decade at least. He saw her graduate, bought her a brand-new camera and gear and went out on shoots with her, freshening up his own portfolio at the same time.

And then something changed. And he spiraled.

She wants him to be that man again. The one who loves life, is a good father and grandfather. But that requires finding him first.

The parkade is halfway down the block, darker than the night she's slogging through. She slows and approaches carefully.

SHERMETO

Rose doesn't take her eye off her kid as he struts across the pavement to a pup tent tucked into a shadowy corner. He unzips the flap and disappears, zipping himself inside.

"Seems like a good kid," Shermeto says.

Rose smiles meekly. Her gaze drops to the ground, to the fire still sizzling beside them. "He's all I got," she says. Her bottom lip rolls under her top teeth. "You have kids?"

No one has asked him that in a long time. It's easy to forget. To shove it into a crack in the back of his mind. "You haven't been out here long."

"Is it that obvious?" Rose's head sinks to her chest. She closes her eyes.

"Should let you get some rest."

Her head pops back up and she studies him, too hard. He doesn't like it.

"You mentioned a Harlow earlier."

"Did I?" He doesn't remember that.

"Someone did." She hesitates, her cheeks narrow, gaunt. "You know him."

On the other side of The Flats a group huddles around a fire bursting from a rusted metal drum. Sparks jut into the sky and dissolve.

"Why do you want to know?"

"He's my brother."

Shermeto's head snaps around. He scrapes his memories for any mention of a family beyond the wife he was running from before the accident.

"Impossible. You got the wrong person."

Rose's head cocks slightly to one side, her gaze boring through him like a fistful of nails, one penetrating stab at a time, knocking him back a mark. *Well, fuck.* Never tell a woman she's wrong.

"Maybe," she says. A train horn blares in the distance, making its way into the train yard. The ground grumbles, the chain link shudders, all the way to his molars. Sirens sound in the distance, too far to be of any concern to them.

The others get up, leaving Shermeto alone with this woman. "I knew a Harlow."

"Knew? As in past tense?"

"He died."

That's not what she expected to hear. Her eyes take on a familiar sheen, her mouth dips. "Maybe it's not the same person." She considers this a moment. "Did he have a scar right here?" She points to her eyebrow. "A wicked thing."

He nods slowly. "There was a scar."

A tear drops from the corner of her eye and slides down her cheek, taking the edges ever so carefully. She might have been beautiful once. Hard to tell between the hard lines, the grit digging into her skin. There's a story there and one that Shermeto doesn't really want to know about. Will do no good him knowing.

The train appears, its headlights carving a path in the dark. The engine looms, stuttering slowly along the tracks, the screech and squeal of metal on metal shattering the quiet.

"He was a good brother." She's not really talking to him, but rather past him, over him, around him. Nothing more than a mere obstacle to get around. "When he disappeared, things got bad. I hated him for leaving us alone, for Reese mostly." She studies the tent where her son is peacefully tucked inside. "I had no choice." The words hover between them. "Do you know what that's like?"

There's always a choice.

"This is no place for a kid. Or you." The women out here are hard, broken. That's not Rose, she's not as broken as she lets on. Hurt, scared, for sure, but scared will get you dead.

"I can't go back."

"Go somewhere else, then."

He knows it's none of his business and he should just keep his mouth shut.

"He always finds us. There's nowhere left to go." She pulls her sweater tighter around her and for a fraction of a second, he sees Harlow behind her eyes. *It's his fault. He let Harlow die.*

A scream shatters the dark. Around The Flats, heads turn, searching for the source. Rose is on her feet, pounding towards the tent. She rips open the flap and disappears inside. Another scream, this one for sure from the tent. Shermeto leaps up quicker than he ever realized he could. Only a few paces and he's there. Rose cradles the kid in her arms. He's weeping into her shoulder, pulling away from her, fighting, tugging on her hair. Shermeto grabs the kid and pulls him off her. Rose's eyes are wide, afraid. The kid gasps for breath, his face and body wet with sweat. Maybe he shouldn't have done that, but it's too late now.

"Hey, hey, hey," he says in a whisper. It's not his place, he knows, but Rose isn't arguing. Confusion and dread wash across her face.

"This has been happening a lot." Rose begins to sob. "I can't lose him, too."

"We need to get out of here. Someplace safe." Does such a place exist?

Rose doesn't look up. "The nightmares go where we go."

The homeless have gathered outside the tent, murmuring to one another about the ruckus. Too many eyes. Shermeto is growing twitchy.

"We have to go." He tugs on Rose's arm, trying to lift her.

"I don't know you. Not going anywhere."

"Look. My friend Jagger, he has a place, out of the rain and cold. Real walls."

Rose seems to consider this for a moment. How can it even be a question? Honest to goodness walls versus the thin nylon tent. Finally, she nods.

KENDRA

The air clamps down like a damp blanket, the fibres soaking up the scent of dust and motor oil. The parkade is darker than she expected, though she's not sure why she thought it might be any other way. All the power has been cut to the city. No backup generator. Then she remembers the flashlight on her phone. She switches on the light, aiming the beam back and forth. There's no one here. She checks every place she thinks a person could hide. There aren't many. A few trash cans, a parking payment machine. She kneels and peeks under the few abandoned cars on this level.

She shoulders her way through a glass door to the stairwell and stops, listening. For what? A cough? A sneeze? The laboured breaths of someone waiting in the shadows to jump out at her? Maybe a skitter or a foot shuffle. The stairwell is silent, yet the hairs on the back her neck bristle.

"Is someone there?"

Her words echo up the shaft. Warning bells clang inside her. *Get out. Run. Back to the car. Drive, fast as possible.* But at the same time her feet seem glued to the concrete. A door sighs somewhere over her head and then clicks shut. There is someone here. She launches up the stairs, taking them two at a time, two floors before she's sure her heart is going to explode from her chest. Her thighs and calves scream at her to stop. *Just stop for fuck's sake. This is going to get you nowhere.*

But it will, a few more floors, that's all. A deep breath and then a step, another breath, another step, until she's up another flight. P4. The whole level is empty except for a grocery cart stuffed full of garbage bags.

"Pssst."

Kendra creeps towards the cart, searching for any sign of movement.

"Where are you?" Her words catch in the muggy air and hover.

"Here." A gloved-hand appears from behind a pillar followed by a whole man. Grisly, gray-hair, a toque pressed down over his head. His eyes dart back and forth. "Don't be so loud."

"There's no one here."

"Shhhh. I'm serious. It's not safe."

The man sits on a concrete block and digs through a backpack.

"Hey. That's my dad's pack."

"Keep your voice down." He zips the pack closed and holds it out to her.

"Where'd you get that?"

Shit. Is he dead? Is that what this is all about?

"He's in a lot of danger." The man drops the bag on the ground and kicks it toward her.

"Where is he?"

The man shrugs. "We all come and go. Never in the same place for too long. That's the whole point, isn't it?"

"Are you a friend of his?"

"Don't have any friends. They call me Old Reuben. And you're Kendra. The first born."

How does this man know this? Is it possible her father talks about her, his kids, his life before?

"How do you know that?"

"A guess. It's usually the oldest ones who come looking."

"Who came looking for you?" Kendra asks.

Reuben squints in the flashlight beam. "We can't stay here."

"Where is my father?"

"I don't know. We were down by the river. I woke up and he was gone. And the water keeps coming."

His eyes begin to twitch.

"You have to give me something more." *What a waste of time. He doesn't know anything.* "You called me," she says.

Reuben takes a deep breath. "If I tell you this it could get me dead."

The wind picks up, carves a path through the parkade. A scuffle. The tinkle of a tin can on concrete.

"When you find him, tell him to watch out for Jagger."

"What does that mean?"

"Tell him Jagger killed Harlow. That's all you need to know. All he needs to know."

"Why didn't you tell him? And who is Harlow?"

"Doesn't matter."

A car engine grumbles. It's coming closer. From the upper level. Reuben grabs his cart and starts to make his way out of the parkade, following the exit signs. "Tell him."

Kendra grabs the backpack and jogs after him. "I need more than that."

Reuben doesn't stop. She grabs his arm. "Please."

"You shouldn't be here. None of us should."

She stomps her foot, clenches her hands into tight fists.

"STOP!" The word comes out as a shriek, but Reuben gets the point.

He swings around fast. "Jesus Christ. Shut up. Someone might hear you."

"There's no one here but us."

The car from above is getting closer. Reuben pushes her behind a pillar just as headlights enter level four, sweep past them and disappear, continuing in a steady spiral down until there is nothing left except their own breaths passing between them.

"Do you hear that?"

Reuben pushes away from the pillar and staggers across the parkade. Kendra follows, unsure what the old man is talking about. They stop at the ledge that looks out over the darkened city and then she hears it, too. The river. Alive, angry, ready to jump the banks.

"We have to get out of here," Kendra says. "Come with me. I'll get you somewhere safe."

"Don't worry none about me. Remember what I told you. Tell him. Promise me you'll tell him." He's sad, giving up.

"Let me help you."

"It's too late for me. You go. I'll be fine." His face twists in the moonlight. "The sun will be up soon. You should get out of here." He turns to her. "Go, before you get stuck too."

There's nothing else for her to say. She can't drag him with her if he doesn't want to go. She pulls the backpack onto her shoulder and backs away. A few steps and then a little faster, she turns and bolts to the stairwell. When she glances back, Reuben is gone. She searches the parkade until she sees him shuffling back to his cart.

What now? She takes the stairs down, two at time. Reuben didn't really give her anything to work with. She's still no closer to finding her father than she was an hour ago when she got the call. She shuts off the flashlight.

When she reaches the bottom of the stairs her phone rings, loud, reverberating off the walls. It's Gary.

"Where are you?" he says.

"Sorry. I had to do something."

"You weren't supposed to go alone."

"I know."

"I called all the shelters I could think of. They're evacuating all of them," Gary says. "I have a list."

"Which means he could be anywhere," she says.

"Tell me where you are, I'll come get you and we can go check the evacuation centres."

"You'll never get down here. There're blocking all the roads. Only letting people out." She steps out onto level one. Firemen scramble along the opposite sidewalk helping people with their belongings. "I'm on my way home, wait for me." She hangs up and tucks her phone into her pocket.

"Need a hand?" A man steps into the street. Too casual to be in a hurry like everyone else. He's wearing a black hoodie and jeans at least two sizes too big and hiking boots.

"I'm fine. Car's just down there."

"It's getting messy out here." Dark eyes study her, his eyebrows shift, coming together above his nose. "Travelling pretty light." He nods to the backpack.

"Could say the same about you."

His beard is neatly groomed, dark hair slicked back. The man shrugs. "Nothing worth saving, I guess."

She takes a few steps forward. The man grabs her arm.

"I'll scream," she says, nodding to the firemen across the street. He drops his hand and she continues, "If you want to help someone, there's a man up there, trapped in the parkade. He's homeless and has no where to go."

"Why didn't you help him?" he says. A smile cracks his lips and disappears as quickly as it appeared.

That's a good question. "What am I supposed to do? I'm only one person."

"Sure you got a nice warm house to go to. Friends to take you in. They've got nothing."

This guy's got a lot of nerve, judging her like that. The firemen are steering people down the street.

"You listening to me?" His voice is louder than it should be.

"Leave me alone."

She tries to elbow past him, but he blocks her.

"That's not very nice. First him now me. What you got against us?"

She can't conceal her surprise.

"Us? What're you talking about?"

"Who's up there?" He nods towards the parkade.

"His name is Reuben. Old guy."

A smile spreads across his face. "You talked to him."

"A bit. You know him?" Kendra is confused. This man doesn't look like the others. "He knows my father but couldn't tell me where to find him."

"Maybe I can help. What's his name?"

"Apparently goes by Shermeto."

The smile melts away. "What else did Reuben say?"

"Nothing. He refused to come with me."

"Stubborn old man." He searches up and down the street. "You have a car?"

"A few blocks down."

"I'll go check on Reuben, see if I can't knock some sense into him, and then I'll take you to your father."

"You know where he is?"

"I do."

SHERMETO

Rose soothes the kid while Shermeto collapses her tent and gathers the pair's meagre belongings. The sun is beginning to rise. Shermeto used to love the awkward angles of light in the early morning. The crisp oranges and yellows. Now everywhere looks dark and bleak even in the sunrise. The sun used to blink. Now it seems to wake in a foggy haze, stretch and wipe the sleep snot from its eyes, peer around and think, *nope not today*. A constant edginess hangs in the air like the toothy blade of a serrated knife. He's living a sandpaper nightmare and getting one hell of a rash.

They pass through empty construction sites, shuffle over gravel where sidewalks will eventually bloom, then pause along the edge of the river, the water rushing around them in a steady hungry roar.

"That isn't good," Rose says. The kid clings to his mother's side. Downriver, the water almost meets the bottom of a bridge.

"Whoa. It's gonna rip out the bridges." The kid leans over the railing, gawking at the swirl.

"Get away from there." Rose tugs him back.

"It won't happen. Watch. Soon it'll be nothing and the city got its britches pinched for no reason," Shermeto says, not really believing his own words.

"I don't know. It looks pretty bad," Rose says.

The kid removes himself from his mother's grasp and rubs his eyes. Rose glances back at Shermeto.

The water is over the pathway in front of them and steadily rising. They climb up hill until they reach an empty parking lot.

"This way," Shermeto says, leading them to the back of the Salvation Army. A blue bin full of donations is crammed full, a dozen black garbage bags and boxes in front of it. Shermeto rips open a bag and begins to dig through it.

"What are you looking for?" Rose asks, standing back.

"Nothing special," Shermeto says. Sometimes he just likes to look. Never know what someone is going to throw away. Shermeto has found coats and sweaters and pants on more than one occasion. Even when they're too big he finds a way to cinch the waist. Suddenly he thinks of Gerard and how he dove into the bags, casting useless items on the ground.

He abandons the sifting when he reaches the bottom of the third bag.

"Cheap bastards today," Shermeto says, wiping his hands on his pants. "This'll do." He holds up a toothbrush—still in the package—and a small tube of toothpaste. "There's a few more."

Rose takes the brush Shermeto offers her. The kid turns up his nose. Shermeto can't help but chuckle. Kids will be kids, no matter the situation. He remembers the trouble of making each of his brush their teeth regularly. Grace had a way of dealing with the defiance and pouty lips.

"You will brush your teeth," Rose says.

The kid scowls. "Oh look." He opens a box filled with kids stuffed animals, most of which are torn or missing eyeballs and look like they haven't seen the inside of a washing machine ever. "Can I take one?"

"Go for it," Shermeto says. "As many as you want."

"One," Rose says.

"Right. Take one," Shermeto echoes. *Fool. Of course, he has no right to speak for this woman.* No claim to the kid, or her, or anyone for that matter.

The kid grabs a mangy looking rabbit with one eye missing.

"Isn't there anything better?" Shermeto asks.

"I like this one." The kid holds the rabbit to his chest.

"Very well." Shermeto rips open his toothbrush and spits on it, then presses a liberal amount of paste across the bristles. He scrubs his teeth. Spits out the dried blood that must have been caked into his molars.

"I'm tired." The kid flops down on one of the garbage bags and stretches out.

"There's got to be a better place than this," Rose says.

"There is. Come on. Let's get out of here."

The city is stretching awake. The sun is starting its pull into the sky. A bus passes on the street. None of the half-asleep bodies he usually sees. It pulls up to a stop with a screech and sigh. The doors open. No one gets off, no one gets on. This will likely be the last bus. Their last chance.

The streets are as empty as the bus. Except for these three weary souls, straggling on, barely able to stay awake. Where did everyone go? Maybe they should've stayed put. Bunk down for the night in the tent, in an abandoned boxcar in the train yard, instead of galivanting all over town, wading through water, for what? A dry place to sleep? A place where nightmares don't exist? If anyone knows if such a place exists, Shermeto hopes they'll tell him.

The kid lets go of his mother and hangs back, tucks his hand into Shermeto's and keeps time with his slogging steps.

"Don't step on the cracks, you'll break your mother's back," the kid sings, hopping over the cracks in the pavement, whatever terrorized him in his dreams long forgotten.

Shermeto doesn't even realize he's smiling until Rose stops, turns around, and smiles back.

***

They stood in the middle of the K-Mart clothing section. Stevie tugged on his mother's sleeve. "Can we look at the toys," he pleaded.

"Not now," Grace said. "Your sisters need new clothes. Go with Dad."

Stevie sulked. "They always get everything."

"It's a girl thing," Shermeto said.

"What does that mean?" Stevie asked.

"It means, never bother a girl when she's trying on clothes."

"Girls are weird."

Shermeto laughed. "They have benefits."

"I'm never getting married."

"Aw, buddy. It's too early to make that kind of decision. You're only seven." His arms began to tire. "And getting far too heavy for your old man to carry you." He drops his boy back on the ground. "Why don't we go take a look at those trucks and let the ladies do their thing?"

Grace mouthed a relieved *thank you*. Stevie slipped his hand into Shermeto's and pulled him through the aisles to the toys. Trucks. Lego. Transformers. Teenage Mutant Ninja Turtles. So much more to choose from than when he was a kid, when there were air rifles, pistols that shot flimsy darts, lawn games, Monopoly and Chinese Checkers. The flow of colours made his head spin, like a seventies drug-induced hallucination. That's when he got his first camera.

"Do you know what you want?" Shermeto asked.

Stevie stood back, arms folded over his chest. His face scrunched in indecision.

"So much to choose from."

"Don't I know it."

"What?"

"Nothing. Pick whatever you want."

Stevie latched onto his leg and peered up at him with wide eyes. "You're the best dad ever."

Then he let go and started touching every toy on the shelves as if his decision could be made simply by how the toy felt against his skin. Too cold. Too rough. Too hard. Too soft. How could one possibly decide?

The minutes ticked away. Shermeto couldn't see his girls buried somewhere in a sea of cotton and velvet and wool. He had it pretty good. He'd seen other fathers struggling to keep up, but there was balance, if it could be found. Mom and Dad. Grace and Del.

"This one." Stevie pulled a large Tonka dump truck off the shelf.

"You sure? That's the one?"

Stevie nodded.

Shermeto tucked the truck under his arm and they made their way back to the clothing section. Grace stood at the entrance to the change room, her face blanched, ready for a fight.

"What's going on?" he asked.

"I'm done. This is ridiculous. You deal with her." Grace pushed past him.

Shermeto grabbed her arm. "Hey."

"She hates everything I choose for her." Her eyes began to glisten. Lily stepped out of the change room, cheeks red and blotchy.

"I don't claim to know anything about girls and their needs, but what if we just let her pick whatever she wants?"

"God. You have no clue. You're so buried behind your camera, you don't see what's real, right in front of your face."

His shoulders stiffened. *What had he done?* "I don't want to fight with you. I'm just suggesting."

Grace stalked around the clothing stands and right on out the front door. Shermeto turned to Kendra who had come to join them. Kendra shrugged. He shook his head.

"Find something you like and let's get out of here."

When they got out to the car, Grace was slouched in the front seat. Stevie, Kendra and Lily piled into the back, their purchases clutched to their laps as if one wrong move, they'd be snatched away from them.

They drove home in silence.

***

"What is this place?" Rose hangs back by the gate.

"We can get some rest. Trust me."

Reluctantly, Rose follows. They climb the back steps to the abandoned house and knock on the window. There's no movement. Shermeto slides open the door and listens.

"Jagger?" he calls. "You in here?"

Nothing but silence.

There's a blanket rolled up in what used to be the living room, where Jagger probably had his way with Tessa and then kicked her back out into the night.

"I don't like this place," the kid says.

"There're rooms upstairs. You two go up. I'll keep watch down here."

Rose leads the kid upstairs. Shermeto can tell she doesn't like it any more than the kid does but she tries not to let on.

"It's only for a rest. Then we can go," she says.

"I'll be here when you wake up." He doesn't think they'll really sleep much.

Shermeto straightens out the blanket and lies down, pulls off his coat and rolls it up as a pillow.

THE RIVER

Onlookers—lookie-loos—stand on the banks snapping photos, gazing in awe at the beast that is the river rolling past them. They have no idea just how much power lays within its depths. Do they think this is a joke? Something to be mocked? Taken for granted? Photographed and pasted on Facebook and Twitter?

"Oh, look what's happening to us," they'll cry to the rest of the world, wanting their pity, for people to say they're sorry, and ask how they can help? They who will stand by in awe, never really understanding the full gravity of the forces billowing beneath the surface.

They should leave. Everyone needs to get far away.

The river pauses for a photo.

Upriver, a man darts into the parkade. The woman is alone on the street. She should go, get away before it's too late.

The river slides up the bank, creating its own path, following, gathering information, surging higher, seeping into buildings, under doorways, through open windows.

Racing up the driveway, level by level, the man stops only long enough for a cursory search. On the third level there's the steady clip, clang of wheels on concrete.

"There you are," he says. "Been looking everywhere."

The river shudders and then begins to roar.

KENDRA

How long is she supposed to wait? Gary is expecting her home, but that was before she got a new lead. This man on the street might be stringing her along. Should she go in there to help him with Reuben? It's already been ten minutes. She checks her phone and sends Gary a quick text.

Got a lead. Will be a little longer.

Not two seconds later the phone rings. "What kind of lead?" Gary asks.

"Found someone who knows exactly where Dad is."

"Where?"

"I don't know yet."

"Well ask."

"I will."

The man comes out of the parkade, walking slowly towards her. To Gary she says, "Gotta go. Will let you know when I know more." She hangs up before he can say anything else. "He wouldn't come?" she says to the man.

"Wouldn't give an inch. Stubborn bastard. Always been that way." He shrugs. "Where's your car?"

"Just down there."

"Show me."

"Who are you?" Kendra asks.

"How rude of me not to introduce myself." He holds out a hand. "They call me Jagger."

Kendra gasps slightly and shakes his hand. "How well do you know my father?" she asks.

"Pretty well. He got me out of a jam a long time back." They reach the car. "This is you?" he asks.

Kendra nods and unlocks the door. She darts around to the driver's side and slides in behind the wheel. It's hard to imagine her father thinking of anyone other than himself.

"Been a long time since I been in a car," he says.

Kendra swings the car into traffic. "How did he help you?"

"Nothing serious. I was in a bad way. He helped me straighten up."

"Get clean? That doesn't sound like him," Kendra says.

"Ha. Shit, lady. No one going to help me do that." He taps his knuckles against the window. "Turn here."

They drive a little farther until he tells her to pull over, but he doesn't get out, only folds his hands on his lap. "There's a lot you don't know about him." He pauses. "My story isn't important, but he, your father, helped me when no one else would. You don't know what it's like, to have no one give two squids whether you live or die. Leaves you empty." He taps his chest with his fist. "Dead."

SHERMETO

Shermeto wakes up, listening to the sounds of the house settling around him. *Have they left him? Was it all a dream?* He picks himself up from the floor and looks out the front window. It's boarded over but through a crack in the plywood he sees the metal fence surrounding the house, the street beyond. Jagger had said the place was condemned. They shouldn't be here. He climbs the stairs, searching room after room for Rose and the kid. He finds them curled up together on the floor, newspapers beneath them, under a blanket. Rose is using her tent as a pillow.

He hates to wake them. It's likely been a long time since they weren't looking over their shoulders. He wants to protect them from themselves, get them some place safe. But this isn't it. They shouldn't be here. But where will they go?

His stomach barks at him, but he doesn't care. He turns to leave. The kid rolls over and opens his eyes. Shermeto brings his finger to his lips. The kid scrambles up from the floor careful not to wake his mother.

"Is this your house?" The kid asks when they reach the main level.

"Not my place."

"Can we stay?" The kid sits on the floor.

"Only for a little while. Are you hungry?"

The kid nods. "Should we wake up my mom?"

"In a bit." Shermeto sits on a milk crate. "You had an Uncle Harlow?" Shermeto asks.

The kid nods. "He was cool."

"What happened?"

The kid shrugs. "We stayed at his house sometimes and then suddenly one day he wasn't there. Auntie Meg, his wife, said he was gone."

"When was that?"

"A long time ago. I was little."

Shermeto smiles.

There's a creak on the stairs and Rose appears. Her cheeks are dusted pink and there's an imprint of a zipper on her cheek.

"What's going on?" she whispers.

"He's regaling me with stories of his childhood." Shermeto winks at the kid.

"What time is it?" Rose asks, plodding across the floor. She stands behind her son, arms folded across her chest.

"Morning. Are you cold?" Shermeto asks.

"Freezing."

"The sun is out. Maybe we go scrape up some grub. The kid is starving."

Rose nods and squeezes the kid's shoulder.

"I have to pee."

"There must be a bathroom around here somewhere."

"I'll find it." The kid springs up from the floor and disappears around a wall.

"He sleep okay?" Shermeto asks, nodding in the direction of the kid.

"Better, I think." She takes in the graffiti covered walls. "Are we coming back here?"

"You don't like it?"

"It's really drafty and I kept hearing sounds like crying coming through the walls."

"It's an old house."

The kid returns. "That bathroom is gross." He wrinkles his nose.

Shermeto laughs. Then Rose too. The sound is like a tinkling windchime in a summer storm, a sound that has been buried so deep in the pockets of his memories that he'd forgotten what joy and humour really felt like.

"Let's get out of here."

He doesn't know where he's going to take them, but he'll deal with that when the time comes.

"Why are you being so nice to us?" Rose says when they're back in the alley. The sun is up, blazing down from a clear blue sky. The heat washes over him.

"Do I need a reason?"

Rose shrugs. "No one does anything out of pure kindness."

"I know how hard it is to trust anyone. But when you can, or do, sometimes it's worth it."

"It's been a long time."

The kid skips ahead of them, kicking rocks, hopping over puddles.

"We all have something we're hiding from."

"What are you hiding from?" Rose asks.

"Myself."

Her lips form a firm line across her face. "How's that working for you?"

Shermeto laughs again. "It's not." It feels good to laugh. He doesn't want to stop.

"At least you're not constantly looking over your shoulder."

Her face registers a faraway glance, remembering something that she likely doesn't want to. How could he be so careless?

They're on the main street, cars are swishing by, loads of people spill out of condos and towers, laden with boxes and bags, eyes wild. Frantic. Shermeto glances around, doesn't understand what's going on.

"In here." Shermeto leads them into a small coffee shop filled with a dozen empty tables, but no customers. A man smiles from behind the counter.

"Two coffees." Shermeto raises two fingers. The kid's face is pressed to the glass covering the pastry shelf. "What would you like?"

"Juice, please."

"Apple, orange?" The man behind the counter says.

"Apple."

"Anything else?"

"What else would you like?" Shermeto turns to Rose.

She leans in and whispers, "How are you going to pay for this?"

"Don't worry about that." He kicks off his boot and pulls the bills out of his sock.

"Bagels would be good," she says.

"Half a dozen bagels. Cream cheese. Butter. And a couple of those powdered donuts the kid can't peel his eyes away from."

The man laughs. "Coming right up."

"What's going on out there? Everyone seems agitated. Did you notice?"

"The city is starting to evacuate everyone."

"What about you?" Shermeto asks.

"Not until they tell me to go or they cut the power here. Power's already out downtown."

Shermeto glances around the small store again. On the street outside, a man is dragging a cooler and a suitcase, like they're heading out for a camping weekend. But their faces suggest something else.

Across the street from the coffee shop is a small green space. Even in the wide open, the homeless are mostly invisible. No one pays any attention to them, but Shermeto sees them. The desperate. The scared.

He'd created imaginary lives for the homed people: mistresses on their way to booty calls, kept women. Kept by married businessmen who can't keep it in their pants. Whose dick is bigger? Let's measure. Judging one another as much as they judged him. Perceived worth based on the size of a paycheck or how many cars fit in the garage. He would bet any one of these snobs live beyond their means, pretending to be something they aren't.

"You should have been there last night."

"Where is that damn portfolio I asked for? I can't wait any longer."
"Hey baby. I missed you last night."

Words: fake, disjointed, without purpose. A stagnant flow of utterances that made him want to barf.

But now it's different. They're as silent as he normally is. Racing away from something bigger than them. No one is perfect. No matter how much makeup they apply, how high they stack their hair, how flat they iron their clothes, the wrinkles and warps are always there. A hair out of place. A smudge of mascara on the eyelid, a cuff un-pressed.

They make their way to the park. Rose unwraps the bagels and spreads cheese across each side. Shermeto sips his coffee. The kid sucks on the straw, barely stopping to breathe between swallows. She offers the first half to the kid and the other to Shermeto. "Go ahead," Shermeto says.

The bagel disappears in a couple of bites. "Can I have a donut?" the kid asks.

"Those aren't for you," Rose says.

"Of course they are," Shermeto says. "Go for it kid."

The kid snatches the bag and silently eats. Rose shoots Shermeto a look he finds familiar. Too familiar.

"At the camp last night when you showed up, you said you were looking for someone." Rose takes tiny bites of the bagel and chews slowly.

Shermeto nods.

"You were angry," Rose says.

Shermeto downs the last of his coffee and crushes the cup. "He's a fuckwad. Nothing you need to worry about."

None of it matters anymore. The kid's head snaps up.

"Shit, sorry. Shouldn't talk that way around the kid."

Rose smiles. The kid starts in on the second donut.

Shermeto catches movement out of the corner of his eye. A group of men have gathered at the far back corner of the park. One of them waves and starts over and then stops suddenly and points. Shermeto turns back to the street.

A police car pulls up to the curb and two officers are making their way towards them. Shermeto stiffens as they approach.

"How you folks doing today?" one of the officers says without a smile. How do they do that? All stern and serious all the time.

"We aren't doing nothing wrong."

One officer keeps his eye on them while the other watches those at the back corner. "Wasn't suggesting you were. We're evacuating the core. You need to find some place to go. It's not safe to stay here."

"Thanks. We're heading out shortly," Shermeto says.

"See that you do. The safety of our citizens is top priority."

Shermeto raises an eyebrow but doesn't respond. The officers make their way across the park to the other men.

"Maybe we should go." Shermeto gathers the bagel bags. "We can eat on the way."

Rose let's out a breath and nods. "Did you see the way they were looking at me?" She pulls the kid to her.

"That's why we need to go."

The group of men have come to meet them. Shermeto knows these guys. "Rat bastard cops. Always getting up in our business," one of the men says.

"Louie." Shermeto nods at the man with slicked back hair, tattoos jutting out under his shirt sleeve, missing the thumb on his left hand.

"You don't like people so much," Shermeto says.

"What's to like? No one is your friend. Especially them." Louie nods to the car pulling away from the curb. "They pretend real well, but in the end, they're cops. Always looking for a reason to haul your ass in, get you in the system. Once that happens, you're done."

Shermeto takes in the other four men standing behind Louie, nodding like marionettes. He's knows two of them, not the others. One guy, tall, dark hair, goggles strapped to the top his head, is staring into the sky, seemingly unaware of anything going on around him. He checks his watch and gazes back at the sky. Shermeto looks up too. Doesn't see what he sees.

"This is Gray," Louie says.

At the sound of his name, Gray's head snaps down and possibly for the first time he notices the others around him. The man steps forward, lips tight and partially buried under a badly trimmed beard and extends a hand to Shermeto.

"I'm Howard. Gray Howard."

Shermeto ignores the offered hand and pulls a smoke from his pocket. He offers smokes to the others. Howard, Gray Howard, snatches one up and pops it between his lips and pats his pockets.

"Musta misplaced my lighter."

Shermeto lights the cigarette for him and then his own.

"Many thanks," Gray says. "These things will kill you."

Shermeto nods and sucks hard on the smoke. Gray Howard leans in close to Shermeto. His breath smells like onion baked fish.

"I'm undercover. Don't tell no one." He brings his finger to his lips. "Completely hush-hush." He flashes yellowed teeth.

"Undercover for what?" The kid pops up beside Shermeto.

"I'm a spy for the government. I've been sent to extract top secret information from the Russian underground."

"Cool." The kid's eyes widen.

"You know you're not in Russia, right?" Shermeto glances past Gray Howard, nods at Rose, who is watching them. She smiles.

"Do you have a car?" the kid asks.

"Dozens. And a plane."

"Must be an impressive estate," Shermeto says, rolling his eyes.

"Oh, yes. Hidden deep in the mountains. No one could ever find it. That's the life of a spy."

"Who are you spying on? What are you trying to find?"

"A key. It's locked in the Mayor's secret vault in the catacombs under the city. I must get the key. Undetected." His voice drops to a light whisper. "Sneaky as a mouse."

Reese's mouth falls open. "Wow. I want to see the secret vault." He turns to his mother. "Can I, Mom? Can I see the secret vault under the—" He turns back to the Gray Howard. "What was it called again?"

"Catacombs."

"Catcombs. Mom, can I?"

Rose shakes her head. "Afraid not." She chews on her thumb.

"No fair. I never get to do anything fun." He crosses his arms and sits down, bottom lip jutting out. The kid's age suddenly more apparent than it's been up until now. He's only a child.

"We should go," Shermeto says.

Gray Howard spins in a circle and then stops suddenly. "I think it's this way." He whistles and points down the street.

"What does the key open?" The kid wraps his arm around Shermeto's leg and gazes at the crazy man.

"It's the Master Key, to the city. It opens every door."

If such a thing exists, Shermeto thinks, *that would be a handy thing to get your hands on.*

"But it's a secret. All in the name of National Security."

Shermeto tosses his cigarette butt in the grass and crushes it under his boot. "Well you better get on with it before someone else finds it first," Shermeto says.

Gray Howard's eyes widen as he considers this. Then he stands up straight and salutes Shermeto.

"At ease," Shermeto says.

Gray lowers his hands and weaves them back and forth in a weird sort of dance.

"What are you doing?" the kid asks.

"It's my car. Do you like it? I just washed it."

Shermeto is about done with the nonsense. Quiet until now, Louie and his gang suddenly burst out laughing. "Come on James Bond, let's get out of here." Louie grabs Gray's arm but Gray swats his hand away.

"Don't touch me." Gray Howard glares at Louie. "And get out of my car," he shouts.

Louie appears stunned. "What car?"

"Exactly," he says then shoves Louie hard. "Invisible. Undetected."

Louie loses his balance and falls on his ass in the wet grass, but springs right back up. "What the hell you do that for? I'll knock out your teeth you crazy bastard."

Gray swerves his imaginary car around Louie. "Catch you later, suckers," he says, waving back at everyone before disappearing down the street.

"Where's he going?" Rose asks.

"Was he telling the truth?" Reese still holds onto Shermeto's pant leg.

"In his mind he thinks so," Shermeto says.

"Who's this?" Louie's gaze falls on Rose and the kid. Rose grabs the kid's arms and pulls him in behind her. "You got yourself a woman, hey there, Shermeto." Louie smiles, nodding in approval. "A fam..i...ly. Looks good on you, old man."

"What do you guys want?" Shermeto asks.

"Hear about Gerard? Damn. Unlucky bastard."

Shermeto feels his skin harden.

"Found over on the other side, head bashed in. Can't believe it."

"I heard."

"Cops all over the place. No face. Sliced clean off."

"Any idea what happened?"

"Those stupid shoes."

Shermeto shakes his head. The shoes were used for their constant amusement, sure. "No one's gonna slice off a face because of shoes. Maybe a few kicks to the ribs and a bruised ego."

"Heard he sucked some guys dick then bit off his pecker." They fall into a fit of laughter.

Jesus. There's a kid here. Shermeto nudges Rose in the shoulder and motions to the kid. She understands and quickly covers his ears.

"Nah. That's wasn't it. Probably trying to suck his own dick and broke his neck. Skinned his face on the rocks."

A gob of snot shoots from Louie's nose. He grinds it into the sidewalk with the toe of his boot. "No. No. He ate the wrong pussy and his face fell off," Louie says, bursting into another fit of laughter. Everyone falls silent and stares at him.

"You're fucking gross."

"Well, screw you guys." Louie folds his arms across his chest and shoots Shermeto a look. "What do you think?"

"No idea." Shermeto takes a step back.

"Leaving so soon?" Louie asks. Then to the kid. "What you got there, boy?" Louie steps closer. The kid pulls back. "Let me see." The kid holds up the rabbit. "That's quite a find. Hang on to that. Everyone needs something to hug." Louie gives a polite bow and rolls his arm in a gentlemanly fashion. "Very nice to meet you, both." Then he turns his attention back to the kid, "You're awfully grown up. How many tattoos you got?"

The kid laughs. "I don't have any tattoos. I'm too young." Shermeto wishes Louie would stop touching the kid.

"Of course you are, kid, of course you are." Louie turns to Shermeto. "You heard the cops. We gotta get out. Thinking the tunnels."

"Is that where that knucklehead, Gray, is off to? Are you stupid? We're on the verge of a flood and you want to go underground where all the water will go? You're stupider than I thought."

"Water's not going to come that far inland."

"Do what you want. It's your funeral." Shermeto turns to Rose. "Let's go."

Firetrucks race by, sirens silent. An ambulance close behind. "Wonder what that's all about," Rose says.

"Can we find out?" the kid asks.

"People die all the time, buddy. Nothing new. Nothing to see," Louie says, folding his arms over his chest. "So where are you guys going?"

"North," Shermeto says.

"That's where the river is. Now who's the dummy." Louie snickers and rolls his eyes. The other three laugh.

KENDRA

They're in an alley on a side of town that Kendra hasn't visited for what feels like forever. She gets out and walks around to the back of the car.

"He's in there?" Kendra asks.

Jagger nods and opens the gate.

She doesn't like the looks of this. The house looks like it might have been condemned but someone had taken away the warnings. "I should call my boyfriend. Let him know where I am." Boyfriend. Had she actually referred to Gary as her boyfriend? She pulls out her phone.

"Do what you got to," Jagger says, latching the gate behind him.

"Careful," Jagger says.

He kneels to move some paving stones out of the way, a rusted bicycle lays on its side in the tall grass. He rummages around in the debris. *If her father is in there, why don't they just hurry inside?* She lowers the phone without hitting send, glances from Jagger to the back door to the gate.

"Dad," she calls out and takes a step forward, and then another. She's at the bottom of the steps when something smashes into the back of her head.

SHERMETO

Shermeto never noticed Rose's limp before. An injury or something less sinister, one leg shorter than the other? It's none of his business, though he's delightfully curious. Rose wraps her arm around his. He fights the instinct to pull away. If there's any truth to what Reuben said, they best get the hell out of here as quickly as possible.

"What happened to you, Rose?" The words slip out, he can't take them back.

She's quiet for a long time. Too long. He offended her. Didn't mean to. Always says the wrong thing.

"Not sure what you mean," she finally says.

"The scar on your face—how'd that happen?" Stupid. Too nosy. "You don't have to tell me if you don't want." That's the right thing to say. Offer an out.

Rose slows.

"A stupid accident," she says. "No big deal."

Shermeto wonders who she is lying to, him or herself. Or both. There's a discomfort in her eyes, the way they search for something to land on, something to find comfort in. Who's he kidding thinking he can help her? He tried that once with his own family and look how that turned out?

***

He remembers the first time he met Grace; knowing the moment he laid eyes on her that he would marry her. He'd never been so sure of anything. She walked, no that's not the right word, floated, into the camera store. He'd borrowed the darkroom in the back and now stood in the main store studying tripods and flash gear, a new lens. Barely out of university and starting to build a portfolio.

In that moment he wished he could capture her movement, her presence, but even he wasn't an experienced enough photographer for that. She bowed her head over the counter, her foot kicked out behind her showing off a thin, sandaled heel.

After a few minutes of studying the equipment she glanced around the shop.

"Do you work here?"

Shermeto lost his words. Not a single coherent sentence formed in his brain. Stunned stupid. That's what she did to him. Her face the colour of pink petals and as soft. The kind of flowers you don't touch for fear they might crumble or be permanently scarred. He should have listened to that fear.

The store owner, Darren, was in the back looking up a stock number for Shermeto. He wouldn't be back for a couple of minutes. "Can I help you find something?"

"It's my dad's birthday." A voice like honey.

"And you want to get him a camera?"

She nodded. "Something simple. Easy to use. He's not a pro or anything."

Shermeto smiled. He used to smile a lot in those days, big toothy grins. All teeth and gums.

"These ones are compact and easy to use. Point and shoot."

"What kind of film?"

Shermeto slipped around the counter and pulled a package of film off the wall. "What kind of photos will he be taking?"

Confusion spread across her face. "Are there different kinds?"

Shermeto laughed. He couldn't help himself, but instantly wished he hadn't. She probably thought he was laughing at her.

"Family gatherings or walks in the park?"

"I guess maybe both."

He dropped a package of flash cubes on the counter. "You'll

probably need some of these too."

Darren came out of the back and stopped, glancing from Shermeto to the woman and back.

"Sorry." Shermeto slipped out to the customer side of the counter.

"He's not bothering you, is he?" Darren asked.

"Not at all. He's been quite helpful." Then to Shermeto, "You don't actually work here?"

Shermeto shook his head. "I might as well though, with how much time I spend here."

"Well. I'll take all of this."

"Don't think I'm going to pay you for you this," Darren said, laughing.

"Not even a discount?" Shermeto winked at the woman. Darren shot him the finger.

The woman paid for the merchandise and started out of the store.

Shermeto should have let her go.

All the should haves, the could haves.

It would have saved her life.

***

Rose clutches Shermeto's arm tighter, like she's holding on to her last possession in the world. He's not worth the effort but if he lets her go, what will that say about him? And if he hangs on, what will that do to her? There's no simple answer. She chews on the thumb of her free hand as they walk.

The kid races ahead. "Look at this." He crouches over the gutter and lifts what looks to be a dead rodent.

"Put that thing down," Rose shrieks. "It could have diseases."

"It's dead."

"I don't care. Drop it."

"It's cool."

"Drop it."

The mouse lands on a rusted grate. Shermeto can't help but

laugh.

"Are their monsters down here?" The kid gets down on his knees and peers through the grate.

"Not the kind you think," Shermeto says.

"Is there another kind?"

"There's all kinds."

Around them the city seems suspended. Cars move in and out, mostly out, but they're becoming fewer as the city empties. And then he notices the lights have blinked out. The traffic lights black, no flashing neon in store windows.

"What's the matter?" Rose squints into the sun.

"I don't know." Shermeto shakes his head. The kid glances up, the rabbit dangling by its ears from his fist, its furry feet wet from rainwater gathered around the drain. "Something doesn't feel right. Do you hear that?"

The kid stands. "You mean that?" He points.

Water rushes towards them, filling the street.

KENDRA

There's a clicking coming from somewhere above her head. All the horror movies she's ever seen are coming to life in front of her. What was she thinking? Of course she shouldn't go anywhere with a man who basically attacked her, even if he tried to take it back. Her hands are bound, hard plastic digging into her wrists. A narrow window sits near the ceiling, above a concrete ledge. Dull light leaks through, not enough for her to make out clearly where she is. Wooden beams crisscross overhead.

And where's her phone? She can't reach her pocket and she needs to call Gary. Anyone to come and get her. Did she scream before she passed out? She can't remember. If she doesn't come back maybe someone will trace her phone. *Do they really do that or is that just in the movies?*

Fuck. James would say he told her so. Only a matter of time before her recklessness got her into trouble. And this officially counts as trouble.

"So now what?" Kendra says to the walls, boxes, a rusted washer and dryer now taking shape as her eyes adjust to the darkness.

"We're fucked."

She whips her head around best she can, searching for the voice.

"Who's there?" The bindings cinch tighter around her wrists as she struggles to shift her body, peer over her shoulder.

"Won't do no good." The voice says. A man. His voice low, raspy. He's gasping for breath.

"Where are you?" Kendra asks.

"Behind you. In the corner."

She cranks her head around, the pain in the back of her skull wrapping around her neck. A man. Older, with gray hair, dark clothes. Shadows form around him, creeping into the stone walls.

Kendra begins to shiver. Panic rises. Her head roils.

"Stop struggling."

She leans her head back, allowing the cold to take her. The man shimmies a few inches, but he's tied too.

"Where are we?" Kendra asks.

"He said she would be here. I believed him."

"Who were you looking for?" she asks.

She thinks about her father. Is he here somewhere?

"But she's gone. So, so gone." His voice sinks to a whisper. "I'll kill you!"

His scream echoes through the basement then his head dips to his chest. He doesn't move, his breathing raspy.

"He's crazy."

The man stretches his legs out in front of him. Footsteps creak above their heads.

"He's back," Kendra whispers, eyeing the ceiling.

"Never left."

Not so reassuring.

A door opens and footsteps crunch down the stairs. First legs appear, then a waist, but the dark hides the rest of him.

"You can't keep us here. Someone will find us." Kendra doesn't really believe her words, but she must try.

Jagger laughs. "No one is looking for you, silly girl."

He's right. No one knows she's here. Her heart sinks, becoming one with the concrete floor, the dirt and mold an extension of herself.

"Why me?" The words whine out of her. She's stupid, weak. "I'm nobody. Can't give you anything."

"You're worth more to me than you realize, pretty lady." Jagger doesn't move from the base of the steps but turns his attention to the man. "But you, Joe. You're nothing. She's worth more than spades to me." He takes a quick step forward then reconsiders.

"Liar. A crook. You'll get what's coming to you. They always do."

"Might have believed that once." The man sighs. "They can try. Once you're broken like me, doesn't much matter." He turns back to Kendra. "But you, Kendra. You have more power than you realize." He wipes his face with his sleeve. "Almost brings a tear to my eye." Then he turns and stomps back up the stairs and slams the door.

His feet shuffle across the floor above, and then there's a sharp scraping like something being dragged. Followed by silence.

***

The stink of chemicals comes back to her, photos hanging like gray ornaments from the lines across the ceiling. She wasn't supposed to go in there, especially without her father. But she needed some glue for her science project. The red light over the door was out. She knocked first but there was no answer. It couldn't hurt if she just slipped in, didn't touch anything and then slipped right out. Dad wouldn't even know she was there. She stood outside, her hand on the doorknob. She hadn't seen him leave. What if he was inside?

Kendra glanced over her shoulder. Her mom had taken Lily and Stevie to the dentist. She'd argued she was old enough to stay by herself. She was almost a teenager. Besides, she hated the smell of the dentist office, all the people wearing those masks. Her mother finally relented but not without a warning. "Leave your father alone. He's busy." He was always busy. But she was busy too. She was trying to put together a homemade bird's nest, but the mud wasn't holding. She needed glue.

The knob twisted easily under her hand and the door opened inward. The smell almost knocked her on her bum.

She left the door open and searched the gloom. Photos hung by clothespins along the length of the room. Black and white with various shades of gray. She often asked her father why he never took pictures in colour. "Colours are distracting. The emotion gets lost. This way, you feel the image."

***

She thinks of her father now, how cold he must be out there on the streets, how lost he must feel. A chill passes through her, air coming from somewhere in the basement. Cold upon more cold. Kendra pulls her knees to her chest and rubs away the tears trickling down her cheeks.

"I'm starving," Kendra whispers, not knowing if Joe is awake or not. "Does he bring food?"

Joe stirs. "You get used to it."

SHERMETO

"Quick, up there." Shermeto pushes them into a stairwell leading to the Plus 15, a series of skywalks that connected buildings around the city without ever having to go outside. His type didn't come up here too much, the pathways reserved for the well-dressed and employed. But this was extenuating circumstances. They stand on the stairs watching the water fill the streets, creeping under doors, filling the sewer, but there's too much water to swallow it all. Rising. Higher.

Rose paces the platform. The kid huddles on a step, eyes wide. Water laps over cars. There are no words. The silence subdued by fear. The rush of water below, eating through concrete and debris, loud enough to dissolve all thoughts. Shermeto's never seen anything like it. The way the water moves, nothing in its way to stop it. A steady surge. The waves roll over top of themselves, in a hurry, as if searching for something.

Rose moves back and forth, back and forth, chewing on her thumb. The first weeks on the streets are always the hardest but throw in Mother Nature's angry whim and he can't imagine what must be going through her mind. Water drips from the eaves above, swallowed up in the fierce roar.

Rose leans over and whispers something into the kid's ear. He laughs and then bursts into tears. This is so far out of his territory he might as well be in Egypt or on another planet. She kneels beside her kid and wraps her arm around him. It's a toss-up who needs who more.

Shermeto hunkers against the wall, legs stretched out in front of him, arms folded across his chest, chin tucked into the collar of his coat. A damp penetrating cold. How will he get them out of this? He promised them safety, what if he can't deliver? His gaze travels up the road, the bridge up ahead, the way layered in water. All they need to do is get to the other side. Simple in concept, reality is something else. He doesn't know the walkways, but how hard can it be?

The wind groans around them, catching in the edges of the stairwell. A potato chip bag flattens against a wall, flapping and crackling against concrete and steel. Nowhere to go.

This is one of those times he misses a bed. A true roof over his head. Falling asleep to the flickering lights of the television, lulled into dream by far away voices. He thinks of his old place, tucked into a pocket of a seedy neighbourhood with drug dealers on one side and an elderly man with a bum leg who always yelled at his dog on the other. And his old roommate Archie. Shermeto wonders how the old goat is getting on. Most of the time Archie was never home. When he wasn't out banging some woman, he worked up north, gone for long stretches. Quite a convenient arrangement. Until he came home and got all up in Shermeto's business.

"You're drinking too much."

"Can't you wash a fucking pan?"

"The rent is late."

Wasn't worth the trouble no more.

Everyone comes from someplace, but that don't always mean they have somewhere to go. He's tired. So very tired.

***

On that last night, he'd gotten into a scuffle with Archie and invited himself to Kendra's. He had no plan. It was what he did every time. Show up when he needed something, not because he really cared. The silence around the table cut hard. James ate slowly. Kendra didn't touch her food.

"When will this stop?" she finally asked.

Shermeto chewed a big mouthful of cheesy noodles and looked at James, who only continued to eat. Had he ever made eye contact with him? Shermeto didn't think so.

"When will what stop?"

"You. These decisions. You're going to end up out on your ass with no place to go. Have you considered seeing a therapist?"

Shermeto laughed, a deep throaty laugh and then took another mouthful of food.

"I could pay for it for you."

James's head shot up, but he didn't speak. He rose from the table, dumped his half empty bowl in the sink and disappeared to another room of the house.

"He doesn't like me much."

"It's not you he doesn't like. It's what you're doing with your life. We're worried about you, Dad."

"I didn't ask for that."

"You don't need to."

Kendra played with the frayed end of her placemat. Twisted the threads between her fingers. He liked to remember these tiny details.

"What happened? You used to be so happy."

Shermeto shrugged. Had he ever really been happy? He couldn't remember a time when he felt real pure joy. Maybe when the kids were born? How quickly they grew though, from those little dependent bundles of poop and fuss to something unrecognizable, not needing him anymore. He knew that parents were supposed to be proud, but when the kids grew and he was parenting alone, the guilt took over. He shouldn't be doing it alone. He'd let them down. Taken something away from them.

"You gonna eat that?" he asked, pointing at her untouched bowl.

She pushed the bowl towards him and he snatched it up before she could change her mind. He devoured the contents then leaned back in the chair. When was the last time he had a meal at a dinner table? Seemed like a lifetime.

"Can I take a shower?" he asked. What had he become that he had to ask for these basic things?

"I'll get you a towel."

Kendra jumped from the table and padded off to the bathroom.

During the shower, he heard them fighting. When he emerged from the bathroom, cleaned up and fresh as he could be, he pretended not to notice. Kendra had already spread a sheet over the couch cushions and fluffed up a pillow for him. A couple of blankets lay folded on top of the pillow. Kendra was in the kitchen, dishes clanking around in soapy water. James had not reappeared.

"I'll be out of your hair by morning," Shermeto said.

"It's no trouble," she said, not looking up. She placed bowls in a drain board, soap still dripping down the sides.

"Can I help?" he asked.

"It's fine. I'm almost done." She pulled the plug and water slurped and gurgled down the drain. She wiped her hands on a dishtowel. "I'm going to bed."

He nodded and sank onto the couch. He spread out the blankets and stretched underneath. He found the remote beside him and flicked on the television. The light warmed the dark room.

Kendra turned off the bathroom light and disappeared to her room. It pained him to think that he was hurting her, but he didn't know how to do any different, didn't know what she expected from him. It was his life to do with what he wanted. What business was it of hers if he wanted to waste himself away to nothing?

There was nothing on the television, so he shut it off and closed his eyes. He didn't think much time had passed, didn't think he'd dozed off, but he woke up suddenly, listening in the dark. Voices emerged from deep in the house. He strained to catch the words, but they were muffled behind the closed bedroom door. Until it opened. Shermeto pretended to be sleeping, kept his eyes opened in narrow slits. Light spilled into the hallway. A shadow stood in the doorway, but light splattered the walls around the void.

"Ridiculous." James was the void. Kendra was crying.

"Don't be like that," she begged.

"When will it end? It's always something."

"I can't just push him out on the streets."

"You can. We wanted a family. And now you won't because of him."

"I can't turn my back."

"I don't expect you to. But you can do both."

"How would I do that? I can't be worrying about him all the time and be focused on a child. One will suffer, and you know it. Why can't you understand?"

"I do understand. That's not the point. You wrap yourself up in caring for other people. I admire that about you, but when will it end? Not until he dies. Is that what you're waiting for?" James sighed. "I would never ask you to choose. But when is our life going to start? He hurts you. All the time. And you still bend over backwards for him. You can't say no."

"I know," Kendra whimpered.

"Come back in here." The door shut, and the hallway fell into darkness again.

Shermeto rolled over, facing the back of the couch. He'd planned on telling Kendra what the doctor said. He owed her that. But now he couldn't. He stared into the dark. *He was holding her back. That's not what he wanted. He needed to leave. To go as far away as possible and allow her to get on with her life.*

Shermeto rolled up one of the blankets and tucked it under his arm. He found his boots and jacket and slipped into the night.

***

The kid begins to sob. Rose pulls him tighter.

"He's cold."

Shermeto shrugs out of his coat and wraps it around their shoulders. A warm wind is winding its way into the stairwell.

"May I?" he asks, nodding to the step on the other side of the kid.

Rose nods and Shermeto joins them, together saturating the kid with body heat. "I've been out here a long time. The dark you get used to. Never the noises."

The kid screws up his face. "You're scared?" There's snot leaking from his nose.

"Always," Shermeto says.

"How do you get unscared?"

Shermeto thinks about this then digs into his pocket. He pulls out the camera and hands it to the kid. "Fear is a good thing. If you're a little fearful you're still alive. I wouldn't want to never be scared."

The kid takes the camera and holds it to his chest, burying his head in his mother's chest. "I don't like it here."

"I know, baby," she whispers. "I know."

"Can he find us here?" the kid asks.

"What did he give you?"

The kid holds out the camera.

"What do you say?"

The kid turns to Shermeto. "Thank you."

"Do you know how to use it?" Shermeto asks.

The kid shakes his head.

"See that there? That's how you turn it on."

The kid flicks the switch and the digital screen brightens.

"You can look through this hole there, or the screen. When you have something you like, just press that button."

"Cool."

The kid aims the camera at Shermeto and snaps a photo, too close to be any good, but it's a start. He hops up and runs up the steps into the walkway snapping pictures as he goes.

Rose turns to Shermeto. "Thanks. It's only an adventure for so long." Her lips form a half smile, her eyes shrink from fatigue. She picks at a stain on her skirt and closes her eyes.

"You're hiding from someone?"

Her eyes snap open and she smooths the wrinkles from her skirt. "It's not as bad as it sounds."

"Humour me."

"His father."

"The scars? From him?"

Rose nods. "We left when he threatened to kill us. He's never done that before. We went to a shelter. Took him a month to find us. Police came. Hauled him away."

"You left."

"In the middle of the night. They promised to keep us safe, but he's resourceful. Seems like he has eyes everywhere."

Shermeto knows the feeling. "Sounds like a dick," he says. "My wife died. Killed herself." Shermeto doesn't know where the words came from.

"I'm sorry." Rose finds his hand in the dark. "Recently?"

Shermeto shakes his head. "It was my fault."

"I doubt that's true," Rose says.

"Wasn't there for her. I should have known."

"Was she sick?"

Shermeto shakes his head. "No. Only sad."

"Sad can be a sickness."

"You're not making me feel any better," Shermeto says. Truth be told, he never thought of Grace as being sick. Even more so, he felt he should have seen it before it was too late.

"How'd she do it?" Rose asks.

"Don't much want to talk about it," Shermeto says.

**

He couldn't remember what they even fought about. There was always something and he'd storm off to his studio. He hadn't taken a photo worth his time in a couple of years. He came inside after a full day, grabbed another beer and sank into the couch. The girls were in their rooms.

After a while he knocked on Kendra's door. "Where's your mother?"

Kendra didn't look up from her book. "In the bath, I think."

Shermeto nodded and shut the door. He slipped into the master bedroom and tapped on the door. "You okay in there?" he asked.

A soft murmur came from the other side and a splash of water.

Taking that as his answer, he guzzled to the bottom of the bottle and fell asleep. When he woke the house was too quiet.

Kendra was on the phone. Lily was in her room. Nearly time for dinner and Grace was not in the kitchen.

"Did your mother come out?" he asked, stumbling to Kendra's room.

Kendra shrugged and waved him away.

Certainly, she should have been out of the bath by now but the door was still closed. He pressed his ear to the door and listened, then lightly tapped. Nothing. No answer. He knocked again, harder. Still nothing. The door was locked. "Grace?" Only silence. Dead silence. He shook the doorknob. "Open the door, Grace."

"GRACE." Panic clenched his throat. Kendra appeared in the bedroom doorway, Lily tucked in behind her.

"Dad. What's wrong?"

"Go back in your room." Shermeto kicked at the door. He rammed it with his shoulder. Finally, the hinges splintered, and he fell into the room.

Red. So much red. Red water. Red streaks dripping down the side of the tub. Red on white. Red swirls. A drooping hand over the side of the tub.

He sank to the floor.

"Daddy?" He couldn't let Kendra see. Not like that.

He rose and pushed her out of the bedroom. "Get back. Both of you. And don't come out until I say so."

They never talked about that day again. Even now, Shermeto has no idea how much Kendra saw. And he doesn't want to know.

KENDRA

"When was the last time you ate?" Kendra asks.

The light has become greyer, the din of another storm moving in.

A scratch of cloth on concrete, a groan. "I lost track," Joe says.

Kendra's throat becomes tight. The sweat and damp pooling inside her jacket, now serving to chill her straight through. This poor man. All of them. Did her father do this to himself? Starve himself? For what?

"Why?"

It's the only word that comes out. There is a lot she wants to know but doesn't know how to ask. She's never been this close to someone....so down on his luck? Someone...her thoughts trail because she doesn't want to think the next words. She's not that person. Refuses to be that person, as if by not acknowledging it, will make her better than the rest. Or is she worse? She can't decide. It's too cold.

"A loaded question." Joe begins to sob

She imagines herself huddled under a blanket, sipping Pinot Noir from the bottle, binge watching *How I Met Your Mother*. Anything to forget. But she can't forget. Can't forget her father somewhere out there, afraid to accept the truth. It crosses her mind that they're not that different, she and him. Dealing with the same crap in a basket. But such different outcomes. Her neck stiffens. She tries to turn but the dark has clamped its fist around her, making it impossible to move.

She imagines coffee. The warm liquid dripping down her throat, warming her from the inside out. The right amount of sweet to take the edge off, but not enough to make it a syrupy sticky mess. "When we get out of here, I'll buy you a coffee."

"I'd settle for tea."

She can't disagree. "How long until he comes back?"

"There's no method to that man's madness. He's more messed up than most of us."

She doesn't respond. The air swirls. The scratch of something behind a box in the corner. It makes her uneasy. A critter. Coming out of the dark. Fuck. She hates the dark. And it's getting darker by the minute.

The scratching grows nearer, running along the wall, the floor, keeping close to the cracks, swerving back and forth. It stops.

"What is that?" Her heart pounds. She doesn't expect Joe to answer. He probably can't see anything anyway.

"Probably a rat." Joe's voice sounds scratchy, weak.

"There're no rats in this city."

"That's what you think." He's giving up.

"Don't die on me." She hates the dark and all that comes with it. She shouldn't have gone to the parkade. She should have done what she was told. Listened to the warnings. Stupid. Stupid. Stupid.

"Nothing else left to do."

"I don't believe that."

"We ain't getting out of here."

Then she has an idea. "Hey, Joe."

He offers a muffled acknowledgement.

"You know my father."

"Did I?"

"Shermeto."

"Short, bald guy. Sat with me and Marie. We were going to get off the streets."

"When was that?"

"Don't remember. A while ago."

THE RIVER

Water careens through the streets. Dirt and debris pressing towards the centre of town. Drains gulp and spit. Choking, rushing into places rainwater goes, and where it doesn't belong. But this is more than rainwater and too much for the streets to dispel on their own. It won't be long. The water snakes through alleys, searching, seeking, filling gutters and drainpipes. The water rises over sidewalks, higher and higher, covering fire hydrants, and ever higher, licking up the stems of parking metres.

The river wraps through the street, curls around the dark parkade. The street lights have blinked their last breath, lost the fight. A mild disappointment clings to the putrid air of the parkade. Automobiles are abandoned as people tread through the streets arms full of their precious belongings. Hurry, before it's too late.

The river winds up the parkade where a dull echo reverberates off the concrete. The haggard man stands behind the cart, eyes wide. Frozen. The cart begins to roll as he crumbles to the ground, the other man hovering over him. He moans and curls into the fetal position, bows his chin to his chest.

"Oh, knock it off."

A boot heel stomps into his cheek. The air goes murky. A kick to the stomach. He can't move and isn't going to try. There's no point. A flick of a lighter and the flames catch on the threads of his pant cuffs, quickly licking up his legs. Fiery tendrils leap at the cloth, devour his pant leg.

The man kicks, trying to roll, but the fight is gone.

Flames slurp at his sleeves, gasping for more, needing more. An insatiable hunger.

The man screams so shrill, nearly enough to shatter, split bones, cause fissures to erupt in the pavement. Seems it could bring down a building. But the screaming subsides as quick as it starts and the body stills.

The river is too late.

SHERMETO

The water is rising fast.

"We can't stay here," Shermeto says.

"But there's no way out." Rose tries a door to the connecting office building but it's locked. Her eyes widen and flash with panic. In his own confusion he sees Grace behind those eyes, trying to call out for him to do something to save her. *It's too late. He's always too late.* He glances from Rose to the kid. *Not again.*

"We're getting out of here."

Warm air hits them in the corridor. Clear glass on either side they stand and watch the water move swiftly through the streets. There's so much power in those waves. Up ahead, on the other side of the bridge he can make out a circle of buses, waiting for straggling passengers. That is where they need to go, but Shermeto has no idea how he will make it happen. From this vantage Shermeto can see the water, swirling, rushing; behind them, it spills onto the side streets and begins to dissipate. And then he gets an idea.

"Stay here." He hobbles to the other end of the corridor and tries the door. It's locked.

"We're stuck." Rose's face sags in defeat.

"Worth a shot. I'll be right back." He heads back to the stairs.

"You're not going out there alone."

"Stay. I'm not going to lose you too."

The kid clutches the rabbit to his chest. There's a sadness in the kid's eyes he's seen before. Rose's lips are firm. Determined.

"You want to just leave us here?" Her body stiffens. "You're no different than all the rest."

Now Shermeto knows this isn't true. He's nothing like all the rest. Whoever the rest are in her mind. At the top of the stairs he stops; he can't abandon them. *Damn it.*

"Well, are you coming then?"

As the pair hurries to catch up, an uncertain smile spreads across Rose's face.

"What's the plan?" Rose says when they reach the bottom of the stairs, the river only a foot beneath them.

"The water is thinner back the way we came. If we stay close to the wall, both of you holding on to me, we can get around the corner to where it's weaker. Move with the current."

"And then what?"

Shermeto doesn't have a clue. "We'll take the long way around," he says.

"We'll get wet," the kid says.

"Yes, we're going to get very wet. But if you do exactly as I say and hold on to me and your mom, we'll be okay." Shermeto wraps his hand around the kid's. "Got him?"

Rose nods.

Shermeto isn't sure if this is the right idea. He doesn't know what lies around the corner. But he can't not try. He takes a step down, and then another. Water gobbles his feet.

"Wait." Rose pulls back. Then to the kid, "Tuck the rabbit under your jacket." The kid does as he's told, Rose closes the jacket so only the ratty ears hang out at the kid's chin. It's a big jacket, but it will do for now. "Okay," she says with a nod and grips the kid's other hand.

"It's so cold."

The kid's right. The water is cold enough to shrivel a testicle. He holds the kid tighter. "Don't let go," he says.

KENDRA

The critter isn't a rat; it's a mouse and now it's hiding between a couple of boxes. She can see its eyes, its nose twitching in earnest. At least it's not coming any closer. Kendra's wrists are sore. Her shoulder blades pinch but she can't do anything to relieve them. Any way she turns only makes it worse.

Joe hasn't spoken for nearly ten minutes and suddenly erupts in a coughing fit. A low, phlegmy rattle that builds until he could possibly be expelling a lung.

Please God. Don't let him die here.

She's sure she won't be able to handle that. He begins to wheeze. Shit.

"HEY!" She screams as loud as she can, not sure if the guy is still upstairs or not. She kicks her feet against the concrete, but it makes nothing more than a dull snap that doesn't even scare the mouse.

"HEY. UPSTAIRS. THIS GUY IS DYING. HE CAN'T BREATHE."

Joe's breathing becomes raspy, short. He's gasping.

"Take it easy. Slow breaths. Calm down."

"She's gone."

"Who?"

"He killed her and now he's going to kill us."

Joe begins to moan, a sad whimper that turns to a high-pitched wail. A sound she hadn't heard since that one photo shoot a while back: a five-year-old threw a temper tantrum and didn't want her picture taken. The mother tried to force it until the kid broke into a shrill scream that could have cut glass. It damn near shattered her skull. This is something like that.

"KNOCK IT OFF!" A thundering voice from the top of the stairs. He is still there.

"Help him! He needs help!"

"I'll help him all right. Stop that nonsense right now before I clobber you."

Jagger comes down the stairs a few steps. Joe doesn't stop. She wishes he would. For his life and for the knife in her skull, ripping in and out.

Jagger reaches the bottom of the stairs and grabs Joe by the collar, hauling him to his feet. Then he shoves him towards the stairs.

"Where are you taking him?"

"You just worry about yourself."

"Don't hurt him. He didn't do anything."

Jagger laughs, pauses a moment. Kendra thinks she might have gotten through to him. For only a moment. But then he shakes it off, stiffens his shoulders and shoves Joe up the stairs. Kendra closes her eyes and fights back the tears. Everything wells up inside her. She can't hold it back. And maybe now she doesn't want to. She's been holding it in for way too long.

***

She remembered the walls, the fence, trees and pathways, always the same. Maybe that's the thing about final resting places. That they never change. Comfort for the dead or for the living. She's unsure.

The sun had been shining that day. The day before Lily left to head out east. The perfect life. And all she wanted was one last chance to say goodbye. Did that mean she wasn't coming back?

"It's beautiful. I don't remember it being so beautiful."

Lily got out of the car. Kendra followed close behind. The temperature had risen at least five degrees in the last hour. Stupid summer.

Creeping down the pathway, Kendra imagined all the ghosts

hanging over their graves, hovering, intertwining with one another in a final dance.

"Do you remember where it is?" Lily waited for Kendra to catch up. Sometimes Kendra forgot how young Lily was at the time. A couple of years younger, it made sense that her memories were blurry.

Stay on the marked path, don't step on anyone. She used to picture bony arms reaching up for her as she passed: one, two, three, four, turn to the right and ten stones up on the left. Those images were still there. She inhaled deep, feet sinking in the spongy earth. The air smells too perfect. Neat. Clean. Nothing hateful. Nothing angry. Only peace.

Her mother's stone was big, more prominent, while her brother's had been laid flush with the ground. She remembered her parents talking shortly after the accident.

"Buy the two plots beside it. Don't leave him alone forever."

As far as Kendra knew that never actually happened because, even though Steven's body lay under the ground at her feet, her mother was cremated. The stone was only for show.

"There," Kendra said.

"We should have brought flowers," Lily said.

"They'll forgive you."

So much time had passed, she thought they didn't belong there. There must be some rule if you don't come visit for, say, longer than two years, you're no longer welcome.

"Do you think they know we're here?" Lily bit at her bottom lip.

"They're dead. So, no."

"You don't believe in an afterlife? Thought you were into all that tarot juju."

"Tarot has nothing to do with ghosts and chatting with the dead," Kendra says.

"What is it then?"

"Therapy."

"What do you need therapy for?"

"Everything. It's my fault." Kendra would never forget.

"What are you talking about?" Lily folded her arms over her chest.

"Steven. It was my fault. All of it. Don't you remember?"

***

November. Her mother's birthday. Kendra had come in from raking the leaves, cranky that she had to do the hard chores while Lily helped her mother with the dishes and Stevie played in a quiet corner, never having to do anything. She was supposed to go to her friend's house, her parents had promised.

"I'm done," Kendra said, dropping her coat on the chair. "Can I go now?"

"Change of plans," her mother announced.

"What do you mean?"

"Your father decided he would take me out for a nice dinner. You have to stay and watch your brother and sister."

She stood, stunned. "You promised."

Her mother swung around. "Birthdays only come around once a year. You can go to Abby's anytime."

"I hate you."

She stormed out of the kitchen and down the hall to her bedroom, slamming the door as hard as possible. She screamed into her pillow and thrashed, pounding the mattress that hadn't done anything to her. It wasn't fair. Why did she always get stuck babysitting? Her childhood was being stripped away one layer at a time. No one even came to say goodbye until Lily knocked on the bedroom door.

"Go away."

"I'm hungry."

"Feed yourself."

She rolled out of bed a few minutes later and padded down the hall. The house seemed eerily quiet. Lily was smearing peanut butter on a piece of bread and getting it all over the table, on her hands, down the front of her shirt. "You're making a mess."

Lily licked one finger at time then held them up for Kendra to see.

"Where's your brother?" she said, grabbing paper towel and tossing it on the table.

Lily shrugged and turned her attention to the jam. *So not fair.* Her parents got to go out and have a good time and she was stuck here, cleaning up after a couple of juveniles. And now she had to find her brother, who was probably hiding in a box somewhere.

Stevie wasn't in his room, though it was hard to be sure under scattered clothes and heaps of blankets. She stepped on a Lego block and screamed.

He wasn't in the bathroom, his parent's room or living room. The TV was tuned to the Wonderful World of Disney. Lily plodded into the living room, set her plate on the table then sank to her knees on the floor.

"Was Stevie watching with you?"

"No." Lily took a bite of her sandwich, jam spilled out the side of the bread and dripped onto the plate.

"Then where is he?"

"I don't know. You were supposed to be watching him."

"Shut up."

"You shut up."

"No, you shut up."

Lily stuck out her tongue.

"Don't drip on the carpet, Mom will kill you."

She checked the closets, calling out her brother's name. No response. No giggle.

"This isn't funny, Steven." The only place left to check was the basement but that seemed absurd. He hated the basement. Too dark. Too cold. She opened the door. The light was on. The stairs creaked and groaned. "Steven, are you down here?" At the bottom of the stairs, Kendra hesitated. She didn't like the basement any more than anyone else.

No response.

He wasn't under the stairs, not inside the washing machine, which he had done once, stayed there for hours until Dad found him and hauled him out. She stood in the middle of the room try-ing to think. If she were an eight-year-old boy, where would she hide? That was impossible.

"I can't find him," she said to Lily.

"He had roller skates."

"What? When?"

"Earlier. Mom told him to stay in the driveway."

"Now you tell me?"

Lily shrugged.

But Stevie wasn't in the driveway either. It was getting dark out-side. She searched the yard but nothing, no sign of her brother. Her parents would be home soon, and if she didn't find him, she was going to be in so much trouble. On the way back into the house, she tripped over a roller skate.

A dog barked somewhere in the neighbourhood.

***

Blame. Guilt. Shame. So closely linked that they were almost one. Deep down she knows it's not her fault. It was just a random act. But still, if she hadn't been such a bitch, so wrapped up in herself, it might never have happened. She hates herself for not being there, for not being able to remember her brother's face, or the way he talked, the way he laughed. It's all so foggy.

Thunder shakes the walls and the small window. The mouse darts past her feet and keeps on going into a farther, darker corner of the basement.

Kendra's tears dissolve into her skin.

SHERMETO

Shermeto pushes through the swirl, testing his footing with each step. The water is up to his knees. Rose and the kid are silent, mimicking his careful movements, jaws tight, a tremble behind their eyes. He can do this. He will get them all out of here and to safety. He must. The water pulls on the kid, so much smaller than them. Shermeto won't let him go.

The kid loses his balance and cries out, his screams buried in the muck coiling around them. Rose screams. The kid goes under. Shermeto scrabbles for the kid's arm and lifts him up, gritting his teeth through his own pain. The kid gasps, his hair pressed hard against his face, water sliding down his cheeks, along with tears fatter than raindrops.

"You're okay. Hang on. Not much farther," he says through laboured breaths. His knees are killing him.

They reach the corner. Shermeto peers up and down the cross street. Nothing looks familiar, even though he's been here a million times before. The lights are out, and he can't tell where the sidewalk ends, or the road begins.

"It looks better up that way." He squints.

"I can't," Rose gasps. She's losing her grip.

"Yes, you can." And maybe for the first time he believes it, or at least he's not going to let on otherwise. "We can. Hold on to me."

Rose wraps her arms around Shermeto's waist, the kid sandwiched between them. The wind whirls around them, raindrops pelting their heads, only it isn't raining.

"Not much farther."

If they can get to the corner, they should be okay. Water thunders around them, drowning out the kid's sobs. Rose clutches his jacket.

"My rabbit." The kid reaches for the stuffed animal, but misses. Another cutting scream shudders off the walls, only he realizes it's him this time, as the weight releases around his waist. Rose reaches for the kid who's thrashing for the rabbit. The kid kicks and screams, struggling from his mother's grasp. Shermeto grabs hard, holds them steady, until the kid regains his feet and clings to Shermeto's jacket.

"I've got you," Shermeto says.

The current is growing stronger, like the hands of the dead writhing around his legs. *How easy it would be to let them pull him under.* Another rush of water hurtles towards them, screaming, angry.

The rabbit snags around a light pole, hovering for a moment. Rose lunges too late for the toy. Shermeto hangs onto the kid and reaches for Rose. She falls, gets sucked under the water. The kid screams for the rabbit and his mother. Shermeto searches around, splashing as if he can part the water and with sheer will get to her.

But he can't. Her skirt is gone. She is gone. He grabs a light pole and holds on. Shermeto thrusts the kid into an alcove. "Stay here."

The kid screams again, a ferocious death rattle, the kind you might expect when faced with a monster in a closet, his face a story of terror. Shermeto pushes into the current and sees the rabbit spinning in a whirlpool in the middle of the street, around and around. He feels under the water, kicking with his feet, his hands.

Rose is gone.

Shermeto watches the place where the rabbit disappeared, searching the surface for any sign of the soggy bunny, or an arm, a piece of skirt, a shoe, anything. Then without warning his legs lift out from under him and he's being pulled down. Water all around him. He thrashes, fighting for breath, the force around him taking him to where he's supposed to go, his life ending just how it should.

His mind muddles, then quiets and for a moment he sees them. The smiling face of his wife, his son next to her. She has her hand on his shoulder and they are both waving.

Shermeto's head emerges from the water, gasping for air and coughing. His back has come to rest up against the side of a building, in the crevice of a doorway. He gathers himself and struggles to his feet.

The kid is across the street but there is no sign of his mother. Shermeto waves to the kid and motions for him to stay put. The kid waves back.

Shermeto has a bigger problem, *how the hell will he get back across the street*?

There's a rumble behind him. He glances over his shoulder. A firetruck is cutting through the water, making its way slowly up the street. Shermeto raises him arm and the truck pulls closer, stopping in the middle of the road. Firemen hang off the side of the truck. They motion to him not to move. Shermeto points at the kid and alarm spreads across their faces. They are speaking to each other in animated spurts and then the driver pulls the truck up further. They're going for the kid first. *Good*. Let the kid be saved and he can slink back into the shadows.

It's too late for that though. He started this and now he's got to see it through. He owes that much to the kid, to Rose, to Kendra.

The firemen attach a rope to the side of the truck and slowly one of them braves the water, making his way to the kid. The water is merciless and even a man as strong as that one, slips and falls. He manages to pull himself up, and he tries again. In a moment the kid is attached to the rope and to the fireman and hauled to safety.

Shermeto wondered for a moment if they would come back for him. They could easily write him off, pretend they don't notice.

But with the kid safely in the cab, the truck begins to back up and they do it again.

"Hold on," the fireman says, attaching the rope around Shermeto's waist. Shermeto holds tight to the fireman and lets himself be taken to safety.

Shermeto reaches for the kid before the rope is unfastened.

"Thank god you're okay." Shermeto wraps his arms around the kid.

The kid's lips tremble but he doesn't speak. The roar of the truck is too loud to hear anything anyway.

"You can let us out here."

Shermeto says, when they round a corner and are surrounded by dryer ground. The truck slows and stops.

"You sure?" The fireman doesn't look convinced.

"Only live over the way."

The fireman nods and Shermeto and the kid hop down. The kid still hasn't said a word. Numb. Scared.

Shermeto waves to the fireman and the truck slowly pulls away from the curb. "We have to go."

"But…" the kid's lip trembles and he's fighting back tears. The kid sinks to the ground, Shermeto with him.

"We don't have much time," Shermeto says. "There's nothing more we can do right now. If she made it, we'll find her."

"She didn't. She's gone."

"You don't know that."

"Stop lying." Tears spill down the kid's cheeks. "She's gone. And it's my fault."

"How could you think that?"

"It's true." The kid buries his face in his hands.

"There's nothing anyone could have done. It was an accident."

An accident. Nothing anyone could have done.

He plays the words over.

Nothing. An accident. No one's fault.

"Come on, Reese. We can't stay here."

Reese seems to be searching the street. Shermeto wants to tell him it's okay, that he's sorry, but he doesn't have the words. Instead, he wraps his arms around Reese and pulls him close. Shermeto feels as though he's been sliced in half. A part of him disappearing into the deluge with Rose. He'd promised to protect them both and once again he failed. How is he going to make it right?

"Your jacket smells like poo," Reese says.

A shred of indignity shudders through him. "You don't smell so great yourself. Let's get out of here and we can both take a shower."

"But…"

"There's nothing we can do right now." For once Shermeto actually believes this.

Reese nods, taking an extra glance back at the water ripping through the streets and then allows himself to be led away.

"I'm sorry." Reese's bottom lip juts out and begins to tremble.

"For what?" Shermeto asks.

He digs in his pocket and pulls out the camera. "I ruined it."

Shermeto tousles his hair. "Is that all?"

**

They trudge through alleys and along sidewalks until they come to a barricade of emergency vehicles letting cars out but blocking their way in. Shermeto stops, studying the police and workers directing traffic while Reese plods on ahead.

"Hold up," Shermeto says.

Reese stops, confusion on his face. "Maybe they can help my mom," he says.

Shermeto considers this a moment. His relationship with civil servants not exactly what it would be with most citizens. Reese is desperate though and Shermeto can't refuse the kid.

The police officer sees them coming and holds up his hand for them to stop. "You can't be here," the officer says.

Shermeto swallows back his fear. "We lost someone back there. The water was too much."

The officer nods and seems to consider their plea but then, "You have to get out of here. We'll send a team out to look but right now it's not safe."

"But she might still be alive."

"We'll look as soon as we can."

Shermeto can't help but think if he looked different, cleaner, they would listen. Shermeto turns to Reese. "Let's go, kid," and steers him through the barricade. They duck into another alley behind a new condo project.

"My feet are tired." Reese slogs through the mud, a steady slosh and slurp.

"There's a spot just up ahead, we'll take a rest."

"I need to pee."

"Me too."

"You take that tree, I'll take this one." Shermeto motions to Reese.

"No peeking," Reese says.

A moment later Reese reappears; his zipper is down. "She's gone." Shermeto gives a gentle nod.

Reese doesn't stop. "What if she's ok? How will she find me?"

He hadn't thought of that. It's possible she snagged a fire hydrant and found her footing. If she's out there, someone will find her.

"We'll figure it out," Shermeto says.

"Do I have to go live with my dad?"

Shermeto doesn't know what to say. Reese isn't his for the taking. But if he's in danger from this man that Rose was so afraid of, then what other choice does he have?

"Not if I can help it," Shermeto says, knowing full well he can't make that kind of promise.

They round a corner and stop. Red, white and blue light splashes across buildings, seeps into the streets. Police, EMS, and fire surround a parkade. Barricades stretch across the street. The water hasn't reached here yet, but it's coming, jumping the banks and slowing creeping along the roadway. It's like it has a mind of its own. Knows where to let up and where to rage full force.

"What's happening?" Reese's eyes widen.

"Let's find out." Shermeto slips into the throng of curious bystanders, mostly his people, held back by yellow tape. The air smells like the many times he singed his hair while lighting a smoke. But there's something else, too. Smoked meat? Hair and smoked meat, Shermeto thinks and instantly can't unthink. Men in uniforms mill, hover, cling in small clusters, whispering. A radio crackles. One officer is on a phone.

The parkade hangs in shadow. Shermeto stands on the sidewalk, pushes into the crowd. He cranes his neck to get a better look but all he can see is a shopping cart pressed against a wall. Murmurs. Rumours. Tangled, nonsensical words, spread fast. Words he doesn't want to believe.

Burned alive. Old Reuben.

"How do you know?" Shermeto turns to a woman with fiery red hair and a large mole on her nose. He's seen her around before begging for change, but they've never shared so much as a word.

"Saw it with my own eyes."

Her eyes narrow, darkening the already deep lines across her face. One side of her face is scarred. She hugs her body tightly, as if holding a newborn.

"What did you see?"

"Two hoods running that way." She points in no particular direction.

"You're high. It was man. Only one. He went the other way." The man scratches his cheek.

"Fuck you." The woman spits in his face. "Don't believe me. That's his cart now, ain't it? He don't go nowhere without it."

Shermeto clenches his fists and stuffs them in his pockets, scanning the group of first responders. He moves closer and sure as shit a kite tail dangles from the cart, unmoving. The kid clings to his side.

"Pig." The woman again.

"You calling me names?" The man is ready for a fight.

The woman motions with her chin to the approaching officer.

"Did anyone see what happened here?" The cop ducks under the police tape then changes his mind. At full height, legs apart, hand inches from his gun, the officer scans the crowd. "Anyone?"

Everyone shakes their heads. Not Shermeto. The cop stops on him.

"You. You see something?"

"No. Just got here." He pushes the kid behind him.

"Any idea who the victim is?"

"How am I supposed to know?" Shermeto says, glancing around at the glossy-eyed crowd. *Why are there so many people still here anyway?* They should be long gone.

The cop shifts from one foot to the other like there's a stick stuffed up his ass. "Recognize this?" The cop holds up Reuben's silver pocket watch, which probably wasn't his in the first place.

All he wants is his wallet and it's probably in that damn cart which is more secure than the fucking Mona Lisa right now. Medics are putting the body on a stretcher.

"Do I know you?" the officer asks.

"Doubt it." Shermeto needs a plan. "It's Reuben."

The cop pulls out his notebook and pen and scribbles on the pad. "What's your name?"

"Don't have one."

The cop eyes him, tapping his pen on the notebook. "Cut the tough act. If you don't want to help, then don't. Unless you know more than you're letting on."

"Nothing to tell. It's Reuben. And knowing my name won't change that."

Was this guy born dumb or does it take training?

"What can you tell us about Reuben?" The cop tucks the book in his pocket.

"He's a thief. Got what he deserved."

The voice cuts over their heads but Shermeto can't tell who it's coming from.

A murmur of agreement threads through the crowd.

"What's going to happen to his cart? Most of that shit belongs to us."

The mystery voice again.

"So, all of you wanted him dead."

That's his cue. Shermeto backs away from the police line and books it out of there before the cops go haywire and haul them all in for no other reason than they have nothing better to do. It's happened before. All minding their own business and the cops stormed their camp, took everyone with them. Not Shermeto though. He got away, hunkered behind a concrete block until the chaos ended.

This is no place for him. Where's Reese? He searches and finds him standing near the back of the crowd, digging in the mud with the toe of his shoe. A hand falls on Shermeto's shoulder. He swings, knocking his assailant to the ground.

"What the hell, man?" Jagger lies on his side. "What you do that for?"

"Where'd you get that stupid hat?" It's a normal ball cap, with the sides jigged with earflaps, stitch marks where a logo used to be.

Jagger pulls the cap off his head, his hair jutting out from his head.

"Found it." Jagger picks himself up and places the cap back on his head, pulling the flaps down over his ears.

"Thought you were gone," Shermeto says.

"Never for long. You know that." Jagger glances at Reese. "Where's the woman?"

Shermeto just shakes his head.

"Drowned," Reese pipes up.

Shermeto's head snaps to Reese then back to Jagger. "We don't know that for sure."

"I do." Reese is relentless, has no filter.

Jagger's face drops. "Oh. Sorry, buddy." He looks to Shermeto for a further explanation but Shermeto won't give it. What happened has happened and there isn't anything anyone can do to change it. Best to keep moving forward.

"Where you going?" Jagger asks.

"Trying to get to the other side of the river, out of this mess."

"Leaving? Are you coming back?"

"Don't know yet. Got some stuff I have to deal with." Reese is staring up at them, waiting. "He doesn't belong out here."

Jagger nods. "I think this belongs to you." He waves a folded square of black leather in his hand. Shermeto's wallet.

"Where'd you get that?" Shermeto snatches the wallet.

Jagger shrugs. "What's so important in there? Not like there's any money in it."

It figures that Jagger checked.

"I'll be damned." Shermeto opens the wallet. The photo is still there, and the letter folded into a neat square, the edges frayed and tired. He pulls it out and tucks it into his pocket.

"Thanks. Really. Thanks," Shermeto says.

The city is closing in on him. What once felt so free is now feeling cluttered, unmanageable.

"Let's get out of here." He turns to Jagger. "You coming?"

"You'll be back." Jagger seems too sure of himself.

"You can't stay out here."

"Can take care of myself." Jagger backs away, dissolving into the dispersing crowd.

A car passes splashing water up and over him. He doesn't even have the energy to flip them the bird. *Fuck*. Pain seizes his chest. He can't breathe.

Reese grabs his hand and squeezes. "Can we go now?" Reese looks up at the sky and the fat raindrops beginning to fall, again.

Shermeto's boots are soaked, his feet slurp and suck at the fluid seeping into his soles. They duck into an alley as the rain pelts full force, then push in under a fire escape between abandoned wooden pallets and bags of garbage. Shermeto pulls a wet piece of cardboard over their heads. A cat slinks into the alley, eyes them then darts away. "I get it, buddy," he mutters.

"Why are we here?" The kid's teeth begin to rattle.

"Wait out the rain a moment."

Razor sharp cold slices at him. Puddles form in the cracks of the pavement, water trickles down the sides of the building and rushes away.

Emergency vehicles are calling out, searching for stragglers, slowly slicing their way up and down the streets, herding everyone out. To safety. He doesn't need safety. He needs to disappear. Forever is preferable but that doesn't seem to be happening, at least not without a little help. Reese is shivering. Shermeto needs to get him inside somewhere.

A white van pulls into the alley and two men hop out. Through a narrow slit in the pallet, Shermeto watches as they rifle through the back of the van, doors slam. With tools and buckets in tow, they disappear into the building. When the door opens a gush of foggy breath escapes. Steam means warm.

"Come on."

He pulls the kid up and leads him to the building.

Shermeto grabs the door handle, half expecting it to be locked but no, it opens slow and easily. He pokes his head inside and looks around. A gust of warm air hits him, but he doesn't flinch. Another door inside hangs open. Murmurs reach him, but he can't make out any words, the clank and bang of a hammer maybe, the steady hum of a fan. They slip into a crawl space under the stairs. Shermeto holds his finger to his lips to keep the kid quiet. No one will see them there.

Shermeto takes off his coat and lays it on the floor to dry out. He kicks off his shoes and sets them neatly beside the coat, then he drapes his socks over the boots. His feet are red and sore. Reese huddles into the corner, fear and fatigue stretching across his face.

"Get some rest. When we're warm and rested, we'll go."

"Where?" Reese can barely keep his eyes open. "There's nowhere to go."

Voices grow louder. The two men are right outside the mechanical room. Keys jangle and a presumably a tool box slams to the floor.

"That's it." A door closes with a click.

"Let's get out of here."

"You really think it's going to hold?"

"Guess we'll find out. They're going to shut down the power any minute."

"Shit. Look at this."

There's a splash of footsteps, a few curses flung into the downpour and then they're gone. Shermeto hears the van engine roar and fade away, then he lies back and closes his eyes. The air is musty but warm. Soon the cold edges away and they both relax.

A vent overhead opens and blasts warm air into the cubby. A

steady *whump whump* comes from the mechanical room, from the stairs above, from everywhere all at once. Shermeto lies back on his wet jacket. Reese curls into the crook of his arm.

Reuben won't even make the news. How fucked up is that? The police won't do jack shit. Written off as an act of circumstance. Maybe a blip on the evening report. People will hear, mutter their *oh my god(s)* and *oh no, that's terrible(s)* over the dinner table but by dessert, he'll be nothing but a dusty memory.

***

They'd gone out for dinner, left the kids home alone. Kendra was a good girl, strong-willed; spirited, but responsible. They would be fine for a couple of hours.

"She's so angry lately," Grace said, as they climbed into the car.

"Teenager." Maybe it was a cop-out response, an excuse.

"You're probably right." She placed her hand on his. There weren't enough of those moments, just the two of them.

He squeezed her hand. "I'll talk to her later if you want."

"I should do it."

They pulled up to the restaurant.

Not an hour later, the waitress came up to them. "Excuse me, are you Del and Grace Shermeto?"

"Yes," he said.

"There's a phone call for you. You can take it at the bar."

"I'll go," Shermeto said and tossed down his napkin.

"Hello?"

"Daddy?" Kendra's voice came over the phone in a desperate sob.

"What's wrong?"

"I can't find Stevie."

"He's probably just hiding. You know how he is."

"No. He's not. I've looked everywhere."

"We're on our way."

"Daddy?" Kendra sounded scared.

"What is it?"

"I'm sorry."

"It's not your fault. We'll find him."

He hung up the phone and headed back to the table.

"We have to go." Shermeto paid the bill and they hurried home.

"What was she thinking?" Grace said. "I gave her one job. That's it. One lousy job."

"Relax. It's not her fault. You know how he can be."

"She always hated him."

"Now you know that's not true. Siblings fight all the time."

The driveway was lit with police cars. The garage light flooded onto the street. Kendra stood in the front hallway, arms folded over her chest. Lily sat on the floor staring up at them.

"Are you the parents?" An officer turned to greet them.

"Where is he?" Grace fell through the door and grabbed Kendra by the shoulders and shook her. Kendra burst into a new flood of tears. Shermeto pulled Grace back.

"Can we go somewhere and talk?" The officer said.

***

Wake up.

Shermeto opens his eyes in a panic. Reese is curled at Shermeto's feet. Shermeto watches him a moment to make sure he's still breathing.

It's time to go.

Where is that voice coming from? Barely a whisper shimmering along the concrete walls. He peers out from around the wall. The doors are closed, the lights flicker.

Shermeto shakes Reese.

Despite the steam, with wet clothes and no blankets, there was nothing they could do to get warm. "Let's get out of here."

Shermeto wraps his jacket around the kid and leads him out from under the stairs. Water seeps in under the door, pooling around their feet. Reese looks up at him, scared, confused.

"Come on," Shermeto says and pushes the kid towards the stairs. "We have to find another way."

DAY FIVE

THE RIVER

Waves leap, the current pulling debris, tree branches, a tarp, rusted tin cans into its mouth in one roaring gulp. It took the woman though it hadn't meant to. A victim of circumstance.

A figure stands on the bank, tired, inconsolable, uncontrollable. He has his own agenda. Will hurt more before the night is out. The river can't reach this man, despite consecutive attempts. Stronger than any malice until now, the hate, the hurt, swirls around like flies on garbage. An attention-seeking soul with no remorse.

The river remembers. It didn't think it could. More of a feeling than an actual memory. This darkness stalked the man named Gerard. Hanging back a few feet until he was secluded enough, then he emerged. Not with the force that darkness can exude, but with a slight tiptoe, rustle, crack of branches. Gerard skipped a rock into the river and plunked himself down on a boulder. He dug a sandwich from his pocket and carefully unwrapped it, balling the plastic and tucking it in his pocket.

The darkness came up behind him with almost no sound.

"Whatcha got there?" it said.

Gerard snapped his head around.

"You." He took a big bite and seemed to consider the boiling sun, giving no mind to the darkness enveloping him. "What do you want?"

The darkness squatted beside him. Hungrier than ten homeless men, but not the kind that could be satiated. Lips formed a straight line, colour sapped from its face. Only the eyes bore down, a stinging gaze, enough to wear the rust off steel. "You're spending a lot of time with Shermeto. And consequently, I can't have that."

"What's it matter to you?"

"Can't have the competition. You and the others put ideas into his head."

"You're crazy. That man don't listen to no one."

The darkness stood, breaking up the light with its shadow.

"He'll listen to me."

It only took a rock larger than his fist. The sandwich disintegrated into the swirling water.

Now, waves snap at bridge bottoms, the river is punching its way further inland, stretching and falling until finally rising to full height and leaping over retaining walls with violent force. It is eating the land as it goes, curling around lamp posts and garbage cans, thrusting cars out of its way, chewing and spitting out patio umbrellas, chairs, tables.

It fills alleys, sweeping, searching, seeping through door frames, filling air vents and basements. The humans run, as they should, slapping through water up to their shins. Its rage knocks them off their feet.

The storm does its part. Rain rips through gutters, swelling and pouring, the pathetic metal unable to accommodate so much power. Sewers swallow the overflow but can't keep up, whirlpools form. Rain and river become one.

Bodies burst from buildings, dart through the streets, crying and screaming, searching frantically for family, friends, arms laden with photo albums, cats in carriers, dogs wrapped in blankets, yanking toddlers by their collars, babies in strollers, car seats, cell phones in pockets, in purses. The water laps at their legs. Pulling. But they fight back. Balancing umbrellas and belongings, fighting against the wind, rain and river. Wild eyed. Afraid.

The river hesitates, takes a moment to gather its composure, sifts through a basement, through long forgotten treasures: an old catcher's mitt, trophies, ribbons, Grandpa Morris' medals from the war. Up a rickety set of stairs, winding around table legs, gobbling up Persian rugs, a dieffenbachia, a child's lettered blocks, the river pours out the front door and into the street.

A scream cracks the air. A man and boy rush into the street from a side door. All the lights are out. The river feels the man's confusion as it wraps around his ankles. His frantic heartbeat. But something else. A need. A drive. The river ebbs backward, creating a path through muddy water, debris. Rain swats their face, relieving him of his muck and grime. The river tells the rain and wind to, "Shhhh," but it doesn't listen.

A siren erupts, the rumble of an engine. A Humvee moves through the streets, tires cutting tracks through the water that immediately fill in behind it. A megaphone strapped to the roof barks out orders.

"Clear the streets. Get to high ground."

The man grabs the boy by the hand and leads him away. Turning one way, then another, stopping every few steps, gasping, sweating. He finds a path not yet engulfed and limps through the street, around a corner and to the bridge that will take him out.

The lower deck is completely submerged under the raging currents; water pulses higher, lower, higher, lower, slaps along the sides of the buildings, rips out the pedestrian paths. Water burbles up from the sewer.

On the upper deck of the bridge, between the pelting rain and clouds, hundreds of bodies move in a slow-motion march. A line of men and women, laden with garbage bags, backpacks—heads down, haggard, disoriented—snakes out of the shelter to school busses, city busses waiting on the other side to take them to safety. Mere shadows, dissolving into the night.

SHERMETO

Shermeto heaves Reese into his arms and falls into the throng crossing the bridge, inching closer to the busses, the headlights. He pads slowly, feeling every muscle, every joint, every piece of cancer surging through his body, all the bad decisions he's ever made. Reese clings solidly to his neck.

"Can you help?" Shermeto calls to a man passing by. The man returns a nod but keeps going.

"Someone needs to help me."

They carry on, slogging up the gentle incline. "Damn it."

Only now he realizes amid the rain pouring down his face are tears, too. Stinging the sores and cuts and scrapes.

And he remembers. Grace. His lovely Grace. They'd met so young, when the world seemed bright and endless. They had babies. Made a life. And then she disappeared inside herself. He should have been better. More attentive. Noticing the signs. The withdrawal.

It was his fault. All of it.

And now Rose is gone. His fault too.

Reese's arms are wrapped tightly around Shermeto, his head buried in his neck.

What must he be going through? Whatever the kid felt, might not be so different from the loss his own kids endured. Kendra was always the strong one, didn't let anything show. Took over the role of caregiver. She was only a kid. Lily didn't seem to notice, thankfully, too young at the time. He should have been there for them. Shermeto begins to shiver, toxic needles, a cold that has been festering for so long. Too long.

He reaches the first bus and sets Reese down. A woman draped in a yellow rain poncho approaches.

"Name?" she asks.

"Does it matter?" he asks, backing away.

"You can't leave." The woman's lips are firm, unsmiling.

Shermeto glances at the bus, the driver. Reese tugs at his pant leg, his little teeth chattering. Warm air reaches for him from inside the bus. He steps back further.

"Take him."

Reese pleads without words. He can't leave him here alone. If he does, who knows what will happen. He'll never be able to forgive himself. It will be the same all over again.

"You can't stay out here. Come on. Let's get you someplace warm. Some dry clothes." The woman steers them towards the open door of the bus.

He knows there's a choice that should be made here. Heat seeps from the bus. His friends, his people, sit in silence in the seats, heads down, hands clasped, teeth chattering. The kid tugs on his arm.

Shermeto pulls his hand back. He peers over the bridge into the water below, rot and debris pressing up against the rails.

"Are you getting on or not?" the woman in the yellow poncho asks.

"Where are we going?" Shermeto asks.

"We have a nice place for everyone." She eyes Reese, knows he doesn't belong here.

Shermeto gives the woman his name and climbs into the bus.

"All full," the woman says, patting the wall. The driver nods and the doors slide shut with a thin whump. The bus hisses and begins to move. Away from everything dying below.

KENDRA

Time stands still in the darkness. Kendra isn't sure if she fell asleep, if the light waning outside is the fall of day or an impending omen of something worse. She hasn't heard anything in the house in a while. Jagger must have left. What did he do to Joe? She shudders thinking of what Jagger might be capable of. She's never known true evil, pure uninhibited hatred. She thought she did, but now realizes it was a hallucination.

For a time, she thought—no prayed—her whole had been a dream, that she'd wake up any moment and hear her mother calling for her, her brother squealing some inconsequential demand, Lily trying to braid her doll's hair. She would bounce out of bed to her parents' smiles, to her daily routine.

But there is nothing routine about any of this.

She tugs on her wrists, tries to wriggle free but it's no use, she's bound and there's no getting out of it. A phone rings somewhere in the house. Her phone? Of course, Jagger must have taken it when he hauled her inside.

She relaxes her arms, no point in struggling anymore.

Kendra wishes her sister was here now. Well not here, because then they'd both be in this stupid mess, but close by. She's all the family she has left and she's halfway across the country. How dare she do that to her?

What if she's stuck here forever? Dies here. Is that what Jagger wants?

A door shudders open and footsteps stomp across the floor, hesitating at the top of the stairs.

"You there?" she yells. "Don't be a pussy and come talk to me."

A soft grunt. Then menacing laughter.

She tugs on the bindings. Tries to stand but it's no use.

All the stories are true. The regret when faced with your potential end. Snapshots of a life.

He clomps down the stairs and sits on the last step.

"You're a cocky one, aren't you? Think you're tough. Nothing can hurt you. A lot of your father in you."

"You don't know my father," Kendra spits out the words.

"I know him better than you think. Been together a long time." He digs in his jacket pocket and pulls out a pack of cigarettes. "Want one?" he asks. "Of course not. These things will kill you. But what does it matter when you're already dead?" He lights the smoke and tosses the rest of the pack onto a nearby box.

"What am I doing here?"

Jagger cocks his head and sucks on the cigarette. "You really don't get it. Of course, you wouldn't. You have everything." He closes his eyes as if studying something far away and then suddenly snaps them open again. "You can't have him back. If you're around, he has something to go home for."

"That's sad," Kendra says.

"You have no idea." He pulls the hat from his head and folds it into his palm. "Killing is easy. You think it will be hard, but once you do it the first time. Kind of like pulling off a bandage."

"What did you do with Joe?"

"He's fine. Don't worry your pretty head about him."

He stands and crosses the floor in two large steps, then leans in really close to her face. She can smell the tobacco and body odor. His teeth are wretched. Kendra stiffens. He runs his hand down the side of her cheek. "You're afraid. That's good. The others weren't afraid enough."

"Kill me if you're going to. I probably deserve it."

Jagger smiles, full mouth, lips spready wide across his face.

"Shhhh. Not yet. It won't be that easy." He turns and stalks back up the stairs.

There's water running somewhere in the house. Not like from a tap but more like water over rocks. Splashing. She peers into the dark, but she can't see anything. Soon she feels it. Her bottom is soaked first. A thin layer swirling around on the basement floor, inching higher. A steady stream spilling in under the window, ground water bubbling up through the floor, all around her.

SHERMETO

Shermeto pushes Reese ahead of him off the bus. They shuffle into the community centre. He recognizes this place, the school next door, the rows of vintage houses. It's only a few blocks from Kendra's house. The building even smells cold though the heat blasts waves over them. They move single file into a gymnasium filled with cots, air mattresses, and blankets. A table of food and coffee is laid out. Children are screaming, racing around chasing balls and balloons.

Most of the cots are already claimed by displaced families and children. Not homeless but forced from their homes by a random act of nature. He doesn't belong here, yet by the look on their faces there's little difference between them. A world of circumstances separates them. The fear, confusion, sadness, it's shared, but one is nothing like the other.

A woman, with a nametag reading "volunteer" hands him a blanket. She smiles but turns away quickly, fidgety eye contact, moving onto the next misfit from the bus. A man approaches with the same volunteer tag stuck to his shirt. He wears jeans, a white shirt and blazer, clothes nicer than anything Shermeto has ever owned.

"Help yourself to food. And there're dry clothes in the back there. Take anything you like."

Shermeto nods. Can't find the words to properly thank him.

He hands the blanket to a passing woman and heads for the clothes room.

"Let's get something dry," he says to Reese who hasn't said a word since they got on the bus. Shermeto elbows his way through the wet and disoriented, finds a sweater with black and white stripes, a pair of green sweatpants and some dry socks, brand new, still wrapped in paper. He tears the wrapping and kicks off his boots, peels off the wet socks and pulls on the fresh ones, then almost tears off his clothes right there before he thinks better of it. He digs through the clothes then notices a pile marked "youth and children". Reese fumbles and finds a shirt and jeans but no shoes that'll fit him that aren't pink or sparkly or light up when he steps.

"Bathroom?" Shermeto asks a short, stubby woman standing in the doorway. She points across the gymnasium and he gathers his belongings, old and new, and shuffles out the door, pulling the kid with him. The new socks feel like a cloud around his feet. In the bathroom he pushes into a stall and drops his wet clothes in a pile and pulls on the new getup. Not fancy, but it will do. He leaves the wet clothes on the floor and exits the stall. He knocks on the neighbouring stall. "You ok, Reese?"

"Yes." His voice is meek. Sad. Shermeto can't blame him.

"Just leave the wet stuff there."

Reese comes out, tugging at the bottom of his shirt. "It's a little tight."

"It'll stretch."

For a moment they look like father and son. Shermeto pulls Reese into a hug. They wash themselves in the sink.

What's he doing? He can't take care him. He can't even take care of himself. What's he trying to prove? There's no going back and this isn't his Steven. There's nothing to make up for. No replacing what he's lost.

"Where's my mom?" Reese asks, his hair hanging over his eyes. "Will they find her?"

"I don't know, kid. I don't know."

Reese stares at Shermeto for a long time, his eyes sad, glossy. "I don't like it here. I want to go look for her."

"We can't."

"Why not?" The kid's lip begins to quiver.

He's not gonna cry is he? Shermeto didn't sign up for that. And why all the questions now? "Let's get something to eat," Shermeto says.

Tears stream down Reese's face. His shoulders begin to shake then he suddenly turns and darts out of the bathroom.

"Hey." Shermeto limps after him. He could have handled that differently.

The kid has disappeared. Shermeto searches the clusters of people playing cards and board games for the children. Panic seizes him, from the soles of his boots to the dead ends of his hair. Where did Reese go? A dizzying feeling takes over as he turns, searching.

Music blasts from a stereo in the corner, one of those Bluetooth contraptions. A television playing the news on a continuous loop. A state of emergency has been declared. Residents have been evacuated from low lying areas along the river, power cut to all areas along the river. More areas are on alert. No ideas when anyone can go back home. Home. Not homeless. Houseless.

There's a difference. Or at least used to think so. The images play over and over, like it's somewhere else, happening to someone else. It doesn't seem real, if not for the evidence all around him, crammed into this room. A basketball slams into the side of his leg and children swirl around him, scrambling for the ball. Reese isn't among them.

"I can't believe I have to tell people this. Stay away from the river." The mayor's eyes are tired. Distraught. Yet there's an undying strength. Shermeto knows that type of fatigue, lets it consume him. It's a special kind of man who can take the tired and turn it into something more. Motivation to serve the people.

Then he spots him. Reese is kneeling over a game of Yahtzee. For a moment he considers leaving him here. Let him play. Let him forget. The last thing Reese needs is some old man trying to tell him what to do. Especially the man who lost his mother.

Shermeto claws his way over. "We need to get out of here."

Reese isn't listening. Dice clatter to the table. A full house.

"You want to play?" A girl with long blonde pigtails asks the kid.

Reese looks to Shermeto for the okay.

"We can stay for a few minutes," Shermeto says.

Shermeto makes his way over to the food table and fills a small plate with buns and fruit, a handful of cheese chunks. He pours a coffee in a foam cup and snatches up a muffin. A woman is helping her own daughter with a plate of fruit. She doesn't want the fruit. She wants chocolate.

Can't blame her, Shermeto thinks.

Across the room, Reese is laughing with the others, a smile spreading across his face.

Despite all that's going on, children are resilient.

Shermeto plods back over to the kid and sits down on the edge of a cot, setting the plate down. The kid grabs the muffin and carefully peels off the paper. It's gone in only a few bites.

"You dry enough?" Shermeto asks.

"Better than before."

"We should go."

"I want to stay here."

They can't stay there. But where else will they go? Then it occurs to him, Kendra doesn't live far away. They could go there. Only for a night, maybe two. Figure out next moves. Kendra would be okay with that.

"I have a better place."

Reese looks like he doesn't believe Shermeto. And why would he? Since they met, Shermeto has done nothing but ruin things. How much damage had he already done? Could it be fixed?

"Where?" the kid asks.

"I'll show you. You'll like it. There's a cat."

The kid's eyes light and he stands.

No one notices them leave.

***

The night is rotting before his eyes. Shermeto feels as though his body is sinking, the ground opening and slowly pulling him down one leg at a time. Kendra hates him, and he doesn't blame her. He did that. Lily, he doesn't even know where she is, hasn't spoken to him in years. He did that, too. He destroys everything.

"I'm sorry," Shermeto says.

"What for?" Reese stoops to pick up a bottle cap and flicks it into the parking lot.

"I couldn't save her."

Reese kicks at the cap but misses.

"I should have left well enough alone," Shermeto adds.

Reese shrugs.

A man with grey speckled hair and jean jacket steps out from behind a tree, staggers over to them.

"Look like you could use a nip." He holds out a flask. Shermeto studies the man, his wiry features, narrow nose, slits for eyes. The flask glows under the pearly light from the streetlamp. Shermeto's shadow stretches out in front of him. The man grins, pressing the flask towards him.

Flask, shadow. Flask, shadow.

"I'm good." He waves the man away. The man takes a long swallow and shrugs, turning back into the night. Shermeto peers out across the parking lot, to the street. It's only a few blocks to Kendra's house. She came looking for him so maybe it will be okay. They can get a good night's sleep and figure things out in the morning. She likely went home when she couldn't find him anyway.

They're barely out of the parking lot when another voice juts from the darkness, this one familiar.

"Sherm. Over here."

Shermeto squints. A man lies in the grass, hands laced behind his head. Only his feet are caught in the spray of the streetlight. It's Louie from the park.

"Where's everyone else?" Shermeto asks.

Louie shrugs. "Got separated." He studies Reese but doesn't say anything. "Sit."

"Can't stay."

"Something better to do?"

For once, yes. "Not staying here." He steers the kid towards the street.

"Better than the alternative." Louie lies back and closes his eyes.

***

The streets aren't as wet here. Dark stains creep into the street, linger in the gutter, but otherwise, you'd barely know anything is going on not so far away. He steps wide of the lines in the sidewalk, remembering the days when he and Grace walked together, she was pushing Steven in the stroller, Lily barely able to walk, racing awkwardly behind Kendra who was always several paces ahead of everyone else, pigtails bouncing. Kendra clasped her sister's hand in hers and pulled her along, hopping over the lines connecting the sidewalk.

Out of habit, Shermeto clings to the edge, half on the grass. Reese struts down the middle, ahead of him, his head lower than ever before. This kid is going to need some help, he thinks. Shermeto shakes his head. *Listen to himself.* Where was all this smartness when he was going through the same thing? When his girls needed support?

The going is slow, his knees crunching and grinding with each step, the pain worsening. But there's a lightness in the way he moves, knowing that for once he will do the right thing. The houses are different. Silent but content, not the frustrated energy felt downtown. He pauses at a hedge and peers into a large bay window, milky light fills the room, a large flat screen hanging above the fireplace; pictures of the river, news anchors, the mayor. He can't read the caption but it's likely the same one he's been seeing everywhere else.

Exhaustion folds around him. Not much farther. He wants to lean on Reese for strength. That's his first problem.

***

Three days. It took the police three days to find Stevie. They got the call in the middle of the afternoon. The police showed up and escorted them to the station. Grace stayed in the lobby with the girls, protecting them from the truth.

An officer led him down a long hallway, with gray sterile walls, to the basement morgue. A steel door hung on hinges.

"Take your time," the officer said, hanging back.

Shermeto approached the window. A woman in a blue mask and surgeon's cap stood on the other side. The officer nodded, and the woman pulled back the sheet.

It wasn't his son. And it was. Gray skin, eyes closed. He could have been sleeping. Shermeto wanted to burst through the door and shake him awake.

"What happened?" The words croaked out.

"We'll know more after the medical examiner is done. But it looks like a hit and run."

***

A car sits in the driveway, but it's not Kendra's. Unless she got a new one, but he doubts that. He climbs up the front stairs, presses the doorbell and knocks. She'll be shocked to see him for sure. He knocks again. The door opens and a man he's never seen before fills the frame. His face is pale, and he's got tiny pinprick eyes.

"Who are you?" the man asks. He glances at the kid standing at the bottom of the steps.

"Is Kendra here?"

"I don't know where she is."

"What do you mean? You're in her house."

The man's face softens. "You're her father, aren't you?"

"What gave it away?"

The man shrugs, relief spreading across his face.

"Come in."

***

"Say it again. Slower." Shermeto's patience is running thin. This,—Gary?—hasn't said anything that makes any sense. And Shermeto doesn't like the way the guy's forehead creases when he's thinking.

Gary takes a deep breath.

"She wanted to go look for you. Both of us, but when I woke up she was gone. No note. Nothing. She called, said she was on the way home. Then a text saying she'd found someone who knew you. That was hours ago. The cops won't do anything. The flood is apparently more important. I don't know what to do. Where to even start."

The man seems distraught. If it's an act, he's convincing.

Reese is on the couch, the cat curls next to him, rolls over and exposes her belly. Shermeto chews on the words. That's what he heard the first two times as well. But this time, they start to sink in. Something has happened to his daughter and again, it's his fault.

"Any idea where she would have gone?" Gary asks.

Shermeto shakes his head. "We can't leave her out there. You'll help?"

"Anything." Gary reaches for his jacket. "We can take my car."

Reese's head shoots up. "I want to stay here," he says. The cat is now laying on his lap.

***

Only a smattering of pebbles ground into the floor mats. The car smells like those cinnamon candy hearts that people pass out in February. Shermeto doesn't know anyone who ever liked those things, but the smell makes him feel like he's dirtying the car by his simple presence. "What's the plan?" Gary asks, backing out of the driveway. "Where to first?"

"Start with the last place we know she was, I guess." Shermeto chews on his thumb. There isn't much nail there, so he moves on to the skin. "It's going to be impossible to get down there. All the roads are blocked."

"So we walk."

Shermeto was afraid he'd say that. "No other choice."

"She said you only thought about yourself."

Gary glances at Reese in the backseat then pulls into a McDonald's Drive Thru. "Hey Reese, want anything?" Reese's head pops up, though he's still resentful they pulled him away from the cat. "Take that as a yes."

Gary pulls up to the speaker and places three orders then passes the bags around. The smell of cinnamon hearts is replaced with fried food.

"Dig in."

Shermeto pulls out a handful of hot fries and stuffs them in his face. The salt rips into his tongue, dries up his mouth, but it's heaven. The heat burns the roof of his mouth, warming his body. Reese studies the food as if he's never seen anything like it.

"You never had fast food?"

Reese lays the food out on his lap. Shermeto, by contrast, doesn't waste any time ripping into the burger. The meat melts between his teeth and is gone in three bites. He must look like an animal, but he doesn't care. His belly is fuller than it has been in some time.

"Where'd he come from?" Gary shrugs toward the backseat.

"Long story." Shermeto swallows the last fry.

***

They approach the city from the east side, back through Shermeto's stomping grounds. It looks different from this angle. The shopping malls, plazas, the Mom and Pop groceries, the specialty shops, all stand out like ornaments. Pockets of teenagers huddle on the sidewalks and in parking lots, wearing tank tops, t-shirts, muscles, midriffs exposed. There's a rush in the air, a sense of needing to be somewhere but not knowing how to get there. So many people, with a heightened sense of self-worth, unaware of the fight going on around them. Shermeto bets there's pain there too. They aren't fooling anyone nor doing themselves any favours.

"You think I don't care?" Shermeto asks.

"No. Not at all. You're here aren't you?"

"We'll find her. She'll be fine. That girl is one of the most stubborn people I know."

Gary laughs. "That's true."

Gary is not James. That's a good thing. He never liked that guy. The way he talked, carried himself, looking down his nose on other people. Not intentionally, Shermeto thinks. A simple reaction to his upbringing. Snobbery. Snootiness. It ran in his family. But Gary seems like good people.

Shermeto recalls the day Kendra got married. The stuffiness in the parents of the groom, their long, pinched noses and the way they silently judged. Sometimes it wasn't so silent. Shermeto had gone inside the house to take a leak, kicked off his shoes at the front entrance, not to mark the white carpet. Under the tall ceilings, he was small. Smaller than the great French artists on the wall, the expensive Chinese vases. All around him, judgement hung. He knew something was off with James the moment he met him; the house explained it all.

"How long you been…you know…with my daughter?"

"Not long. A few weeks; off and on. Nothing too serious."

"You obviously care."

"It's who I am, I suppose."

"Let me guess, she's keeping you at arm's length?"

Now Gary really laughs. "You know her well."

"She wasn't always that way."

"A victim of circumstance."

"Something like that. Oh. Turn right here." They turn onto another street, houses and four-plexes packed close together, cars practically copulating with the curbs. "Over there."

The car crawls along the street. Shermeto searches the grimy darkness. Gary pulls up to the curb under the shadow of a mock orange bush. A brick half wall runs the length of the street separating the road from the housing on the other side. Houses that would have all been evacuated by this point due to their sheer distance to the river. *The water won't come this far,* Shermeto thinks.

Up the road a team of trucks with flashing hazards block the road. Pick-ups and vans full of sandbags. A dozen men move back and forth, lugging the bags to the river bank, piling them high and going back for more. There's determination in their steps, a smoothness of knowing what needs to be done and doing it. No questions.

"What about Reese?" Gary asks.

Shermeto takes a deep breath and considers. "We won't be long. Can you stay here?"

Reese nods and curls onto the backseat, his eyelids already closed before his head hits the seat.

"He'll be okay, right?"

"Don't see why not. Do you want me to stay with him just in case?" Gary slows. "I can stay if you think that's better."

"No, no. I need your help." Shermeto ducks his head inside the car. "Don't open the door to strangers."

"Take this." Gary shakes a blanket from the trunk and lays it over Reese.

***

Shermeto and Gary follow the sidewalk to where the workers are busy building up the barricade. A little too late for most of the city. Police cars block all traffic into the core, firemen with their uniform sleeves rolled up help with the sandbagging, orders flying around. *Take that there, this over here. Hurry. Hurry. Hurry.*

The police turn the curious back. Nothing to see.

An officer catches sight of them and hurries over.

"You can't be here," he says.

This is what he expected to hear, and he doesn't have a plan.

"We want to help," Gary pipes up.

The officer studies them, looking like he might turn them away anyway, but then decides against it.

"See that guy over there?" Along the bank a man in a yellow rain poncho is building a rock wall. "Go talk to him. He'll find you something to do."

"Thanks." Gary pulls Shermeto by the arm.

"What are you doing?"

Heat rises in Shermeto's face. This is not what he had in mind.

The man in the yellow poncho looks up. Kind eyes. White teeth. Gary crushes his hands in his pockets.

"We want to help."

The man nods. "Bring those rocks down here." He points to the back of a truck loaded up with slate and other landscaping rocks. Gary pushes Shermeto towards the truck.

"I don't see how this is going to help."

"Trust me."

Shermeto hates a lot of things, but what he hates the most is anyone telling him to trust. Those are the ones to stay as far away from as possible.

"Looks like he thinks he's building a garden instead of a wall," Shermeto says.

Gary grabs an armful of rocks and takes them down to the guy in the poncho. They share some words. Shermeto grabs a couple of rocks in his hands and carries them down.

"The power's out," the man says.

"Won't be long," Gary says. "In and out."

"Don't know how you'll get past those guys." A cluster of officers has formed.

"Give me a reason to go over there," Gary says.

The man thinks about this a minute, then says, "Empty the back of the truck."

They move back and forth, slowly but efficiently. Mud streaks down Gary's face as he digs in, hard. In less than an hour the truck is empty.

The man in the yellow poncho twists his face and throws them bottles of water. "Over there." He points to a pedestrian crossing underneath the blocked bridge. "Be careful." He points at the cops. "And be fast."

"Thanks." Shermeto limps to the pathway before Gary can say anything.

They stay close to the bank, hidden by the overgrown brush and duck behind the trees. Soon they are crossing the surging river. Shermeto pauses and for a moment thinks of Harlow and what he used to say.

When the river gets riled, stay the fuck away. It ain't worth it.

Up the opposite bank they climb a narrow path and emerge into a neighbourhood broken like him. An ominous quiet dangles from the window frames, hanging from broken downspouts, gutters. In the distance, high-rises, construction signs, cranes, balconies ten stories high, all silent. None of the usual chatter, the grumble of a too busy city. Time stands still now, waiting for no one, especially not him.

"Where are we going?" Gary says.

Shermeto holds his finger up to his lips and points to the apartment complex. "In there." His voice drops to a whisper as if anything louder will interrupt the silence.

"What's that?" Gary points to a sewer grate. Water bubbles and stirs and begins to flow upward and out of the drain, backing up into the street. Water curls around their feet, rushes to nowhere, all the sewers blocked, overflowing, regurgitating muddy water like an afterbirth. Across the street, Shermeto catches a glimpse of a black hood and dark pants, disappearing between a growth of trees. The water is everywhere.

"We gotta go. I know a short cut."

The apartment building is different from this side. At one time it might have been a nice place to live. A canopied entry leads to two large glass doors, an intercom inset into the concrete wall, wires hanging free, most of the buttons gone. The odd name remains, *D. Smart*, mostly faded. Others, empty or simply read Occupant. There haven't been occupants in this building since the city shut it down several months ago. Condemned. Supports not supporting. The residents forced out without consideration.

The door needs some convincing, but finally it stretches wide. Shermeto clambers in, over broken out walls, trash buckets, old dishes, magazines. He retreats down a hallway, the air is musty, abandoned. Gary keeps up as they press through another door leading into an abandoned courtyard and across through a narrow opening in the walls and out into the street on the other side.

It's a blistering mess. Water moves in streams, curling around fire hydrants. But he can see the parkade.

THE RIVER

The river can't find him but knows he's there. His pain shudders all the way through its molecules, to the pavement, up the walls of buildings.

The river takes one street and then another. Hurry. Before it's too late. Around a corner and there he is. The boy's face is pressed up to the window of the car, the man stands with his hands on his hips.

"Come on. You can't stay here."

The boy rolls the window down a crack. "I'm supposed to wait."

"There's a better place. He'll know where to find us."

The car door opens and the boy allows the man to take his hand, lead him away.

The boy nods. Comfortable. This is no stranger.

"Oh, don't cry."

Kids have a way of giving a little heart yank.

"It'll be ok. Trust me."

KENDRA

Kendra tugs on the bindings. It's getting her nowhere. The water is now up to her hips. She tries to stand, to wiggle her way up, but her legs are locked, and the bindings have pulled so tight she can't move. There's nothing she can do except panic.

This isn't supposed to happen. Is this what true hopelessness feels like? Is this how her mother felt? Easier to lay back and die than fight. She kind of gets it, but it doesn't make it okay. And no matter what, Kendra still has some fight left in her.

Her body begins to vibrate. From cold or fear, she can't tell which.

"Do you believe me now?" Lily's voice rips through her. That was just after the birthday party, when her father showed up a complete mess. That day, their father became dead to Lily. Nothing Kendra could say would make it better. It's why she left.

She misses her sister. When she gets out of this mess, she'll go visit. The break would do her a ton of good.

***

Kendra and Lily stayed home that day. He hadn't spoken in hours, laying on the couch, eyes closed but not really sleeping. Every few minutes he would take larger breaths, wince as if in pain and then settle.

"Where's Mom?" Lily finally asked.

So little, Lily wouldn't understand. Kendra had been praying the question would never come, practicing over and over for when it did. But now that the question was out there, hanging between them, none of the words seemed right. And they jumbled together, falling like a water balloon into the pit of her stomach.

"She's dead." Her father stood in the doorway.

The balloon exploded.

Lily's head darted between the two of them and then tears spread down her cheeks, faster, faster. She fell into Kendra's arms and didn't move. Rage boiled inside her. "How could you?" She glared at her father.

She didn't mean it how it sounded. Her father turned and stalked down the hallway, the backdoor slamming behind him.

Lily fell asleep on her lap. Kendra lifted her carefully onto the bed and shut the door behind her. She stood in the doorway again of her parents' bedroom. The bathroom light still on.

One step then another. It seemed to take forever to cross the small bedroom. A half empty cup of water sat on the nightstand on her mother's side of bed. A half-read book, balled up tissues. On her father's side, nothing but a thin layer of dust. She sat on the bed, on her mother's side, slowly laid down and curled into a ball, burying her face in her mother's pillow. The smell of her still lingered.

She lifted her head and listened to the silence. The steady click, click, click, of the clock in the living room, the house settling. Every creak. Every shift. She felt it in her bones. Lily still slept sound, blanket pulled up over her ears, head buried in her favourite stuffed puppy they called Molasses because he was dark and sweet.

Kendra roamed through the kitchen without much intention. She checked the answering machine. A message from a neighbour who had heard the news, offering their condolences. The kitchen spun, she sat down, stood up, opened the fridge, closed it again.

She couldn't avoid it any longer.

Nothing could prepare someone for the aftermath of a death. Didn't matter how much experience lay behind them. She'd seen it plastered on the faces of the officers and the medical examiner. Under the whispers. Inside the sad glances.

"What about the kids?" They shook their heads. "So sad."

Indeed.

Kendra took a deep breath and stepped into the bathroom. Initially, she'd only planned on shutting off the light, told herself not to look, but she couldn't help it. Red water filled the tub, towels tossed beside the toilet probably from her father trying to clean up the mess. No one had even emptied the tub. A metallic stench clung to the air, the walls. Not some gory death scene like in a horror movie, but it wasn't far off. The bath mat had a brownish red footprint dried into the centre of it.

For a moment she froze and then the rage she felt earlier returned and she stomped into the kitchen, grabbed an empty trash bag, rubber gloves her mother used to wash dishes, a rag and bleach and Mr. Clean. Back in the bathroom, she pulled on the gloves, closed her eyes and pulled the plug. The water gurgled and groaned, gulping, slurping, it couldn't swallow fast enough.

The towels, the mat, all went in the garbage. She pulled down the shower curtain and stuffed that in the bag. Bleach and cleaner and a lot of scrubbing, the bathroom smelled like lemons. Not a hint of red. She scrubbed the shower tiles, between each tile. Nothing could remain. And then when she felt like she was done, she stripped off the gloves and tossed them and the rag into the bag. She tied it closed and took it out to the garbage can.

When she got back inside, the phone began to ring. The sound vibrated her skin. Made the queasy nerves come out in full force. She snatched up the phone. Maybe it was her father. Or her grandmother. Had they even been notified? Heat began to rise in her cheeks. The room became blurry, her head a flurry of white noise. Pressure grew behind her eyes; the phone heavy in her hand.

"Who's this?" A man's voice came through the phone. Music blared in the background, a mash of cheers and laughter.

"Kendra. Who's this?" Her words felt thick, pasty.

"There's a man here. Someone needs to come get him."

"Who is this?" Kendra repeated.

"Fred. Dewey's Pub. Says his name is Del. You know him?"

And then it became clear.

"I can't get him."

"Someone's got to."

"I'm only fifteen."

"What about your mother?"

Did he have to say that? How dare he even suggest it. "I'll come."

"He's outside, anyway."

Kendra hung up the phone and pulled on her shoes. Her sister was still asleep. She could get there and back before she woke up. Kendra ran out the door.

True to Fred's word, her father sat on the curb in front of the bar, his face buried in his hands.

"Dad?"

Her father looked up, his focus aimed somewhere behind her, through her. Then his eyes settled on her. "You shouldn't be here."

She's couldn't agree more. "Let's go home." She grabbed his arm, tried to urge him to his feet.

"Get off me." He shrugged her arm away.

"We need to go home."

"What does that even mean? Home. A joke." He hung his head, traced lines in the dirt with his finger.

It wasn't the first time and it wouldn't be the last.

**

The water isn't slowing. The whole bottom half of her body is wet and getting wetter. Kendra pulls against the bindings. Her wrists burn. She struggles, moves. Finally, the bindings give a little but not without cutting into her skin. She tugs harder, moving her feet up and under her. One slow inch at a time, she begins to stand. Not going out like this even if it means losing a wrist.

There's a pop and pain rips through Kendra's shoulder but she's standing. Her legs quiver in the water surging around her ankles, reaching up her calf. She searches the room, the darkness having slightly cleared into a grey haze. She cranks her head around, biting through the pain. She shifts around the pole that's holding her hostage to get a better view. Her shoulder has other ideas. Her head begins to pound, a faint burn in the back of her throat and she leans forward to puke. The tears roar from her then. All the years, rushing to the surface. And she's going to lose.

She sees her mother, floating like a cloud over her, the sadness a milky drizzle that makes it hard to breathe. Her brother hangs by the delicate threads. And her father, below it all, gazing up, unmoving. Frozen in concrete, unable to react, or choosing not to. Her sister, rushing off to something better, clawing her way out, and making it.

Then James. Reacting to the anger that she's kept down for so long. Seeing her fear, her rage and unable to do anything about it. She wouldn't let him. This situation, inevitable. Always trying to help, always ending up worse because of it.

"What else am I supposed to do?"

She screams into the empty basement, into the water billowing around her feet. No answers.

Not her fault. She's heard it all her life. But isn't it? Her jealousy, her anger, brought them all to this point. All the people she cared about leaving in one way or another. She needs to pull herself together. Make a choice. Let the outcome be what it will. Cause and effect.

A door crashes shut upstairs. Footsteps hard against the floor. She listens, tracks their movement through the house. He's returned. So now what? Is this the end?

The stairs creak, feet, legs, a torso, arms appear on the stairs. She realizes she's not so much afraid anymore, than she is angry, but that anger isn't going to get her anything but bloody, torn wrists. She's going to have to appeal to Jagger, connect with him somehow.

Jagger stands at the bottom of the stairs. He's clutching a child by the back of the shirt.

"What am I going to do with you?" he says, glancing at Kendra. He crosses the basement, splashing through the water, leaves the child at the base of the stairs. Is he talking to the child or her?

She wants to yell at the child to run—get help—but Jagger would be back on top of him so fast, wouldn't he? "You're not going to get away with this," she says.

"Probably not and I'm okay with that. But I don't think you're enough of a lure. The kid though. He'll do the trick."

The boy lowers his head, picks at his fingers.

"Life is not all balloons and white picket fences," Jagger says, pulling a ziptie out of his pocket. He hovers over the kid, his back to Kendra. "No one understands, I had to let them know. Shermeto was my friend, but he betrayed me, going off with the others, talking about me behind my back. They snickered. Made fun. I told him everything." Jagger snaps around to face her. "I'd never done that, and he threw it back in my face. Do you know how that feels?"

"I'm sorry," Kendra says.

"Are you? Are you really?" Jagger studies her for a minute. "I don't think you're any different." He stands and grabs the boy by the arm, pulls him to where Joe was tied up. The boy kicks and screams but it's no use.

"Where's Joe? Did you hurt him?" Kendra asks.

"I should have."

"You let him go, then." Kendra pulls against the bindings. Maybe there's a chance for her then, for the both of them.

"Against my better judgement."

"What kind of monster are you?"

"The worst kind."

The boy lays motionless on the floor.

"Never had anyone who cared about me the way he cares about you."

"I don't know what you're talking about," Kendra says.

"And you care about him." He shakes his head. "What does that even feel like? To care about someone so much that you'll drown in the sewers to save them."

"What are you going to do to him?" she asks.

"The same thing I've done to all the others."

SHERMETO

"So now what?"

Shermeto clutches his stomach. A thousand needles coming at him from the inside. He knows he's running out of time.

"Go back to the car. Get the kid. And figure it out." He groans and falls to his knees.

"You okay?" Gary takes his shoulders. Tries to lift him.

"It's nothing."

"Not nothing. Come on, let's get out of here."

They follow the sidewalk. The water seems to have retreated some. They cross back through the apartment building and back to the street. The water is bubbling out of the sewers, carving a path through the grass, leaping the curbs. They tread carefully, knee deep. Shermeto holds Gary's arm.

A Hummer moves up and down the cross street as they stumble back to Gary's car. The police don't even remember who they are, pay no attention; they're too busy building up the banks. Higher. Wider.

Shermeto swipes his hand across his face, touches the scab on his lip. Seems like forever ago he was in the hospital. His mouth is still tender, though the wounds are healing. The swelling seems to have gone down and he imagines the myriad of angry colours buried under the new beard of the last few days.

Mud lines mark the spot the water reached but didn't linger. *Or it's already receding?* The rain doesn't last long this time. *Let the wa-*

ter worry its way back to the river, like a spray of waddling ducks chasing after their mother.

A magpie squawks from a nearby roof, hopping, telling him off.

At the end of the street, a man staggers onto the sidewalk and collapses to the pavement. Gary runs to meet him. Shermeto limps.

"Joe?" Shermeto says.

Joe lifts his eyes to Shermeto. "I'm sorry."

"What the hell for?"

"I couldn't stop him. He took Marie. He took everything."

"What are you talking about? Who took Marie?"

"The only thing left to live for. Gone." Joe sits up. His head resting in the palm of his hands. "Time to die." Joe emits a soft moan. "Go away. Let me die."

"You're not going to die today. What are you doing here?"

"Says you. Death is but a step. Another door to pass through."

"Seems pretty final to me."

"That's what they'd have you believe."

Gary tries to pull Joe up.

"Get back!" The man spins, appearing ready to bite anyone who gets too close. "Alright. Alright. Calm down." Shermeto holds up his hands. "I'm not going to stop you. Let's talk a bit."

The man's eyes narrow to slits, his face pinches. "Don't want to."

"Where's Marie?"

"I told you. He took her."

"Who?"

"Black. Dressed in black. You know him."

"What man?"

"Black eyes."

"Who?" Shermeto knows who, he needs Joe to say it.

Joe shakes his head like a mutt shaking off water.

"Jagger. He has another one."

"One of us?"

"No. This one's pretty."

"Where are they?"

"A house. So much water."

Shermeto turns to Gary. "I know where they are."

***

They scramble back to the car, dragging Joe with them. The air is oddly silent. No electric hum, no flashing lights, nothing to distract. In the distance are the sirens attached to the army vehicles, fire trucks, police, milling through the streets, the megaphone calls asking if anyone needs help.

"Where's Reese," Gary asks when they reach the car.

"What the hell?" Shermeto scans the area, behind trees. "Where could he have gone?"

They run up and down the alley calling his name but there's no answer. *Not again,* Shermeto thinks. *This can't be happening again.*

In the dirt, halfway up the alley, Shermeto spots something on the ground. He approaches slowly. The camera. It's still intact. He snatches it up and turns it on. The screen brightens and Shermeto flips through the photos. *Shit.*

"We have to go now," Shermeto yells back at Gary. Joe is leaning against the car.

"Did you find something?" Gary asks.

"Jagger has him too." Shermeto waves the camera at him and climbs in the car.

Shermeto leans his head back against the seat, peers out the passenger window. Joe breathes slowly in the backseat, his head against the window. sunken and for the first time he can remember, he seems ashamed. They should all be ashamed. How could he have been so selfish all this time?

Between his panic, his need to protect the boy and Kendra, he realizes this is it. The last time he will swagger along the streets. The last time he will go ignored. A part of him will miss it but he's got more important things to deal with now. Not the daytime noise but the quiet of night where he can slide around without a worry. Like being tucked in at night.

The car rumbles over train tracks. A searchlight sweeps back and forth. Joe doesn't move, but Shermeto shrinks deeper into the seat. Where will he go? Where will any of them go?

Shermeto thinks about Reese, then Steven and his edges begin to unravel. So much has gone unsaid. Undealt with.

Reese isn't his. What will happen to him? Nothing good, he's sure. Shermeto can't protect him.

"Over there." Shermeto directs Gary to the alley. He pulls in front of a garage, behind Kendra's car. They get out.

"I'm not going back there." Joe folds his arms over his chest like a defiant child, his eyebrows pinch together.

Shermeto won't let him come anyway. *Since when does breathing hurt so much.* It's not in the lungs exactly, or maybe it is now. No way to know. But each time his chest expands and deflates his guts begin to grind, picking off little pieces of him one bit at time. Shermeto falls onto the hood of the car and rolls to the ground.

"Hey. Shit. Come on. You have to get up." Gary leans over him.

Why? Why does he have to get up? He stares at the sky, at the gray, at the small patches of blue and wonders what it would be like to float down the river, not knowing where it will end.

"Kendra's in there."

There's a determination behind Gary's words that hurt worse than any beating that's ever been laid on him. Worse than a frigid, frozen night.

"She needs you."

Shermeto rolls over and pushes himself up from the ground. She only needs him this one last time. He owes it to her.

Joe sticks his head out the window. "If you don't mind, I'd like to die now."

"Not yet you won't."

Joe stares hard at Shermeto, clenches his jaw and begins to sob. Joe's eyes are red, tears splotch his cheeks.

"Jagger," he says.

"I know."

"No." Joe points.

Shermeto and Gary turn. Jagger stands in the middle of the alley, hands stuffed deep into his pockets.

KENDRA

"You awake?" Kendra whispers into the dark. She tries to turn her head but her shoulder's pinched at a stupid angle. There's a rustle of movement but the boy doesn't speak. "Where'd you come from?"

"Out there." His words scrape out.

"How old are you?"

"Nine."

"That's a good age."

"I guess."

"How'd you get here?"

"I came with him."

"Do you know him?"

"I guess."

"How'd you meet him?"

"By the fire. He had weird eyes, but the nice man was friends with him, so he was okay."

"What nice man?"

"Shermeto."

Kendra's head snaps in the direction of the boy. Pain shoots up her back. "What did you say?"

"Shermeto. He was nice to me and my mom."

"Where's your mom now?"

"The river."

She's not sure what that means but is a little worried to ask. "Where's Shermeto?"

"He's not coming back."

"Why do you say that?"

"They never come back."

"Of course, he is. He said he would."

"They lie."

"He's not like the others."

"That's what my mom said."

"Your mom sounds like a smart woman. What were you doing with Shermeto? You and your mom?"

"He said he was taking us to his daughter. She would know what to do."

"Where's your dad?"

The boy doesn't answer. The water is up to her knees now. It must be even higher on him. "You still there?"

"Kinda hard to go anywhere."

Kendra laughs. She knows she shouldn't, but she can't help it. "What's your name?"

"I'm not supposed to talk to strangers."

"Kind of late for that."

The kid is silent for a moment. "My name is Reese."

"I'm Kendra. Where's your dad?"

"I don't have a dad. I did. But he was mean."

"I'm sorry."

"Do you have a dad?"

"I did. He was the best dad anyone could ask for. But then for a while he wasn't."

"Why not?"

"He got hurt really bad."

"Did he heal?"

"I'm not sure. I hope I get to find out."

She pulls against the binding. It's become slightly looser, enough to move her arms up and down. But there's plastic and she's sure they'll never snap by shear will and determination. "Hey Reese? Can you do me a favour?"

"I'll try."

"The water is getting really high. We gotta get out of here. I want you to scream as loud as you possibly can. Can you do that?"

"I can do that."

"Good. On three?"

"Ready."

"One. Two. Three."

SHERMETO

"Thought you weren't coming back," Jagger says.

"What are you doing, man? Is what they're saying true?"

Jagger shrugs and nods towards the house. "See for yourself."

"I'm going to fucking kill you if you do anything to her."

Shermeto takes a step forward, pain shoots up his right side.

"I'd like to see you try, old man."

Gary pushes past Shermeto to the house.

"You're too late." Jagger spits on the ground, shifts from one foot to the other. Gary practically crashes through the fence. A hinge busts.

"You asshole." Shermeto lunges at Jagger. *What's he got to lose*?

Jagger steps out of the way and Shermeto crashes face first on the ground.

"Pathetic." He stands over Shermeto, one leg on either side of his body. "You should have trusted me."

"I did trust you. And look what happened."

"You tolerated me. None of it was real."

"What are you talking about? I did everything for you."

"And yet, at the first chance of a way out, you were going to take it. Leave me here."

"Is that what this is all about? I never talked about leaving."

"You did. Everyone did. And you were there."

Suddenly the truth steamrolls over him.

"You killed Gerard. You killed them all."

"Harlow was the first."

Shermeto begins to rage. He balls his hands into fists and begins swinging at the air, at Jagger's legs. All the people he ever cared about, and who cared about him. And Harlow? All this time, Shermeto thought he was to blame.

"You won't get away with this!"

"Watch me." Jagger pulls a switchblade from his pocket and flicks it open.

This is it, Shermeto thinks. *This is how it's going to end.* He won't even make it out of here, won't have his death on his terms. He lays back and closes his eyes.

"Do it already."

Footsteps. A commotion. Jagger is on the ground, Joe on top of him. The knife wielded only inches from Jagger's throat.

"I'll slice you. You killed my wife. My Marie." He brings the blade down into Jagger's shoulder.

"Jesus, fucking Christ." Jagger cries. "You stabbed me."

There's a crash from the backyard.

"And I'll do it again." Joe stabs him in the other shoulder.

Shermeto pushes himself up and staggers to the fence. His legs sink into water up to his shin. It fills his shoes. Gary is on his back beside the deck. The railing beside him. Blood covers his arm and shirt.

"You okay?" Shermeto asks. "Should have warned you about the railing."

"Go get her. I'll be alright."

Screams split the air. "Do you hear that?" Shermeto says.

"Yeah. Go."

Shermeto slides open the door. The screams cut through the gloom. He takes more steps than he would like to cross the kitchen and then down the stairs, too slow. Halfway down the screams stop.

KENDRA

Kendra clamps her mouth shut. Reese does the same. It takes her a second to orient herself. Someone is on the stairs. She watches, careful. She thought she heard yelling outside but through the din of the water pouring in, she couldn't be sure.

"Who's there?" she calls to the stairs.

"Kendra? Jesus. I found you."

Her father. Her mind swims. She pulls against the bindings.

"Dad, I can't move."

"Where's Reese?"

"I'm here," Reese says. "You came for us."

"Thank God. We're going to get you out of here."

We? He didn't come alone? More footsteps on the floor above.

"Down here," Shermeto calls up.

"I got his knife."

"Gary? Is that you?"

Tears begin to well. Her chest feels heavy. She doesn't know whether to cry or laugh.

"We're coming."

Her father splashes through the water towards her.

"Get him first," Kendra says. "The water's too high."

In a moment the kid is free and standing in front of her.

"He's your dad?"

Another second and the bindings release. She rubs her wrists. There's blood and they sting like all hell.

"Come on, let's go."

"Is he gone?" Kendra asks falling into her father's arms.

SHERMETO

Joe is sitting in the middle of the alley. He looks up as they approach. "Can I die now?"

"You will not die today." Shermeto holds out his hand to the man and helps him off the ground. "Where'd he go? Did you kill him?"

"Nah. Only scared him a little." A smile spreads across Joe's face. "Maybe I don't want to die. Can you take me home instead? I need to tell my kids about their mother. See my grandkids."

"I think they'd like that," Gary says.

"You don't know them at all."

They all pile into the car, Gary and Shermeto in the front, Reese in the back squashed between Joe and Kendra.

"Do you need a doctor?" Shermeto says.

"No. It'll heal."

Shermeto turns to Reese in the backseat. "You might be needing this." He hands over the camera.

***

Gary parks under a tree across the street from the address. They all peer at the front porch, the grass, the clean sidewalk. The bright windows.

"It's nice," Shermeto says.

"What if they don't want to see me?" Joe grumbles in the backseat. "I smell really bad."

"Do you want someone to go with you?" Gary asks.

"No."

He opens the door and saunters across the street. On the sidewalk he turns and offers a salute then goes up to the front door.

"Should we go?" Gary asks.

"Not yet."

Joe rings the doorbell and looks like he needs to pee. He keeps glancing back at the car. After a moment the door opens, and he disappears inside.

DAY SIX

THE RIVER

Jagger sits on the bank of the river, his shirt covered in his own blood. The river wants to laugh. This man who tried to tear and destroy everything that meant something and failed. He can't be allowed to get away with it. That wouldn't be right. That wouldn't be the happy ending a story deserves.

Are there ever really any happy endings? the river wonders. *Maybe only new beginnings.*

Jagger climbs down the bank and dips his hand in the water.

The river gasps and finally understands. Feels everything he has ever felt. The neglect, the mistrust, the abuse. It's not his fault and yet, he feels the complete weight of it pressing down on him like the mud and rocks giving out beneath his feet. He catches his balance in time and rights himself into a crouch.

Sad and alone. That's all he is. Never anyone to tell him he was enough, lacking the confidence to make a difference.

Jagger had never met Shermeto before the night Harlow died. He knew Harlow though, had watched the way he buzzed around the community, taking in the lost souls—but weren't they all lost?—Jagger wanted to be taken into his embrace but when he'd approached him, it didn't pan out like he expected. Harlow didn't trust Jagger and Jagger thought Harlow too high on himself. Didn't drink, didn't smoke (at least not the good stuff) but never turned his nose down at anyone. Except Jagger.

Shermeto came along and he got everything Jagger wanted.

They'd seen each other once, in the lineup at the shelter. Harlow came up to him and out of nowhere, "You don't belong here. Go home."

What did Harlow know that no one else did?

Jagger didn't know what that meant. He had as much right—need—to be there as anyone else.

"Take your maggot face out of here."

Not kind words. Not the type he gave to everyone else.

He saw Shermeto and Harlow out there, under the old trailer. Jagger was out of money, desperate. Freezing. He only meant to take some cash from Shermeto's boot—he'd seen him tuck it in there earlier—but Harlow woke up, challenged him. They struggled. Harlow pushed Jagger. Jagger pushed Harlow. Harlow fell, his head smacking on a landscaping boulder. Hard. When the man didn't move, he dragged his body back under the truck.

He doesn't think it's his fault. Why shouldn't he pay?

And then…Jagger begins to cry. The river doesn't know what to do with this. Simple tears turn to drops. When Jagger begins to hiccup, the river reaches out a tentative ripple, wrapping gently around his feet and ankles and then more, up his shins, his knees, his thighs, his waist and then, it takes Jagger by the hand and welcomes him home.

KENDRA

"He won't stay," Kendra says. "He never does."

"Give him a chance. He might surprise you." Gary pulls clothes from the laundry basket and folds them onto the bed.

"Reese means something to him."

"Speaking of that. Has he told you where he came from?"

"Not really."

"So weird."

"He's a good kid."

"We can't keep him. He's not ours."

"I don't think anyone is looking too hard for him."

"I can't believe you just said that."

She throws a towel at him.

"Breakfast is ready," her father shouts from the kitchen.

Gary and Kendra share a glance.

"Don't question it," he says. He pulls her to him and she knows she's safe.

Her father has cooked a heaping pile of scrambled eggs, toast stacked on plates.

"You look good." Kendra leans against the kitchen counter.

Her father runs his hand over his face, "Amazing what a good razor will do."

"Are you staying a while?" Kendra asks.

"Is there a time limit?"

"No. Of course not. It's just that…"

"Eat your eggs."

SHERMETO

Kendra and Gary are heading out to help with the cleanup. Shermeto has an appointment with the oncologist. He knows what he's going to say; Kendra insists and for once he wants to do right by her.

"Sure, you don't want me to go with you?" Kendra hesitates by the front door.

"Go. I'll be fine."

Reese is already in the car. They'll give it a few days, then see what options are available but from what they can tell it's not optimistic.

"You're really going to go?"

He realizes the trust is going to take longer than he's got left but he plans on going out on a positive note. "I'm going."

He peers out the front window until they pull away. Kendra waves from the front seat.

***

It's been a week. They're sitting in the living room; Kendra next to Gary, her head comfortably on his chest, Baby Spice curls on Shermeto's lap, and Reese sits cross-legged on the floor.

The room is warm and full. No one speaks; they don't need to. There's a comfort level that Shermeto hasn't felt in some time. He takes in the moment. The results of his latest MRI burning in his pocket.

Lily called last night. Awkward conversation, but conversation nonetheless, full of apologies and undeserved forgiveness. Whether sincere or not, Shermeto will take it.

The news shows images of the flood. The water receding but no one can return home yet. There's so much clean up to do, it'll take months, but they're committed. A whole city coming together to help each other. Rubber boots sit by the back door, a full load of dirty, muddy clothes spun through the washer, now drying, ready for tomorrow.

The fatigue is real. A sense of accomplishment, doing something for someone else. People treat him differently too. Now he's just another man with a name and face. Not disgust and abhorrence.

It's there when he goes out on warm evenings to walk. His knees ache but he doesn't want to sit still; neighbours pass him with a nod and a smile or wave from their yards. And every time he heads for the door, Kendra tenses, wondering if he's coming back. But each time, he's never gone far, and he always comes back.

Reese scratches the floor, trying to encourage the cat to play; she's old and won't have any of it. She lifts her head lazily and then slowly sets it back down.

"I like dogs better," he says.

"Did you have a dog before?"

Reese shakes his head. "A long time ago. *He* kicked it. And it died."

Shermeto and Kendra's eyes connect. She shakes her head, Shermeto extends a sympathetic smile.

"Looks like the worst is over." Gary stands. "Who wants ice cream?"

He's talking to Reese more than anyone else.

The kid's eyes light up. "I do." He glances at Shermeto, then adds, "Please."

He's resilient. Young enough to let the sadness be just that, sadness. It doesn't need to linger. He doesn't need to suffer.

***

"You coming?" Kendra calls down the stairs.

"My knees are killing me. Don't think I'm going to make it to-day."

Shermeto can't get out of bed. He unfolds the letter again. He can't read it. Won't.

He closes his eyes. Sees himself wandering alone along the river.

Harlow's waiting for him. Gerard. Marie. Scissor. And in the background, there's Grace, holding tight to Stevie's hand.

KENDRA

Kendra glances at Reese in the back seat. Gary is driving. She filed paperwork last week to be his foster parent. Never in a million years did she imagine this happening but how could she turn him away? He's been through enough and helping him feels like penance for her own wrongs. Also, she's grown to love the kid.

They pull into the parking lot. The sun is high and bright; so much heat. Hard to imagine that only a few weeks earlier they had been wrapped up in relentless rain. A few puddles remain, the ground squishes under her feet and the heat is almost unbearable.

They wind through pathways that she's travelled many times before. Gravel kicking out under her feet. The grounds are so well kept, it's hard to imagine this place untouched. They approach the graves. Two have now become three.

Last week's flowers have wilted, dried out from the sun. They replace them with fresh ones and stand back, linking hands. Birds flit from tree branch to tree branch, a cat rolls on its back in a patch of clover.

Kendra's cell phone rings. It's Brenda from Child Services.

"They found her," Brenda says.

Kendra glances in the back seat at Reese who's playing with the Nintendo DS Gary gave him.

"Are you sure," she says.

"Pretty sure. Someone from the women's shelter ID'd her body."

"Now what?" Kendra asks. "Does this change anything?"

"No. The paperwork will be processed." Brenda pauses. "We located his father and he's given up any rights to him. He can stay in your care for now."

"Thank you."

Kendra palms her phone.

"Everything ok?" Gary pats her leg.

Kendra smiles. "Perfect."

THE RIVER

The river creeps over the weir and south. How far it will travel, how much more destruction it will unleash, is anyone's guess.

Anger doesn't last forever. The river's aching bones are stretched and still expanding but it will return to what it once was, or a similar version of its previous self. As the days turn to night, an infinite circle of time, the river gathers itself and settles. For now, its content.

Never the same. Ever changing. Stretching out to eternity. It understands now where it came from, but never where it's going.

THE END

ACKNOWLEDGEMENTS

Lifelong gratitude has to go, first and foremost, to the Alexandra Writers Centre Society, for without the support of this amazing organization I'd still be writing really shitty first drafts and thinking them gold. To my first instructors at AWCS: Ellen Kelly, Betty Jane Hegerat, Caroline Russell-King, Eileen Coughlan, those early years for me were some of the best as I found my voice and learned to tell a really good story. All of you have shaped me in one way or another.

Naomi K. Lewis & Kari Strutt knew Shermeto before he was "this" Shermeto and knew he had so much more to say than I was letting onto the page. Rosemary Nixon simply made me a better writer. Lauren Carter and Ian Williams gave me confidence in this story and myself and forced me to see the bigger picture.

Sarah Butson helped me shape this idea in the first place. Without you, there wouldn't even be a story.

My cheerleaders—there are so many of you and I'm sorry if I forget anyone—Jason Pearce who has been there from the beginning when I didn't know the difference between show vs tell; Alex Benarzi, Drew Henn, Jaclyn Adomeit, Meghan Way, Natalie Vacha, Nick Friesen and Sarah E Johnson for your support through this whole manuscript and your friendship beyond the words; Theanna Bischoff, Ali Bryan, Bradley Somer, Sandra McIntyre, Darren Flach, Philip Vernon, Robert Bose, Rona Altrows and Lee Kvern for just being awesome and excited for me when I didn't really show it.

You all mean so much to me.

Especially grateful to Sarah L. Johnson, who has been the best writing partner and friend a girl could ask for, knowing exactly what I needed to hear whether words of encouragement or ripping apart sections of a manuscript, challenging me to do better and always there with a bottle of wine and wise words when I wanted to cry and give up.

Thanks to Stonehouse Publishing: Netta Johnson, Julie Yerex, and Lisa Murphy-Lamb for understanding what I was trying to say and believing others needed to hear it too.

Obviously, to my family, Arie and Julianne, for your patience and support, leaving me alone on weekends to pound away at the keyboard, telling me to get back to work when I toddled around the house looking for anything else to do. To my fur babies: Pekoe, my precious kitty, who left this world way too soon, for keeping my lap warm on so many days and nights, purring your encouragement and then promptly sitting on the keyboard and deleting everything. Skittles, who doesn't give a shit what I'm doing because…feline, and Stella, you crazy dog, for the endless walks to get me out of my head for a little while, sometimes too long.

To Shelly, my best friend for more than half my life, I finally get to use the pen.

And, of course, my mom and dad, who I literally wouldn't be here without, for instilling in me a love of books and stories from an early age. The Hobbit is the first book I remember you reading to me.